KYZER'S DESTINY
A Novel of Historical Fiction

JON HOWARD HALL

iUniverse, Inc.
New York   Bloomington

KYZER'S DESTINY
A Novel of Historical Fiction

Copyright © 2009 Jon Howard Hall

All rights reserved. No part of this book may be used or reproduced by any means, graphic, electronic, or mechanical, including photocopying, recording, taping or by any information storage retrieval system without the written permission of the publisher except in the case of brief quotations embodied in critical articles and reviews.

All characters and places in this novel, with the exception of persons and places of actual history, are fictitious and a product of the author's imagination.

iUniverse books may be ordered through booksellers or by contacting:

iUniverse
1663 Liberty Drive
Bloomington, IN 47403
www.iuniverse.com
1-800-Authors (1-800-288-4677)

Because of the dynamic nature of the Internet, any Web addresses or links contained in this book may have changed since publication and may no longer be valid. The views expressed in this work are solely those of the author and do not necessarily reflect the views of the publisher, and the publisher hereby disclaims any responsibility for them.

ISBN: 978-1-4401-7286-1 (pbk)
ISBN: 978-1-4401-7287-8 (cloth)
ISBN: 978-1-4401-7288-5 (ebk)

Library of Congress Control Number: 2009936411

Printed in the United States of America

iUniverse rev. date: 9/15/2009

For Paula

KYZER'S DESTINY

CHAPTER 1

Kyzer wasn't a handsome man, but women seldom recognized it when they heard him speak or watched him walk across the room. Bronze skin and dark brown hair complemented the tall, lean physique he possessed. Dellanna always said it was his eyes. His deep brown eyes captivated her the first time she saw him, but that was a lot of love making and three babies ago.

Late in the evening, Kyzer sat in the rocking chair on the veranda overlooking Kellwood. He lit his pipe filled with rich Kelsey tobacco and gazed toward the setting sun. While the silent wind blew its gentle breath, a fragrance of magnolia blossoms permeated the air, and the soft breeze lifted the sweet perfume to his nostrils. The smoke from his pipe swirled above his head, mingling in a marriage with the magnolia.

Lydia, almost six, came running from the doorway, across the veranda, and launched herself into his lap. Bouncing red curls cascaded down her back from a blue satin hair bow.

"Grammy said I could come sit with you before supper."

"I believe that would be just fine with me," he said. "Where's your brother?"

"Jared is taking his nap," she answered. "Father, would you tell me the story about the time Papa Kelsey found you on the porch?"

"I suppose you'll want to hear the truth, the whole truth, and nothin' but the truth, so help me jumpin' June bugs," he laughed. The sparkle in her eyes said it all. He couldn't deny the pleading request while he held her in his arms.

Kyzer believed there was no such thing as destiny — only different choices. At thirty, Kyzer had endured many hardships. However, the fulfillment of his destiny was apparent while he realized it was all within his control. Was Kyzer's destiny simply a choice? Could it destroy him or would it mold him into the man that God fully intended? Kyzer thought about these things while he relaxed in his chair with Lydia. "Listen, while I tell you the story my father told me a long time ago."

In 1841, life in rural Georgia continued as it always had in the past. Located several miles to the south of Atlanta, Jonesboro had survived the cold bitter months of winter. With the arrival of an early spring, the encircling spirit of the thriving, prosperous little town suddenly emerged like the cones on a southern pine.

The wind had a slight chill in it, while the setting sun cast its willowy shadows onto the street where he walked. It was almost dusk on that April evening while the young doctor walked home. The moment he turned down Main Street and saw the house, he knew this summer it must be painted. He felt the tiredness in his feet when he reached the last step of the front entrance portico. A slight turn of his hand adjusted the wooden plaque mounted to the right side of the door when he approached it. The sign read *Dr. John Kelsey, M.D.* It had been a permanent fixture there for nearly two years.

He reached for the front door latch when the door suddenly opened and swung back. There was Sylvania, looking rather anxious while she charged through the doorway. Her white ruffled petticoat swirled under a flowing black skirt and made a final swish when she halted. Two large bright eyes widened above the plump cheeks on her worried chocolate brown face.

"My Lord, have mercy, Dr. Kelsey!" She began to wring her hands together while her feet shuffled in place. "Miss Elizabeth done fainted two times today a gettin' ready for the move. I tells you, she just not able to be doin' all this liftin' and packin'."

"Where is she, Vanie?"

"Sweet Jesus, she restin' in her room. Wouldn't even let me send for you this mornin', the first time she felt poorly."

"Well, I thank you for taking such good care of her. You go ahead with the supper, and don't worry about anymore packing this evening. I'll go and look in without disturbing her."

"Yah suh, Dr. Kelsey. Vanie call you when supper's ready." Sylvania always preferred to be called Vanie. She was a pleasant and free spirited soul most days unless something upsetting happened out of the ordinary. God forbid!

While he paused a moment before ascending the staircase, John remembered how difficult it had been for Elizabeth during this pregnancy. Now, at six months, she remained weak and tired, nearly drained of all her energy. Dr. John insisted upon complete bed rest while he kept a close watch on her. Elizabeth lay resting well upon the bed while John entered the bedroom and stood at her side. A single candle glowed by the bedside, and with the firelight, the room gave off a golden hue which made her face appear angelic.

Elizabeth had long raven black hair, often worn in a chignon or simply piled up and pinned off her neck, especially during the hottest months of the Georgia summertime. Her eyes were crystal blue set into the flawless complexion of her beautiful face. She wore only a pinch of red rouge on her cheeks and lips with a hint of dusting powder on her face and neck. Her magnolia white skin was smooth and soft covering her medium framed body. She spoke with a gentle voice — soft, sweet, and slightly accented.

Not desiring to awaken her, John slipped from the room and down the stairs to the parlor. He felt that sleep provided the best medicine. Surely, she was just tired. A bit of rest was all she needed. John poured a brandy from the decanter on the sideboard into a cut crystal glass and took a seat in his chair. He put his feet upon the hassock and leaned his head against the chair back. It felt good to sit down. While he sipped his brandy, his eyes focused upon the fireplace and the fire that Vanie had started a few minutes earlier. He sat back and relaxed. The fire began to catch up, and he watched a spark while it suddenly popped onto the hearth. While the flames began to lick the wood, the smell of hickory soon filled the room as the fire began to crackle. John's thoughts turned to Kellwood.

Since his father's death during the past winter, plans were to move the family to Hastings to live with his mother. Their children, Susannah and Rob, anticipated the impending move, but somehow John felt Elizabeth wasn't happy about the situation. He knew she cried a lot. He never believed her alibi, 'just pains caused by the baby'. Thoughts of having to leave home were distressful to her. He figured that had to be the reason. The children often spent several weeks during the summer with Papa and Nana at Kellwood. John felt a permanent move to Virginia suited them, especially for a seven and a five year old.

"John," she spoke in her soft whispered voice from the doorway of the parlor. "John, darling, please help me."

He bolted upright in his chair, realizing Elizabeth needed him at once. Quickly rising to his feet, he raced across the room and caught her as she collapsed into his arms. He dropped to the floor with her and rolled a corner of the carpet back to support her head. She cried and clutched onto him with a death grip. John soothed and calmed her, while he assessed Elizabeth's sudden situation. He saw the front of her nightgown was drenched with blood. John gazed toward the doorway, while he noticed the continuing trail of bloody footprints leading from the staircase into the room.

"Vanie.. ... Vanie, come here at once," John yelled.

"I've lost our baby," Elizabeth whispered.

"Don't talk, my darling. Don't say anything more."

While he called out for Vanie once again, Susannah and Rob came running into the room. Seeing their mother lying there on the floor, they began to cry aloud. John felt the sudden drops of perspiration trickling down his face.

"Susannah, run out to the kitchen and get Vanie. Rob, you go with your sister. Tell Vanie to hurry and come quickly."

Vanie was there by his side in an instant. Now, in a panic, she tried to regain her composure.

"Poor Miss Elizabeth. What can I do to help?"

"I want you to take Susannah and Rob out of here," he said. "Bring me some towels and hot water. I need you to remain calm, for the children's sake."

In a moment, Vanie was back. "Here's the towels. I'll be back with the water as soon as I can."

John grabbed a towel from the stack, and lifting Elizabeth's gown, he applied enough pressure to finally stop the bleeding. She had grown limp while she lay there, lips slightly quivering. Elizabeth's crying was reduced to an occasional whimper. While he reached over her, he picked up his brandy glass from the table. Raising her head, John placed the glass to her lips. She took a few sips and then her head fell back.

"John, I hurt so badly," she said while looking into his eyes, now widened deep with concern.

"I know, darling. I'm going to take care of you. Don't worry." John continued with the necessary medical attention to his dear wife. He was amazed at the strength it took for her to make it down the staircase.

"I love you so much," she whispered while her eyes closed.

Vanie returned with a basin and kettle and placed them on the floor nearby. "Miss Susannah and Massa Rob are in the kitchen. I's give them a biscuit and some milk to drink."

Vanie and the doctor spent the remainder of the night attending to Elizabeth. He stripped her naked on the parlor floor while Vanie bathed her. She was almost finished drying her by the time John returned with a clean nightgown. Vanie helped him dress Elizabeth into her long flannel gown. He carried her upstairs and put her into the bed in the guest bedroom in complete darkness. He fumbled in the dark until he was able to light a lamp on the night stand beside the bed. When he left the room, he met Vanie at the bottom of the stairs.

"Dr. Kelsey, you go see the chillin's. Vanie will clean in the parlor and change the bed linen in Miss Elizabeth's room."

While he crossed the back porch into the kitchen and opened the door, there was Susannah and Rob seated at the table. Rob had some milk on his upper lip and Susannah's eyes were red from crying. "I want Mama," she sniffled.

John stepped over the bench and sat between them. He took her on his lap. With one arm, he pulled Rob closer to him. "Children, your mother is going to be all right, I promise. She lost the new baby she was going to have for us, but we still have her," John uttered with as much assurance as his deep voice could muster.

"I want to see her," Rob cried.

"All right, son. Finish your milk. You may help me build a fire in her room, but then you will have to go to bed."

On his way back into the house with the children, John gathered an armload of firewood and a few sticks of kindling to take upstairs. Rob helped stack the wood onto the andirons while John placed the kindling underneath and ignited the fire. Susannah was at her mother's bedside, stroking Elizabeth's hair with her small fingers. Elizabeth was awake, and while the fire slowly began to catch up, John could see the glazed look in her beautiful blue eyes. She made a feeble attempt to smile at him while he walked over to the bed and leaned down to gently kiss her forehead. She put her arms onto his broad shoulders and pulled him downward just enough to kiss him on the lips and squeeze her hands on the back of his neck.

"Darling, the children wanted to say good night to you before I put them into bed. I'll be back to see you. Get some rest."

A feeling of calmness came over the room while they hugged and kissed their mother. Moments later, when John left Susannah's room, he passed by their bedroom and looked inside. There were spots of blood on the floor and the bed sheets were saturated in places. A pair of bloody scissors lay on the floor. One heavy spot was located on the bed covers halfway down. John walked over and while pulling the coverlet aside, he gazed upon the bed, sadly now to see a small crumpled mass of flesh and blood lying there

John wrapped the dead baby in the sheet he tore from the bed. He took it and held it against his chest. When he passed the parlor, he could see Vanie on her knees cleaning the carpet stains. She never saw him walk by. When he reached the back door, he opened it and gazed into the night. He could see the outline of the tool shed in the glistening moonlight. He closed the door gently behind him and stepped onto the porch. He stood there for a moment. John grieved over the loss, especially for Elizabeth's sake. He knew how much she was looking forward to having this baby. What if Elizabeth had died? He didn't want to think about it.

While his saddened eyes adjusted to the night, he walked down the back stairs and headed toward the shed. Just inside the door, he reached for the shovel. That night in the dark, John buried his son.

◀▶ ◀▶

Vanie surprised John when she met him unexpectedly at the back door to announce his supper was ready. John walked into the dining room and poured from the pitcher sitting on the wash stand into the bowl. He immersed his blood stained hands into the clear water and watched as it changed to red. While he washed, he thought about the baby and how he nearly lost Elizabeth.

For the next two days, Elizabeth continued to recuperate upstairs in their bedroom. She was unaware that John caught her crying from time to time while she kept her sorrowing thoughts quietly to herself. It was a relief when he told her about the baby. John buried him under the big oak tree out back. He promised to show her the little grave when she felt well enough to take a walk. She told John she had named the baby, Michael Shane, her 'little angel boy'.

On the third evening, Elizabeth joined the family in the dining room for supper. She was slowly regaining her strength, and John thought it was good to have her moving about the house as they headed toward the parlor. After spending time together with their parents, Susannah and Rob were hurried off to bed by Vanie. Elizabeth was hemming a dress she had made for Susannah several weeks ago while she engaged John in small talk about the day's events. He settled back into his chair and began to go over his journal as he was accustomed at the end of each month.

When he glanced toward Elizabeth, he loved watching her sitting there with her sewing. God, she was beautiful. John's thoughts returned to their wedding day at the All Saints Episcopal Church in Jonesboro. The wedding was long remembered as very elegant, and it was said that Miss Elizabeth was the most beautiful bride that had ever been seen anywhere in Clayton County.

John walked to the foyer to check the door latch, as was

his ritual before bedtime. Tonight, the familiarity of his action reminded him that, despite the loss of the baby, he still had Elizabeth and two healthy children to care for. In the silence of the night, he heard a faint baby's cry. Was his mind playing tricks on him? He stood quietly, listening. The sound came again. He opened the door to discover a squirming bundle at his doorstep. Good Heavens, what is this?" He bent to lift the bundle. An infant. He looked out into the darkness, but there was no sight of a desperate mother fleeing. Whoever had left the baby was gone. Quickly, he thought of the women he knew who were near to giving birth, but he could imagine none of them doing such a thing. He looked toward the parlor, cradling the infant in his arms. Should he tell Elizabeth? Would the sight of this infant lift her despair or deepen it?

"Elizabeth, I am sorry to tell you this," John said, "but some unfortunate has left a child on our porch. I will do all I can to return the infant to his mother, but until then … ."

Elizabeth sat up in her chair, her eyes bright and interested. "Until then, we shall see he is taken care of. Abandoned?" She shook her head and held out her arms. "Poor thing. Give him here."

John marveled at her generous heart after her own loss. Once again, he was reminded of why he had married her as he gently laid the infant in her arms. He hoped she would not find it too difficult when he had located the boy's mother.

The baby continued to cry while Elizabeth began to sooth him and unwrap the tattered blanket. When she drew the tiny infant closer, within a fold in the blanket, a small fragment of crumpled paper fell to the floor. John reached down and retrieved it between two fingers. Turning it over in his hand, he found only one word written on the torn paper. Scribbled on it in charcoal were simply the letters — *KYZER*.

"Oh John, who would leave such a precious baby boy with us?"

"I don't know, but whoever it was surely must have been desperate."

"What are we going to do?" Elizabeth asked.

"The first thing is to get him warm and fed, and then we can talk about what we are going to do. Do you think you could try to feed him?"

"I'll go upstairs and find a fresh blanket. I remember seeing some of Rob's baby things only yesterday while I was packing," Elizabeth said. "Let's pray that my milk has come in."

John returned to the parlor and put away his journal. The end of the month business matters would have to wait. He felt stunned while he thought about his patients who were expecting. He could only think of two women. He was certain that neither of them would give up her baby, but he would find out tomorrow. He would check with Dr. Harlan at the hospital. Maybe he had delivered a baby in the last few days. This baby was just a few days old, maybe a week.

John walked across the foyer to his examining room and lit the lamp on the table. Elizabeth, so natural and radiant, appeared at the doorway while she held the baby. "I was able to feed him."

"Bring him here, and let's have a closer look." He motioned her to enter.

Elizabeth placed the baby on the table and removed the blanket. "What a beautiful baby," she sighed.

While he lay there content, the baby reached out with each arm and kicked with his legs and feet. Clenched fists opened and closed, revealing his long fingers. His eyes were dark, and his head was crowned with thick brown hair. He had a darker complexion, the overall skin tone not very pink as compared with many newborns. When the doctor finished his examination, he found the child to be in good physical condition. In fact, he was a perfect little boy with the exception of a strawberry shaped birthmark on his back near the right shoulder.

"That's a fine boy," Dr. John said.

"I cannot imagine who left this baby on our porch," Elizabeth said.

"Well, my dear, there's not anything else we can do about this situation tonight. Darling, take the baby to our room while I get the crib out of the attic."

"Won't Susannah and Rob be surprised?" Elizabeth left to prepare for bed.

To lose a baby three days ago and suddenly find one on your doorstep was more than John wanted to think about while he opened the door to the attic. He thought about the note he had found and left on the table in the parlor. "Who are you, little one?"

The dawning of the new morning started early for John and Elizabeth. They were awakened by a wet and hungry baby. It was Sunday, and Dr. John had no scheduled patients to see in the office. Hearing the cries of the newborn, the couple realized the dilemma they faced. They prayed things would work out.

"John, have you decided what we need to do?"

"After breakfast, I am going to call on Mary Sinclair and Kate Davidson. I want to make certain they're still carrying their babies."

"What about the hospital?"

"I'll ask Thomas and others around town before I return home. We won't be attending the church this morning. I'm sure God will understand."

"I've awakened Susannah and Rob and told them we have a surprise for them at breakfast," Elizabeth said. They both walked down the staircase with the baby.

The couple sat at the table, and Elizabeth held the baby. Vanie was serving when Susannah and Rob burst into the room. John saw their eyes widen in excitement when they caught a glimpse of their mother and the baby on her lap.

"Oh Mama, a baby," Susannah exclaimed. "Is it a boy or a girl? Where did you get it?"

Rob didn't say anything, but he moved closer for a better look. Elizabeth told them how their father discovered the baby boy on the porch last night. They were amazed while they listened to her.

"Can we keep him?" Rob asked.

"That's what your father is going to have to find out this morning. For the time being, we will be keeping him here," Elizabeth said.

John spoke up. "I'm pretty sure that his mother is missing him so I'm going to try my best to find her this morning. Children, let's have our breakfast."

"Does he have a name?" Susannah asked.

"We really don't know anything about him yet, except that he is strong and healthy. We think his name may be Kyzer," Elizabeth said.

"Could we call him that?"

"Why yes, Susannah, I believe that would be all right. He'll probably like that very much."

"I'll be taking the carriage this morning while I make my rounds. Might as well stop by your sister's on the way to the Sinclair place," John said. "Katharine will be anxious to hear how you're doing, Elizabeth, as well as the news of the baby. Rob, run upstairs and get dressed. You can help me hitch up ol' Dan, if you want." That sent Rob scampering off momentarily while John kissed Elizabeth and Susannah goodbye for the morning. "You are a fine boy," John said while he touched his forefinger to the baby's nose and lifted his hand to pat his head as he left for the carriage house.

Later that morning, after John left for the countryside, Vanie appeared at the doorway of the parlor to announce to Elizabeth that she had a visitor, the widow Rachel Petersen.

"Good morning, Mrs. Rachel. What a pleasant surprise to see you."

"And you too, my dear. I must say you're looking well. I brought you this fresh apple pie."

"Thank you very much. It looks really wonderful. Vanie will take it from you and please, have a seat." Excuse me, I must look a mess."

"Oh no, dear, you look fine. I hope you don't mind me coming by unexpectedly. I felt I needed to offer my condolences in the loss of your sweet baby. I'm very sorry, Elizabeth."

"I appreciate your kind thoughts. My heart is saddened with Michael's loss." She paused to wipe away a tear. "I don't guess you've heard about the abandoned baby boy left on our porch last night?"

"Heavens no, dear. Really? You'll have to tell me all about him."

Elizabeth told Rachel Petersen all about the events of the previous night and invited her upstairs to see the sleeping baby Kyzer. After a nice visit together, Elizabeth walked Rachel to the door.

"I've got to get back home and check on my servant girl. She's been sick all week," Rachel said as she waved goodbye to Elizabeth.

"I'm hoping we will be able to come back to Jonesboro for Christmas this year," Elizabeth said.

"That would be just wonderful, my dear," Rachel said while she headed down Main Street.

By this time, John had arrived at Katharine and Will's. When he drove ol' Dan into the yard, Katharine met him at the corner of the porch. She was excited to hear the news about the newly found baby, and relieved that Elizabeth was doing well.

"I'm out here to check on Mary Sinclair and the Davidson woman," the doctor said.

"I saw Mary two days ago washing clothes in her yard, and I can tell you, she was barely able to bend over the pot," Katharine said.

"If you and Will hear anything, let me know. I'm sorry if I alarmed you by coming here so early."

"I'll be going to see Elizabeth in a while," she said. "Will is out hunting and I don't know when he will be home. Elizabeth is expecting me today, but I don't imagine she will be packing this afternoon."

"Before I go, Katharine, how's your shoulder? Elizabeth told me you had recently taken a fall."

"I'm much better," she said. "It's a little stiff this morning."

"Let's go inside. Maybe I need to take a look at it," he said.

John didn't give Katharine any time to respond while he ushered her into the house. She pulled against him, not wanting him to enter. Several fragments of broken glass lay there on the floor. Walking to the doorway and looking into the dining room, John saw the long knotty pine table overturned on its side. A broken chair lay against it and a small bench looked as though it had been thrown across the room. Shattered plates and broken bowls were scattered in pieces all over the floor. Portions of dried food were splattered on the wall and spilled onto the floor all around the table.

"My God in Heaven," John shouted. "What has happened here, Katharine? I cannot believe it."

Katharine broke into tears. "It was Will," she said. "Will came home drunk and did all of this."

"That son of a bitch," John yelled. "Where is he now? Are you sure you're all right?"

"Oh, I'm all right now. Please, sit down. I'll tell you what happened."

When John turned the table back onto its legs, he positioned it with Katharine's help. They each pulled a chair to the table and took a seat. John sat there shaking his head while he continued to look around the room.

"Will hasn't always been like this, you know, but drinking isn't his only problem," she said.

"What do you mean?"

"I mean, he's changed." She reached down and picked up the handle from a broken pitcher and placed it on the table.

"Kat, I nearly forgot about your shoulder. Please, let me take a look at it." He stood, reaching down to touch his hand to her shoulder.

Katharine gave out a sigh while she allowed him to begin to examine her. "John, I know that my Will is a good man. He has provided me with a generous living since we've been married. He has worked many long and hard hours every day down at the lumber mill." She hesitated for a moment.

"It has been my misfortune to be unable to bear him any children."

"Does he want children now?"

"I'm sure he must, but he never says anything about it."

"What's got into him? Has he just gone to the devil? Oh, your shoulder should be better in a few more days, no broken bones. Sorry for the interruption, please continue."

"It started about a year and a half ago. Will began to make deliveries by wagon load from the mill to Atlanta. Those times gradually continued to be more often and for longer periods of time. I started to worry when he came back home and had been drinking heavily. That was something he hadn't done for several years. I found cause to become suspicious when I discovered a distinct perfume smell in his clothes that wasn't mine. I didn't want to believe he was seeing someone. Eventually, I needed to know so I asked him about it. He became so angry. Rushing toward me, he slammed me to the floor while he tripped and fell. That was my chance to get away from him while I jumped up and ran from the house. I hid in the corn crib until I saw him mount his horse and ride away into the night. Will's actions were shocking, so unlike the man I married. When I returned to the house, this is how I found it."

Katharine was trembling while the tears welled up once again and flowed down her cheeks. John held her in his arms while he tried to comfort her. He offered to drive her to visit her sister when he completed his stops out in the country. He left, promising to return for her soon. It took him a short time to confirm that Mary Sinclair and Kate Davidson were definitely with child. John's thoughts began to fill his mind to the point of being overwhelmed with emotion over the past few days while he drove back to Katharine's. Elizabeth's sudden miscarriage, burying his son, finding the abandoned baby, trying to find the mother, and now the situation between Katharine and Will. He wondered what else could happen? When John arrived at Katharine's, she was waiting for him on the porch.

"I'm ready to see that baby now," she said while she walked down the steps, around the front of ol' Dan, and climbed into the carriage.

CHAPTER 2

When John entered the front door of the hospital, he turned down the main corridor and walked down the hallway. His timing was precise. He met Doc Harlan coming out of the supply room.

"I didn't think you were coming in today, John."

"I need to talk with you, Thomas, that's all. Do you have a few minutes?"

"Go into my office. I'm taking a few supplies to the operating room."

John waited on his return. The doctor took a seat behind his massive oak desk. "How's Elizabeth and the children?"

"They're fine. Elizabeth came down for supper last evening and Susannah and Rob are quite excited with what I'm about to tell you."

"And what's that, John?"

"Then you haven't heard what happened last night at our house?"

"Well, I guess not. I retired early to bed last night and arrived this morning at the hospital at daybreak. I haven't talked to anyone today."

"Late last night, someone abandoned a week old baby boy on our front portico."

"Goodness gracious, John. I'll be damned."

"I was wondering if you have delivered any babies, maybe last week?"

"Why no, I haven't, but what about … ?"

"I've already checked on the Sinclairs and Davidsons. They are all right," John interrupted.

"I don't recall any patients with a current due date," Thomas said. "Say, maybe the mother isn't from Jonesboro."

"Anyway, we're left with the responsibility of a new baby until we can find his mother. Elizabeth and I weren't expecting this just three days after losing our own son."

"I wish I could help you more. It may be quite difficult to track her down. I would suggest that you talk with some of the townspeople, just to see if they know anything," Doc said.

"I planned to do that on my way home from the hospital," he said.

"I'll be listening for any information concerning this matter. Looks like to me that you have a new son after all, John. Good luck, my boy."

"Why don't you come by the house on your way home today to see Elizabeth and the baby?"

"I may do that, John."

"Plan to have supper with us," John said remembering that Thomas had lost his wife last year.

"So long for now," Doc said.

When John left the office, he knew Jonesboro would be deserted today, except for the few church folk and townspeople who gathered there on Sunday afternoons to socialize and gossip. When he approached the vicinity of the square, John stopped the carriage across the street. He walked to the bench where he observed a few men gathered in hearty conversation.

"Hello, Dr. Kelsey, remember me?"

"Yes, Billy. How's that arm since your accident?"

"I'm doing well, sir," he answered, "but I haven't been able to do much good at the mill on my regular job. They've got me on clean up detail right now."

"Any arm broken in two places will take much longer to heal," Dr. John said. "Take care, Billy."

An elderly man from the church approached him. "We missed seeing your family this morning at the service, John. What brings you here this afternoon without Elizabeth and the children?"

"I don't expect any of you are aware of what has happened to us during the past few days," he said as he made his way around the square. Hoping to glean any possible information, he told about Elizabeth's sudden miscarriage and the discovery of the baby on the porch. As a result, no one could recall anything out of the ordinary concerning a week old abandoned baby boy named Kyzer. Nothing, absolutely nothing, except several of the women now offered to help Elizabeth care for the baby. Although discouraged and upset at the moment, John felt somehow he would soon find the baby's mother. Maybe tomorrow. It was getting late in the afternoon and John headed ol' Dan toward the house. John was met at the door by Vanie who motioned him to the parlor. When he walked into the room, there were Elizabeth's parents, George and Mary McArdle, her sister, Katharine Jackson, Susannah, Rob, and Elizabeth, sitting there laughing and talking. Their talking and actions ceased as they appeared frozen in place. All eyes were upon John as they waited for him to speak.

"Good evening, everyone. Sorry I'm late. I meant to arrive sooner." He walked over to where Elizabeth was seated and bent to kiss her on the forehead.

"Hello, darling," she whispered to him. "I'm glad you're home."

John stood and turned toward everyone while Susannah ran to her father. He lifted her to his chest and kissed her on the cheek. "How's my big girl?"

"Hello, Father," she said, putting her arm around his neck. "The baby is asleep now, and I've been helping to take care of him."

"Thank you, Susannah. You're a good helper." After John put her down, he reached to pat Rob's head as he walked to him. "Hello, son. Have you been a good boy today?"

"Yes sir," he answered while he returned to his toy on the floor.

George McArdle arose from his chair, and John walked over to shake hands with him while he gave a slight nod toward Mary and Katharine.

"What did you find out today, John. Is there any news?" Katharine asked.

"I'm afraid not," he said. "I've talked with Doc Harlan and so many people today. Not a clue."

"Somebody must know something," Katharine said. "Jonesboro isn't that big."

Elizabeth spoke to her husband. "What are we going to do now?"

John looked toward her and smiled. "I've been thinking about this situation all day long. The townspeople and the church people I've talked with now all know about the baby. Doc Harlan and the hospital staff now know as well. Whoever left the baby certainly knows that we have him. We are going to have to be patient ourselves and just wait it out."

"What about the move to Virginia, remember? You're taking my daughter and grandchildren to live there in Hastings in two weeks," Mary said.

"What choices do we have? Our lives will have to go on as usual," John answered.

Vanie appeared at the doorway to announce that supper was ready to be served. Elizabeth's parents declined her invitation for them to remain for the meal as they prepared to leave the house. Katharine was encouraged to stay overnight at her sister's insistence since Will had not yet returned home. After supper and the children's bedtime, John hoped that he would be able to talk more with Katharine. Presently, the family gathered around the table for an enjoyable supper together. When a knock at the front door came, Vanie returned to the dining room announcing Doc Harlan. John stood from his chair and walked into the foyer to meet him.

"Good evening, Thomas. It's good of you to come, but I'm afraid you're a little late. We have just finished our supper."

"That's quite all right. I didn't come to eat. I've already had my supper. Can we talk privately?"

"Let's go into my office." John motioned Doc to follow him. While they were being seated, there was a faint knock at the door, and it opened slightly to reveal Elizabeth peering through the opening.

"I know you two have business to discuss, but I wanted to say hello, Thomas. I'm glad you stopped by. Would either of you care for some coffee or brandy?"

With that offer, they both requested their unanimous choice — a brandy.

"Very well," Elizabeth said. "I'll have Vanie bring you each a glass. I'll be in the parlor with Katharine and the children. Thomas, you'll be sure to see the baby before you leave, won't you?"

"Yes indeed," he replied as the door closed. "How is the boy, John?" Doc asked while they settled more comfortably into their chairs.

"He is doing well. Fretful at the beginning, but he is adjusting to us, I think. I find him to be a strong, healthy baby."

"That's good," Doc said. "Let me tell you what I found

out late this afternoon. When I was going home today, I was stopped by Lucas Finch. He told me that he had been at the town square when you were there earlier. After learning about your inquiries, he asked me to tell you about something he recently witnessed."

"What's that?" John asked.

"A few days ago, he remembered passing by a horse and buggy stopped along the side of the Jonesboro Road. It was a rig that he had never seen before in town. He assumed it was visitors returning home to Atlanta. There were no occupants in the buggy while he approached it, but he saw a tall man and a woman in a black dress walking from the woods as he rode past. He said the man resembled Will Jackson, but he didn't recognize the lady. He only caught a glimpse, not paying any mind to them. However, one thing he did remember was the spokes on the buggy. One of the spokes on the left rear wheel had recently been replaced. He could tell at a glance because it didn't match the others."

They were interrupted momentarily when another knock was heard. It was Vanie who had brought their brandies. With a quick nod she acknowledged Doc Harlan as she set the small tray on the corner of the desk nearest him and made her way out while closing the door behind her.

"John, I need to be getting along home. Tomorrow begins another week at the hospital," Doc said as he stood to leave.

After finishing their drinks, the two doctors walked into the parlor. Elizabeth and Katharine sat on the sofa with the baby between them.

"Good evening, ladies. I must be off, but I did want to see the baby before I left," Doc said.

Elizabeth picked up the baby and uncovered him so the doctor could have a good look at him.

"John tells me that he is a fine, healthy boy and that I can see for myself. Maybe in a few more days we will learn the whereabouts of his mother. May I say, Elizabeth, that he looks so natural with you as you hold him there."

Elizabeth smiled back at Doc. A small tear appeared at the corner of her eye as she pulled the baby to her and held him close. "He feels like he belongs to me."

After Doc Harlan left, John joined Elizabeth and Katharine for the rest of the evening. The three of them recalled the events of the last few days until they soon tired.

"Vanie informs me that the guest room is ready for you, Katharine. Visit with John for a while longer if you wish as I bid you both a pleasant good night," Elizabeth said.

After Elizabeth retired, John got his chance to talk more with Katharine.

"John, I haven't told Elizabeth entirely my suspicions about Will. I believe he is seeing someone in Atlanta. He's drinking more heavily now, and that brings on his sudden fits of anger whenever I try to talk to him. It is getting to be unbearable to remain with him, but I still love him so much. When is this going to stop? I just keep asking myself." Katharine sat there softly crying.

" Wish I knew what to tell you, Kat. Sounds like it's going to come down to another confrontation to get him to admit what's going on."

"All I know is that I'm so upset and don't know what to do," Katharine said.

"I know our time here is short, but Elizabeth and I will come to see you before our move to Virginia. You can count on that."

"Thank you for your concern, John. I'm tired and need to go to bed. Good night."

It was morning and Elizabeth and Katharine were packing the china in the dining room. Their work ceased by the interruption of the sound of Vanie singing to herself while she answered the loud knock at the front door. They both recognized the familiar voice they heard shouting for Katharine. It was

Will, and amazingly, he sounded sober. Will came bounding in behind Vanie. The commotion was enough to bring John to the dining room.

"Katharine, I've come to take you home." Will took her into his arms to lead her from the room.

"Hold on, just a minute, Will," John said. "You can't come barging into my house to grab Katharine like that."

"It's all right, John," Katharine said. "I'll go. We do need to talk."

"She is my wife." Will responded with a glare.

"I'll come back later to help you with the packing. Just give me a couple of days," Katharine said.

Elizabeth and John followed them onto the front porch where Katharine gave Elizabeth a hug. She turned back toward Will. He took Katharine by the arm and helped her down the steps and put her up into their wagon. Elizabeth stood there in silence and watched them drive away.

John took Elizabeth into his arms and held her close to him. For a few minutes, they stood on the porch in a deep embrace. His arms were around her waist while she held her head against his chest.

"What was that all about? I'm worried about Katharine," Elizabeth said.

"Now there, don't go worrying your pretty little head about those two. They'll both be all right."

"Wish I could know that for sure. Will's acting mighty strange," she said.

"Too much heavy drinking messes up a man's mind. I'm probably going to have to talk with our dear brother-in-law before long," John said.

"Did you notice Katharine? She was practically shaking the whole time he was here. Her hands were trembling," Elizabeth said.

"At least, he was sober. I don't believe Will has the guts to hit her again and let me find out. Not now, not ever," John said. "Katharine can take care of herself. Please, don't worry."

"I guess she told you plenty last night," Elizabeth said. "What did she have to say?"

"She's just deeply concerned about Will's excessive drinking right now. Katharine asked me not to talk about it. So, you see, I have to respect her request."

"I need to go inside and check on the children. Kyzer should be ready to wake up from his nap. You coming, John?"

"Darling, you go ahead. I think I'll sit on the porch for a while and have a smoke."

Two days passed when Elizabeth decided it was time for John to drive out to Will and Katharine's place. He closed the office for the morning but planned to be back for his afternoon appointments. One of the ladies from the church came by to help Elizabeth with the baby. John headed down the back porch steps toward the barn for ol' Dan. The sky grew dark and the wind began to rustle the leaves of the nearby trees as he hurried to lead Dan from the barn to the carriage house. Large raindrops started to fall. John had finished the last strap and jumped into the carriage when the whole sky opened up in a tremendous downpour. He sat there while the water cascaded down in sheets of blowing rain and puddled the ground all around. The storm soon passed, and John started toward Will and Katharine's. When he pulled Dan to the side of the house, Katharine came out and met him on the porch.

"Good morning, Katharine. How are you?"

"I'm all right."

"Is Will here?"

"He's down at the mill. Been gone about an hour, I reckon."

"May we talk?"

"Yes John, but remember, please don't tell anyone what I tell you."

"Why certainly, you know I won't."

Katharine sat on the bench and placed her hands on her lap. She was about to speak when a sudden gust of wind blew across the porch. It passed through her long brown hair, several strands blowing against her face. She took her hand to push the hair back into place, repositioning herself on the bench. John leaned upon the porch railing while he listened to Katharine.

"When Will came for me the other day, I felt afraid although I tried not to show it. I couldn't believe that he would ever try to hurt me. That night, after drinking so heavily, was the only time he has ever lifted a hand to me. I have never experienced that much anger from Will since I have known him. It was like someone else had taken control over him completely. All I could think about was just to get away from him that night. On the ride from your house, Will didn't have much to say. We agreed to talk when he had finished eating and taking a nap. Will claims that he knows nothing about the baby or who the mother is. He finally confessed about seeing that woman in Atlanta."

"Is that all he would tell you?"

"Yes, he told me that he didn't know anything about the night you found Kyzer on the porch. He apologized for mistreating me and tearing up the house. He promised it would never happen again."

"That's good to know," John said.

"He told me that the affair is over between them. She is the wife of an Atlanta businessman. They met when he delivered a load of lumber to their estate."

"Let's hope that it is really over," John said.

"What else can I say? Will won't talk about it," Katharine said. "Now, just to mention it makes him angry."

"Your secret is safe with me, Katharine. We'll have to pay attention to any further developments," he said. "Well, I need to get back for my afternoon appointments. See you in a few days."

While John drove back into town, he couldn't help but think

about the possibility of Will's involvement in this situation. He openly admitted to the affair with the Atlanta woman. Could she be the mystery woman seen by the proprietor of the livery stable, Lucas Finch? Was Will Jackson the father of Kyzer? It was definitely something to think about as John drew closer to home.

The day before the Kelsey family was to leave Jonesboro, Dr. John was finishing some paperwork at his desk. He heard the door to the office quietly open. He was surprised to see the girl standing there awaiting his acknowledgment.

"Hello there. What brings you here? You're not sick, are you?"

"No sir, Dr. Kelsey. I's not sick. I just needs to talk to you," she said.

"Please, come on in and have a seat. I'll be right with you," he said.

She closed the door while she slowly walked toward the chair by the desk and sat looking at the floor. "Thank you, sir, for seeing me," she said.

"How's Mrs. Rachel?"

"She fine."

"Now, how may I help you, Delilah?"

Big brown eyes glancing toward him, she placed her hands on her lap across a pale yellow muslin dress. She paused for a moment waiting for the words to come. "Kyzer … … … … my baby."

"What's that you say?" John couldn't believe what he had heard.

"Yes sir, I say Kyzer my baby. I's left him on the porch that night."

"Dear God in Heaven! Girl, how can that be?"

"I look at my baby. He white. I's scared, so scared. Don't know what to do."

"Oh my God, Delilah, what has happened to you?"

"My baby, I name him Kyzer. I know he don't have a chance 'round here lessen you and Miss Eliz'beth take him. Please sir, will you take my baby?"

"Delilah, who did this to you? You've got to tell me. I promise to help you get through this."

Tears were rolling down the face of the seventeen year old light skinned negress. She sat there trembling in the chair. Once again, she made her plea. "Please take my baby, sir."

"All right, Delilah, listen to me. Please try to control yourself and tell me exactly what happened. Don't be afraid. No one's going to hurt you anymore," the doctor said.

Relaxing somewhat in the chair, she began her story as Dr. John listened intently.

"Dr. Kelsey, I's a good girl. I stays close to my Mama Rose while we work for Mrs. Rachel. One day, 'fore my mama dies, I's in the barn milking the cow. I see Mrs. Rachel's son lookin' at me all the time. His name Mister Matt Petersen. She call him Matthew. All at once, he standin' there with his pants dropped to his knees. He say 'come here, gal, you gonna make me feel good.' I say 'oh, no sir, I can't.' He say 'oh yes, you are,' and he slips off his belt and beats me. He make me do things to him. He hears somebody comin' so he push me down in the hay and holds his hand over my mouth saying 'You better not make a sound, you hear?' The milk pail gets knocked over while he slip out through the side door of the barn. That night, I's scolded by Mrs. Rachel for spillin' the milk. Some time ago, after my mama die, we's alone in the house one day while Mrs. Rachel gone. That day, he take me on his bed and force hisself inside me. I cry out and he put his hand on my throat and he say 'If you scream or dare tell anybody, I'll kill you. I promise, I will do it, gal'. Later on, he leave home for a long time. I's relieved for a while. I hear Mrs. Rachel say that Mister workin' on a river boat in New Orleans."

"Do you need a drink of water?" Dr. John asked.

"No, thank you sir. I finish tellin' you 'bout my troubles. Last summer, Mister come home unexpected for a few days. I's scared again. I stay close to Mrs. Rachel. One night, he drunk after Mrs. Rachel bedtime. I's in the kitchen puttin' away the supper dishes and I hears the door open and shut. There stand Mister lookin' wild. I's back up against the wall while he grab me around my shoulders and push hisself on me pinning my arms backward. I's want to scream, but scared to do it. He tear the front of my dress open while he throw me down onto the kitchen table. With one hand on my throat, he begin to undo his pants while he pushes them down. Then, he lift up my skirts and he on top of me. I just lay there. If he kill me, I don't care. I lay there quiet and let him do his business. Not long, he through and fall into the chair. I hears him breathin' hard and pullin' his pants back on. 'Nigger, if you ever tell anybody, I swear I kill you'. He stagger out the door and that the last time I see him. Later on, I feels sick and find out, I's gonna have a baby. My Kyzer, he like his father, he white. I want my boy to have a better chance than me. That why I's plead with you to take him and raise him white. Never tell anybody, 'cause nobody know. Mrs. Rachel, she don't know I have a baby, her grandson. Mrs. Rachel git her neighbor girl to come sit with me. She think I's sick. Girl named Lettie. She help me have my baby. Lettie say, 'Oh Dee, you's got a white baby — a boy'. But I don't tell her who his daddy is. She don't know. She say she won't tell."

Stunned, John didn't know what to say. He was shocked beyond belief at Delilah's confession. What could he really do to help her? He prayed silently as he sat there, bewildered and distraught. During his professional career, John had never encountered such a uniquely surprising predicament, although young female slaves had babies all the time. So many of them were often fathered by their masters.

"Delilah, I'm so sorry, but we just can't take the baby. We're moving to Virginia tomorrow."

With that, she broke down into uncontrollable sobs as she bent forward clutching her stomach and rocking up and down in the chair. "Please help me," she cried.

The concerned doctor reached into his coat pocket and offered Delilah his handkerchief. John Kelsey sat there at his desk as he thought about the surprising news he had just heard from the trembling girl. Oh, he knew about Matthew Petersen all right, only too well. Rachel's boy had quite a reputation around town. Matt was always the favorite topic of discussion of local gossip. With handsome good looks and his seemingly uncontrollable lust and desire for women, he had ruined many young girls. That was common knowledge. Coupled together with his taste for fine whiskey, it appeared there was no stopping him from his so-called amorous adventures.

John remembered delivering at least two of Matt's bastards only a few years back. The most prominent just happened to be the Methodist preacher's daughter, Miss Lida Rose Greenwood. It was rumored at the time that Matt had to pay a considerable sum to her father from his recent gambling winnings to save him from the fate of an upcoming rape charge. Although Matt Petersen contended that his romantic encounter with the daughter was consensual, everyone knew better. The final outcome turned out like a wildfire roaring through a hay field. That summer, Pastor Greenwood sent Lida Rose and her blond headed baby boy to live with relatives in Boston, and the Jonesboro Methodist Church got a new steeple. Doctor Kelsey scratched his head while Delilah sat waiting on his answer. Could Matt Petersen be capable of such an accusation?

"Let me think about it and see what I can do."

"Thank you, sir. God bless you and my Kyzer." Delilah closed the door on her way out.

The next morning, John awoke early. Today was moving day. The rising sun continued to awaken the rest of the town. It was a beautiful morning in May with birds chirping and the occasional barking of a dog. The events of the past week had been quite busy leading up to the Kelsey's final day in Jonesboro. The family had been given a farewell party at the hospital, a reception at the church, and numerous friends had stopped by the house during the week. Dr. John made sure that the furniture and personal belongings had been loaded and delivered to the railway station in Atlanta for transport. Just yesterday, he sold ol' Dan to Lucas Finch. He was saddened to see them drive away. George, Mary, Will, and Katharine had joined Elizabeth and John for breakfast while Vanie prepared her last meal for them. Vanie was in a quiet mood this morning. She knew that she would be moving to the McArdle house. John and Elizabeth realized this move would be quite an adjustment for all of them. They would definitely miss Sylvania. Susannah and Rob were accustomed to the servants, Aurelia and Jesse at Kellwood, but John could only imagine how much they would miss Vanie in the days ahead.

Elizabeth had Kyzer in her arms while she entered the parlor and took a seat beside John. She looked beautiful in her pale blue Sunday dress while she opened the family Bible that she had failed to pack. John recognized that Kyzer had on one of Rob's baby togs as he held their new baby boy.

"What are you writing, Mama?" Susannah asked.

"I'm adding your new brother's name to our Bible. Now, you see, we will have a record of his birth," she answered.

"May I see the page?"

"Yes, Susannah. See, I have written his name here. *Kyzer John Kelsey born April 25, 1841 — Clayton County, Jonesboro, Georgia.*"

After tearful goodbyes, Dr. John and his family loaded into the wagon with Will and Katharine who would drive them to the railway station. When it pulled away, they waved to George, Mary, and Vanie who remained standing on the porch. They continued to keep each other in sight until the end of Main Street when the wagon turned onto the Jonesboro Road. Standing there along the road, Delilah waved goodbye. John was the only one who noticed the tears in her eyes. His thoughts were for her while he kept Delilah's secret deeply embedded within his soul.

At last, John had made his final decision. He would try his best to grant Delilah's plea by taking her son and raising him as white. John realized that now Kyzer's destiny was also his destiny, while they drove to Atlanta that day. They would have to hurry now to make the train by noon.

CHAPTER 3

Kellwood Plantation was originally a one hundred twenty-three acre tobacco farm in Chesterfield County near the small town of Hastings, Virginia. Hastings was located about sixty miles south of Richmond near Petersburg. Toward the east lay the James River. The area and climate of the region proved suitable for tobacco farming there and it flourished.

John's father, Robert, was the first generation of the Kelsey family to settle near Hastings. While a young man, he learned how to grow successfully large crops of tobacco from his father in Richmond. After several years on his own, he purchased sufficient acreage to increase his tobacco fields. Business soon became extremely profitable with the continual demand for tobacco prevalent in regions all over the north and south. Robert Kelsey eventually made his own good fortune when he formed the Kelsey Tobacco Company of Virginia.

During the past winter, Papa Kelsey died suddenly with an apparent heart attack. He had been in declining health for the last two years, enough that his tobacco company, including over one hundred acres, had to be sold. The main house and twelve remaining acres had been deeded to his devoted widow, Sarah Louise Johnson Kelsey, now mistress of Kellwood. She was alone except for her house servants, Aurelia and her boy, Jesse. Sarah was eagerly anticipating the time when her son, John, and his family would be coming to live at Kellwood.

"Look yonder, Jesse," Aurelia said gazing over her wash pots. "Bless my soul, I believe that's Mister John a comin' down the road. Run and tell Miz Sarah they's nearly here." Aurelia left her soiled apron there on the ground while she made her way toward the front of the house. In a few moments, she was joined on the veranda by Sarah, rushing through the main door to stand by Aurelia.

John's wagon turned onto the oak tree lined drive while Susannah and Rob waved to Nana. John could remember, as a small boy, the big house where he played countless times on the landing of the upper front portico. He imagined being a military general and spent hours spying out the land for the enemy. Often he would give the order to fire the cannons to stop the threat of an imposing attack. At other times, he would day dream or sit back and take in visually all the beauty of the land viewed from the second floor vantage point. He found it to be the best place to play when it was raining and he couldn't go outdoors. It was so serenely beautiful there on the grounds with the towering white columned Greek Revival called Kellwood presiding over the magnificent landscape. The wagon stopped near the front steps. As John looked more closely, he observed the neglect of the house over the past couple of years when he had last visited. Later, he would get a few shutter boards replaced, and fresh paint would do wonders. Right now, he wanted to jump down and hug his mama.

"Hello, Mama," John said while he lifted her and swung her around three times.

"Now, I'm dizzy, son. Put me down this very instant," she said.

He kissed her cheek and made sure she was steady on her feet. Susannah and Rob were next with their hugs while John helped Elizabeth and Kyzer from the wagon.

"Hello, my dear Elizabeth. Welcome home to Kellwood," Sarah said. "So, this is baby Kyzer. What a fine looking boy."

"Good to see you, Mister John, Miss Elizabeth. You chillin' sure has grown," Aurelia said. "I gets Jesse to help with your things."

"Why Aurelia, you're as pretty as ever," John said.

"Aw, Mister John, get on from here. I's an old lady now. Jesse soon be fifteen."

"Fifteen, I can hardly believe it," he said.

"That boy's never 'round when you needs him. Y'all go on in the house while I go find Jesse."

"Let me take the baby," Sarah said as she motioned everyone into the house and took Kyzer from Elizabeth.

A much younger John recalled sliding down the bannister of the winding staircase while they stood in the great hallway. He imagined Kyzer doing the same thing one day.

"John and Elizabeth, this is now your home as well as mine. Please make yourselves comfortable. There are a couple of rooms upstairs from which you are welcomed to choose for your bedroom. Susannah already knows her room. John, you know Rob always stays in your old room. Will the baby sleep with you?" Sarah asked.

"For the time being, that will be fine," John said. "Later, we can put him into another room, or he can just bunk in with Rob. Don't worry about it now, Mama."

"Aurelia should have Jesse around to help you before long," Sarah said. "In the meantime, go upstairs and refresh yourselves. Children, you may want to play outside. I'm going to lie down for a while. Remember, supper's at six. I declare, Kyzer is such a good baby." She handed him to Elizabeth before they walked upstairs.

Aurelia found Jesse out back and made him unload the Kelsey belongings into the hallway, pull the wagon around to the barn, and unhitch the mules. After settling in later that same evening, the family met in the parlor.

"Mama, in the morning after breakfast, I'll be going back into Hastings. I have to report to the infirmary, return the borrowed wagon, and make arrangements at the railway station to have all our things delivered. Don't know how long I'll be," John said.

"What all do you have?" she asked.

"Maybe a couple of wagon loads, I reckon. I'll need to take one of the horses along for my ride back."

"Certainly, just tell Jesse. Now, about the house, you can put your things anywhere you please. There's plenty of space in the attic if something needs to be taken out and stored, you hear? I really don't mind," Sarah said.

"Mama, you'll remember our house in Jonesboro was owned by Elizabeth's parents, including many of the furnishings. Well, George McArdle already has plans to turn it into a boarding house. He always has a keen eye for business when it comes to making money," John said.

"Your father also had a good business sense. I miss him so much," Sarah said.

"I know, Mama. I miss him, too," John said.

"You were married for a long time, weren't you?" Elizabeth asked.

"Yes dear, almost thirty-seven years. I married Robert in this very room on March 11, 1804. In the morning, we can take a walk out by the cemetery, if you want."

"We'll see. Right now, I'm nearly exhausted. John darling, we need to get the children ready for bed," Elizabeth said.

"Ring for Aurelia if you need anything. She stays in the

small room off the kitchen since Robert has been gone," Sarah said.

"Good night, Mama," John said. "Are you ready for bed?"

"I'm going to read my Bible for a while. Aurelia will help me to bed. I hope you all sleep well. Good night."

Early in the morning before breakfast, John took a walk to his father's grave. The Kelsey Family Cemetery was located there on the grounds about three hundred yards from the big house. The grass had nearly covered the grave while it still awaited the missing headstone. John remembered his mother saying that it was due to ship from Richmond within the next few weeks. He stood there looking down at the other two graves. John thought about the sisters he had never known. He read the inscription on their markers — *Zulah Caroline born Jan. 15, 1805 - died Jan. 17, 1805* and *Anne Marie born Jul. 19, 1806 - died Mar. 28, 1808*. John sat on the bench and recalled that his father had constructed the little family cemetery just before he was born.

The joy and happiness felt by Robert and Sarah Kelsey after the birth of their first baby daughter was quickly diminished in sorrow. On the second morning of her life, Zulah was dead. Sarah found the lifeless little infant in her crib. She was buried in a plot near the flower garden. A year later, Anne Marie was born. She was a beautiful child, they said, with long black ringlets and big blue eyes. When she was two years old, she died from scarlet fever, and Robert and Sarah were heartbroken. They buried her alongside Zulah's unmarked grave.

In the next few weeks, Robert Kelsey traveled all the way to Richmond on the train to have a special monument created by the Pennbrook Monument Company. He ordered a large stone cut from granite and engraved with the name KELSEY. At the center of the stone, an urn was to be mounted on the top for flowers. On either side, there were to be statues of beautifully winged angel cherubs. Robert anticipated the completed structure would be truly magnificent.

The first pieces to arrive home came within six weeks. These were the inscribed headstones that were placed on the grave site of the two girls. After another few weeks, the large monument and the two angel statues arrived at the railway station in Hastings. It took a team of mules and eight darkies to unload all the statuary from the train and onto the wagon. Mr. Robert made the decision that the large stone would be delivered first, followed by the angels on the second trip. Although each piece was crated separately, special care had to be taken to insure that nothing would be broken or damaged. When everything was in place at Kellwood, Robert Kelsey had a local iron works company to construct a black wrought iron fence. The twenty foot perimeter fencing, along with the ornately designed gate bearing a golden letter K, evolved into the little cemetery. Robert granted his wife's wish by having a small magnolia tree planted at each corner outside the fence.

On a Sunday afternoon in August, several family members, along with a few close friends, gathered at Kellwood for an informal dedication of the new addition. Later, that same afternoon, Sarah had to be put to bed. The activities of the day proved to be too much for her. That night, August 14, 1808, John Robert Kelsey was born.

Jesse suddenly stood outside the cemetery gate.

"Good mornin', Mister John. My mammy says to tell you it almost time for breakfast, sir."

"Thank you, Jesse. I'll be along in a moment. Could you have a horse saddled for me to take to town this morning after breakfast?"

"Yes suh, Daisy be waitin' for you in the barn. She Massa Robert's favorite mare. I hitch the mules up and you can just tie Daisy to the back of the wagon when you's ready."

John thought about ol' Dan while he headed toward the house. He had already prepared himself for the busy day that lay ahead for him. He set out for Hastings soon after breakfast. The task of opening baggage and the few small crates fell to the women of Kellwood. Aurelia helped the mother-in-law and daughter-in-law while they unpacked and put everything away. A much larger job awaited them when the furniture and all the other things would arrive.

Elizabeth asked Aurelia to take charge of Susannah and Rob while she took a stroll with Sarah. They stopped and took a seat on the bench inside the cemetery. Elizabeth held Kyzer on her lap.

"I come here every day, Elizabeth. I know Robert's not here, but I feel drawn to him at the place of his physical remains," Sarah said.

"That's understandable. I know John misses his father. We've talked about him several times," Elizabeth said. "I'm sure it's been really difficult for you."

"Robert left me quite well, but it's been lonely here with just Aurelia and Jesse. I'm so grateful that you and John will be living with me," Sarah said while she began to weep.

"There, there Mrs. Kelsey, just let it all out. It'll be all right."

"Thank you, darling girl. You might as well start calling me Sarah or even Nana."

"I'll call you Nana," Elizabeth said.

"Now, precious, you'll have to tell me all about the baby."

"Not much to tell. Kyzer was left abandoned on our porch. We still don't know the whereabouts of his father or mother, who they are, or even where he came from. John and I adopted him, and we will be rearing him along with Susannah and Rob."

"I'm so sorry for your loss of baby Michael. I felt completely helpless, being so far away," Sarah said.

"Now, I try to believe that God took our son from us in order that we could take Kyzer. John has already said that we will rear him as our own. He's given up trying to find the parents."

"Well, I think the baby looks like both of you. With your

dark hair and John's dark skin, he looks a lot like Rob when he was a baby."

"You think so? Look here, he has a little birthmark on his back," Elizabeth said.

"So, I see," Nana said as Kyzer began to fret a little. "I smell rain in the air. We'd better get back to the house."

Several weeks passed while the Kelsey family settled into their new lifestyle at Kellwood. Two wagon loads of furniture and personal belongings had been delivered to the estate. John's desk and chair, medical supplies, and trunks bearing clothing, china, crystal, and silver arrived in good condition. Each item had been unpacked and put away into all the newly created areas in the house. Elizabeth placed her china cabinet in the dining room directly across from Sarah's. John stored the present furniture of one small bedroom in the attic and converted the room to an office by adding his desk and chair.

It wasn't long until things were more or less routine. Aurelia did the cooking, washing, and housekeeping. Jesse helped her prepare the food, milk the cow, and take care of the horses. Sarah was pleased to have John assist her in making decisions necessary in running the household. Elizabeth took care of her children, along with Sarah and Aurelia's help. John would take Susannah every morning to the public school house on his way to work while they both rode horseback on Daisy. In the afternoon, Jesse had the buggy ready for Elizabeth to drive into town to pick up Susannah after school. Dr. John kept busy at Collins Infirmary by seeing his new patients and assisting the young Dr. Geoffrey Vincent, the resident doctor.

The headstone arrived on a Saturday. John and Jesse took the wagon to the train station to collect the small crate. That afternoon, John placed the marble marker at the head of his father's grave. The inscription simply read — *Robert Thomas Kelsey — 1783-1840.*

◀▶ ◀▶

Summer days turned into weeks, and the weeks passed into months. It was now December, and soon it would be Christmas. Returning to Jonesboro wasn't going to happen this year, but an alternate plan was in the works. Elizabeth was overjoyed that her parents would travel by train to be at Kellwood in time for Christmas Day. She had also received a letter from Katharine with hint of a special surprise and promise to come. Hopefully, Will could take a few days off work to come with her. Thoughts of the first Christmas at Kellwood with the entire family made Elizabeth very happy. It would be the first time to see her parents since the move from Jonesboro.

The snow was falling that morning on Christmas Eve. A light dusting of white lay on the ground while the smell of bacon and eggs sizzled from the frying pan in the kitchen. The aroma quickly spread throughout, waking the sleeping house. Aurelia was busy at her work while Jesse came in with a fresh pail of milk. Susannah sat on the bed in the bedroom of John and Elizabeth while they were dressing. Kyzer was still asleep as well as Rob. The McArdles were waking up in the guest room while Katharine shook Will in Susannah's room in an attempt to awaken him. It wasn't long until everyone assembled in the dining room. Sarah remained in her room until time for breakfast. She was the last to be seated while she took her place at the table.

"It is so good to have everyone here. George and Mary, Will and Katharine, I hope you rested well last night after your arrival yesterday. Enjoy your breakfast. We have much to do today."

It was part of the Kelsey family tradition at Kellwood to cut the tree and place it into the parlor on Christmas Eve. The task had always been performed by Robert Kelsey so this year, Sarah asked John to have that honor in memory of his father.

John and Will pulled on their boots and fastened their coats while donning hats and gloves in preparation to leave. The men walked toward the barn where they met Jesse who finished putting the bridle on Daisy. John picked up an axe while he and Will headed into the nearby woods. It was their job to find the perfect Christmas tree, cut it down, and have Daisy pull it back to the house.

From the branches of the old magnolia tree out back, Jesse sawed several small bunches of leaves. He carried them inside to his mother. Aurelia attached them to the main staircase bannister with pieces of baling wire. It was Sarah who always positioned the large red velvet bows into their proper place among the magnolia leaves. Elizabeth and Katharine sat on the parlor floor sorting through a box of old paper ornaments and smaller red velvet bows.

The heavy front door swung open, amid the fierce blowing snow, while Will and John pulled the eight foot scotch pine into the great hallway. Moments after a brief rest, they placed the tree into the handmade stand in the parlor. The women began their task as they added the decorations. Additional candlesticks and candelabra adorned with red berries, holly, and mistletoe were placed throughout the hallway, parlor, and dining room. It would prove to be a beautiful sight that night whenever the candles were lit. In the meantime, Will and John relaxed in the parlor while the women left for the kitchen to help Aurelia with her cooking and baking for the Christmas Eve dinner. Throughout the meal, it was all Katharine could do to keep silent and hold her secret surprise.

Christmas morning found Susannah and Rob the first to arrive downstairs. Under the tree, there was a new doll for Susannah and a broomstick horse for Rob. They had emptied their stockings which hung from the fireplace mantel filled with apples, oranges, walnuts, and peppermint candy. On the hearth lay a small stocking on top of a blue baby blanket for eight month old Kyzer. By this time, the rest of the family gathered there waiting for Sarah. She arrived at the doorway wearing her favorite Sunday dress while she handed her Bible to John, asking him to read the Christmas story from the

Gospel According to Luke. When he finished, Sarah took a seat at her harpsichord while she played and led the family in the singing of "Silent Night, Holy Night." With the last gift opened, Katharine stood near the beautifully decorated Christmas tree to finally present her surprise.

"I feel so happy and blessed to be able to share this time at Christmas with all of you, the ones I hold so dear to my heart. With grateful appreciation to Sarah for having us all here at Kellwood, thank you for your kind hospitality. For my dear sister and her husband, John, and the children, Susannah, Rob, and now little Kyzer, what joy you always bring to my life. To my dear parents who have been there to guide me along life's pathway, thank you so much. And lastly, to my dear Will, for his promise to start anew while we both try to forgive and forget the past, I love you, my darling husband. I wish you all a very Merry Christmas as I tell you about my greatest gift, and Will already knows this … … … I"m pregnant! The baby is due at the end of the summer."

Joyous laughter and shouting rang out and filled the room while everyone embraced and offered their special blessings and congratulations to the happy couple. Christmas had indeed come to Kellwood that year.

Looking back, John knew he had made the right decision by adopting Kyzer into his family.

CHAPTER 4

In the summer of 1842, the *Dixie Belle* left the Port of Natchez, starting its journey down the mighty Mississippi. The gigantic paddle of the river boat churned the rolling river, causing a fine mist of water spray to rise high above the revolving wheel.

At a poker table in the saloon sat Matt Petersen. His medium length blond hair fell across his forehead accenting his bright blue eyes. He was dressed in black gaberdine trousers with a matching waistcoat. A powder blue silk shirt lay open down to the top of his unbuttoned black satin vest. He had removed his neck tie which he placed inside his coat pocket. At thirty-two, Matt was still perceived as an attractive and handsome man. However, his alcoholic lifestyle was beginning to take a toll on him. Small lines were now formed around his eyes and mouth.

A game of five card stud was about to begin whenever Monsieur de la Valois arrived at the table. Matt had met Charles in a café in Natchez and invited him to join in a game of poker whenever the river boat was underway. Matt was growing impatient with the tardiness of his new friend until he spotted him in the doorway. A glance across the crowded room revealed the sudden disappearance of the woman Monsieur Charles recently held in his arms. Matt knew her as a former lover, a dancer named Lily Lamour.

"Pardon. Good afternoon, monsieurs. I apologize for being late," he said approaching the table.

"Gentlemen, may I present Monsieur Charles de la Valois," Matt said. "Charles, this is Louie Cordova, Wiley Hagood, and Joe Mack Heaton, all friends of mine."

"A pleasure for me to make your acquaintance," Charles replied.

"What did he say?" Joe Mack asked Wiley.

"Pull up a chair, Charles. Let's order another round of drinks before we start," Matt said. "I could use another whiskey."

The poker games continued all afternoon. The men halted briefly for a quick supper, resuming play that lasted well past midnight. It turned out that Matt was the big winner, taking the table for a mere five grand as witnessed by the four men. By this time, Matt was so drunk that he had to be carried to his room by Louie and Wiley. Joe Mack remembered the time, around two in the morning.

The next morning, Matt Petersen was found lying on his back across the bed, wallet missing, and his throat slit ear to ear. Monsieur de la Valois and Lily Lamour were not to be found on board. Word quickly spread about the murder while the river boat continued its journey down the Mississippi River. Soon after the grisly discovery, Angelina, another dancer, came forward with the information that she had overheard in her dressing room — Lily plotting with the Frenchman to rob and kill Matt for his refusal to marry her. It seems Lily had planted Charles in the café in Natchez to meet up hopefully with Matt. After the invitation for Charles to board the river boat with Matt, the plan for revenge became the plot for murder. It seemed so perfect, since Matt had initiated the poker game in the first place. In part of the conversation overheard by Angelina, Lily assured the Frenchman that certainly she could swim. Logically, it seemed to the Captain of the *Dixie Belle* that following the brutal killing and at some point during the cruise the two would have to go overboard and try to swim to the river bank. Whether they made it or not, nobody knew. The Frenchman and the dancer were never seen again.

In Jonesboro, Rachel Petersen received the devastating news. Her only son, Matthew was found murdered on a river boat somewhere along the Mississippi; and she, to her credit, was totally shocked and grief stricken. Delilah remained at her side, day and night, while numerous friends came and went during their sympathetic visits. When his body was released for burial, Rachel had Matt brought into her home and laid out in the parlor. Matt looked peaceful in a blue suit as he lay in the pine coffin. The undertaker had done his best by placing a dark blue silk scarf around Matt's neck to offer concealment of his fatal wound.

For the next two days, a wake was held. Those in attendance were George and Mary McArdle as well as Katharine who sat each night with Mrs. Rachel. It was slightly uncomfortable for Katharine during this time. She felt the need to be with Mrs. Rachel even though her baby was due anytime. Earlier, George McArdle sent a telegram to John and Elizabeth informing them of Matt's death. The funeral was set for Friday at three o'clock. It was to be a grave side service.

Delilah walked over to the coffin with Mrs. Rachel after the undertaker had removed the lid. Rachel bent down to kiss her boy while Delilah stood trembling at her side. Only for a moment, Delilah looked closely upon the face of the father of her baby. She was truly sorry for Mrs. Rachel, but Mister would never hurt her again. She retreated to a corner and took a seat while Mrs. Rachel talked with Doc Harlan. After a while, Delilah's hands began to tremble in her lap while she sat in the darkened corner of the parlor. She saw the Kelseys enter the room. She swallowed, producing a big lump in her throat. She looked at Dr. John Kelsey standing there with Miss Elizabeth at his side. She held Kyzer in her arms. The other children were not present. "My baby, my own precious boy," Delilah whispered under her breath.

Rachel stood to greet them as John threw his long arms around her while offering comfort. "I'm truly sorry. We came as soon as we could."

"Thank you for coming. My heart is broken," Rachel said.

Elizabeth hugged Mrs. Rachel as John walked over to the room's darkened corner.

"Hello, Delilah. How are you?"

"I fine."

"We've brought our baby Kyzer with us. Would you like to hold him while we visit with Mrs. Rachel?"

"Oh, yes suh, Dr. Kelsey. I take care of him."

"Let me just get him from Elizabeth and you may take him outside if you want. Kyzer really loves the outdoors."

"Thank you, sir. I be careful with him and I never forget your kindness to me."

After a while, following the visitation, John found Delilah on the back porch rocking her baby. It was time for John and Elizabeth to go. They planned to spend the night with her parents.

"If it's all right with Mrs. Rachel and Miss Elizabeth, I think I may be able to persuade them to have you keep Kyzer for us tomorrow while we attend the funeral."

"Oh, thank you sir. I's want to do that, more than anything."

"Delilah, that will have to be the last time you see him. We'll be leaving early the next morning on the train back to Hastings."

"Dr. Kelsey, I so happy that my Kyzer, your Kyzer. God will grow him into a very fine man. I just knows it."

After the funeral, a supper meal was prepared by her neighbors and members of her church's congregation for Mrs. Rachel at her home. She invited John and Elizabeth, among others, to take the meal with her. John quickly accepted her gracious invitation, also knowing this opportunity gave Delilah more time to see her son. When the time finally came for John and Elizabeth to leave with Kyzer, Delilah excused herself from the room. She quickly ran up the stairs to the front bedroom and drew the curtains back, her hands fumbling with the tiebacks. Delilah stood at the window with her eyes taking in every movement as she watched the Kelsey family as they were leaving. While John and Elizabeth walked toward the street, John took the boy and placed him facing backward on his shoulder so that Delilah could see the face of her son. She began to wave frantically, trying to draw Kyzer's attention to her. She would always believe in her heart that he really saw her standing there waving to him.

Then, the tears came.

◆▶◀▶

It was two weeks after the funeral, and Katharine had her baby in the Jonesboro Hospital. Doc Harlan delivered a healthy boy weighing almost eight pounds on August 2, 1842. The baby was named William Walter Jackson, and he would be called Walt.

Katharine could hardly wait until Elizabeth got the news from her letter. Will and Katharine were overjoyed at the birth of their son.

CHAPTER 5

Elizabeth sat alone on the back porch as she read the letter from her mother. She could hardly believe that it had been almost five years since she had last seen her at the funeral of Matt Petersen. Her mother was faithful to write several times during the year to keep her informed of the news around Jonesboro. Elizabeth was happy to know that her mother and father were in good health. Vanie was doing well, sending her love to Miss Susannah, Massa Rob, and little Kyzer. Despite her present condition, Katharine and five year old Walt were doing well. Two more doctors had recently been hired at the General Hospital, and Doc Harlan was considering his retirement. Sadly, the letter ended with the news of the death of Mrs. Rachel Petersen. She died from pneumonia during the winter around the end of February. Her servant girl, Delilah, was sent to live with a family in Atlanta.

A scream. It grew louder, coming from inside the house. Aurelia suddenly emerged from the back door onto the porch.

"Miss Elizabeth, Miss Elizabeth, you gotta come quick! Something awful done happened to Miz Sarah."

"Where, Aurelia?"

"She layin' almost at the bottom of the stairs."

"Oh, my God," Elizabeth yelled as she ran toward the doorway, her letter falling to the floor. She ran up the grand staircase where Sarah lay motionless, Aurelia was right behind her. Elizabeth dropped by Nana's side, leaning upon her breast to listen while she felt her wrist for a pulse. She didn't feel anything. Sarah's twisted body lay on her back, crumpled against the bannister with her legs in an upward position, one arm dangling through the railing. Her head was pressed down against the step, turned sideways. Elizabeth thought she heard a moan, but Nana didn't appear to be breathing.

" God Almighty! Miss Elizabeth, I just turn in time to see her fall down all these stairs. What we gonna do?"

"Where's Jesse? Get Jesse to take the buggy and go for Dr. John at the infirmary. He is to say that he is needed at home and to come quickly. I'll stay here with her," Elizabeth said. "Please, hurry."

"Yes'um, I gets Jesse to go right now."

Elizabeth held on to Nana, talking quietly to her and knowing she didn't dare attempt to move her. All she could do was to wait on the doctor to get there. Still, there was no response from Sarah. Elizabeth was crying while she sat there waiting on the staircase.

The front door slammed back against the wall as John burst into the great hallway. He saw his mother lying there on the staircase with Elizabeth at her side. He rushed immediately toward them, praying that everything would be all right. Had Sarah just fainted there on the steps? Dr. John knelt as he touched his mother in several places, ending his examination with his hand placed under her chin. He tried to turn her head slightly, then stopped, withdrawing his hand. "She's gone," he said. "Her neck has been broken." Without another word, he picked her up into his arms and carried her up the stairs and placed her on the bed. Elizabeth followed her husband and stood at the doorway of the bedroom in silence. "Someone needs to go get the children from school," he said.

"I'll go, my darling. Be back in just a while," Elizabeth said. She walked over to him and put her arms around him, kissed him, and turned to leave. "John, would you want me to stop by the funeral home on the way and have them come to the house?"

"Yes, that would be fine. Tell Uriah I will come in the morning to make the arrangements."

Reality set in very quickly for John. As a doctor, he had experienced death in many and various ways. However, it felt so different for him now to lose his own mother. He lingered in her bedroom a few moments longer and retreated to his upstairs office for a brandy. He remained there until he realized that Elizabeth was home with the children. John came down and gathered his family in the parlor.

"Where's Nana?" Susannah asked, noticing her absence.

"She's in Heaven. Your Nana had a terrible accident today, and now she's gone to be with Papa Kelsey," John said.

They all cried while they hugged and tried to comfort one another. Aurelia came into the room and announced the meal time, but no one had much of an appetite. It was a sad day for everyone. It was nearly dusk when Uriah Priester arrived at Kellwood for Sarah. John had Elizabeth and the children remain in the parlor with the door closed until the body was removed from the house. When John returned inside, he passed by the dining room. Aurelia was gathering the dishes from supper.

"Aurelia, Miss Elizabeth told me that you witnessed my mother's fall. Could you tell me what happened? Please, have a seat at the table," John said.

"Thank you, sir. Oh, Dr. Kelsey, I's so sorry. I never should have left her side. It all my fault." Aurelia pulled the bottom of her apron upward to wipe her watering eyes.

"It's all right, Aurelia, I'm not blaming you. Just tell me what you remember."

"I's takin' Miz Sarah upstairs for her afternoon nap, just like I always do. When we's almost to the top of the stairs, Miz Sarah say, 'Aurelia, I forgot my knitting bag. Would you get it for me?' Yes'um. I's nearly to the bottom when I hears her scream out. I turns around to see her fall backward and tumble down the stairs. I runs to the back porch to get Miss Elizabeth."

"Was she already falling when you saw her?"

"Yes suh, she already fallin' when I turns around. I's can't believe she gone."

"Thank you, Aurelia. That'll be all for right now," John said.

John opened the door to the parlor where Elizabeth and the children were waiting. He spent the rest of the evening with them while he sat on the floor playing games with Susannah, Rob, and six year old Kyzer.

On the morning of the funeral, Uriah Priester delivered the body of Mrs. Sarah within close proximity to the gate of the Kelsey Family Cemetery promptly at eleven o'clock. The glass paneled black hearse was drawn by four black horses. Each horse had a large black ostrich feather attached to its head. On the white pine coffin lay a spray of greenery interspersed with white lilies. Earlier that morning, Mr. Priester sent two boys to Kellwood to dig the grave. Two wide oak planks and two lengths of rope lay across the open grave.

Dr. Geoffrey Vincent assisted John, Rob, Jesse, Priester, and Richard Braxton from the nearby Chandalar Plantation while they slid the coffin from the rear of the hearse. It was carried about thirty yards toward the gate and then placed onto the planks extending over the grave. Priester, the undertaker, laid the flowers aside and removed the lid while the family and friends took their final viewing. Afterward, replacing the lid, Priester nailed the coffin shut with the small hammer and nails he carried in his coat pocket.

John stood with Elizabeth at his side while she held onto Kyzer's hand. Susannah and Rob stood in front of them. Next to John was Dr. Vincent and his wife. Across from them was Richard Braxton and his wife, Anne, holding their young daughter. Aurelia and Jesse remained outside the fence with the two grave diggers and Uriah Priester. Several church folk and friends pressed inward at the request of Reverend Will Jennings who began the brief grave side service. 'Dust to dust, ashes to ashes' ... . concluding with the Twenty-third Psalm, 'Surely, goodness and mercy shall follow me, all the days of my life, and I shall dwell in the house of the Lord forever'.

Following the service, the family and friends were asked to return to the house. John remained there with Rob who would not leave his side. Dr. Geoff, along with Mr. Braxton and the undertaker, stood together at the grave site, taking their positions. Priester asked Rob to pull the boards away while the four men bore the weight of the coffin onto the ropes as they lowered Sarah Kelsey into the ground.

"That's all, gentlemen. You may drop the ropes. Everyone may return later after the grave has been filled," Priester said.

Rob thought it sounded like small pebbles being thrown against a barn door while shovels of dirt rained down upon the lid. Such an empty, hollow sound. John placed his hand upon Rob's shoulder as they walked toward the house.

Later that evening, John spotted it. Just a few feet in front of him right there on the stairs. He looked down in disbelief, now staring at his discovery. It was a torn piece of fabric, matching the dress worn by his mother on the day she died. It hung there caught on a loose nail. With all of the excitement of the past three days, surprisingly, no one had even noticed. Not until now. So, that's how it happened. As Sarah was walking up the stairs, her dress must have caught on the nail and whenever she took the next step, the snag simply pulled her over backward, sending her down the staircase. John reached down and pulled the nail and fabric from the step and put them into his pocket. If only he could have made his discovery earlier. He would always remember that the life of his dear mother was given as a result of a simple nail that cost less than a penny.

Six months later, Rob helped his father place the marker on Nana's grave —

Sarah Kelsey — 1786-1847.

Following the death of his mother, John Kelsey at thirty-nine years old, inherited Kellwood and its twelve acres. The next few months were spent in the dispensing of Sarah's personal effects, and making various room changes, thus transforming the household into the home of Dr. John and Mrs. Elizabeth Kelsey. Aurelia even moved back into the servants quarters out back with Jesse.

In the years that followed, Dr. John Kelsey and Dr. Geoffrey Vincent acquired more patients than they had ever anticipated. Elizabeth usually managed her volunteer work at the infirmary whenever she wasn't busy with the children. Susannah, Rob, and Kyzer spent most of their days involved with their school activities while they continued to grow mentally and physically. As far as spiritually, Elizabeth saw to that. She was always quoting the scripture to them, and practically every Sunday found her family in church at the Episcopal Church of the Ascension. Just like their parents, the children all believed in God the Father and Jesus Christ the Son; and for the most part, they tried to live according to the teachings in the Bible. Rob, however, couldn't understand why everyone had to go to church every Sunday. He thought he could worship just as well on the creek bank either fishing or swimming down at Moss Rock Creek.

Susannah had a different idea. She liked to attend the church and the socials. It gave her the chance to be with the boy she loved. At seventeen, she was about to finish school, hoping that Henry Hollis would soon ask her to marry him. After all, he was two years older, working for his father at Hastings Mercantile and extremely handsome. He had kissed her three times already.

At fifteen, Rob had two more years at school, but he already had his sights set on attending Virginia Military Institute at Lexington. He had always been interested in studying about the Revolutionary War and its great battles. Rob promised his father that he would work hard if he could continue his education there and become a soldier. John Kelsey was already putting aside the funding necessary for his son's future.

As for ten year old Kyzer, with a much older sister and brother, he sometimes felt like an only child. He longed to do many of the things that Rob was doing, like secretly smoking rabbit tobacco, or swimming naked in the creek with his friends. He had tried doing to his private parts what he had seen Rob do several times, but nothing happened. How could Rob seem to enjoy something so useless and disgusting? Kyzer was perfectly content to take his slingshot, line up old tobacco tins at the back of the barn, and take them down with his steady hand. He always tried to keep a pocketful of rocks in his pants. With his slingshot kept in his back pocket, he was always ready for unsuspecting birds, rabbits, chipmunks, and squirrels. Sometimes, when it was raining and they couldn't go outside, Susannah and Rob would play games with him. They played hide and go seek, ball and jacks, and checkers. If Susannah and Rob didn't want to play with him, Kyzer usually sat on the back porch steps and whittled with the knife he got for Christmas last year. He had already carved out another slingshot and made lots of spears to throw when he played outside. Still, he looked forward to the day when he would be as big as Rob and Susannah.

After supper on that April evening, Elizabeth surprised Kyzer with a chocolate cake she had baked for his eleventh birthday. When the celebration was nearly over, John and

Elizabeth told him they had a present for him out in the barn. Kyzer was overjoyed to have his very own horse, a year old stallion that was black as midnight.

"That's what I'll call him," he said, "Captain Midnight." He was so happy about his horse. Why weren't Rob and Susannah happy for him? He didn't understand.

"In the morning, we'll saddle him up; and you can go for a ride, son," John said as he and Elizabeth returned inside the house.

"You always get everything," Susannah blurted out.

"Yeah, my father never gave me my own horse," Rob said.

"He gives you lots of things," Kyzer said.

"Like what, Kyzer? You just tell me," Rob said.

"Daddy gave you Papa Kelsey's rifle last year. Mama sews dresses for Susannah all the time."

"So what," Susannah said. "You get a birthday cake every year."

"That's not true, and you know it. I don't get a cake every year."

"You do, too."

"I do not."

"Mama and Daddy always cater to your every whim. Their precious little son can do no wrong. They always have to treat you extra special just because you're … .," she stopped.

"Oh yeah, because I'm what?" Kyzer yelled back.

"Shut up, Susannah," Rob shouted.

"Go on, tell me," Kyzer said. "Because I'm what?"

"Because you're adopted!" Susannah began to cry when she realized what she had just said.

"I am not! You're lying … . … you're a big storyteller."

"Oh Kyzer, I'm so sorry. I never meant to say that."

"You don't know. You're just saying that to be ugly. Rob, it's not true, is it? My daddy would have told me."

Rob was speechless. He didn't know what to say. "I don't

know.. … maybe." With that, Kyzer tore out in a hard run to his room, crying all the way.

"Now, you've done it," Rob said to Susannah as they followed Kyzer hurriedly into the house. They could only imagine what they were in for when they saw their mother and father.

"Rob, Susannah, come here you two. What's the matter with your brother? He just came running to his room like he had been crying or something," John said. Susannah just broke down while Rob began to tear up.

"Oh, Dear God, what's the matter with you both?" Elizabeth asked.

"Mama, I was angry at Kyzer; and I told him … … I"m so sorry. I told him he was adopted."

"You said what? Susannah, how could you?" her father asked in disbelief.

"Yes, sir. I didn't mean to, but I told Kyzer … . he was adopted."

"Dear God in Heaven! I thought we all had an understanding about this. You two knew better than to mention this ever, and now it's too late. It's me, God. Let it fall on me. I should have told the boy already. You both will stay here in the parlor until I come back to deal with you. Elizabeth, we need to get upstairs, and I mean right away."

When they entered his room, Kyzer was stretched across his bed, lying on his stomach with his face buried in the pillow, arms folded underneath. He stopped crying momentarily.

"Kyzer, look here, son," John said. Kyzer lay there still and quiet. "Please, listen to me."

"How can you call me your son when Susannah says I'm not?"

"But you are, dear boy. That's what your mother and I want to tell you about. Will you let me talk to you?"

"Why should I? Why should I believe anything you both tell me?"

"Because I love you so much," Elizabeth said weeping, tears falling on his bed.

"Kyzer, please turn over and look at us. I want to tell you honestly how we have come to love you so much. Won't you listen to me?" John asked.

Kyzer rolled over and sat up on the side of the bed. Elizabeth sat beside him, trying to place her arm around him. He leaned away, not wanting her to touch him. "It's all right, son," she said, sitting there, hands folded on her lap. John remained in his position on the floor by the bed.

"Look at me, Kyzer. Look me in the face, and I promise to tell you the truth, God as my witness."

Kyzer slowly raised his head while he looked into the eyes he had thought belonged to his father. At last, he decided to give him a chance. He didn't know what else to do. He waited for words to come that he thought he didn't want to hear again. 'Please God, don't let him tell me that I'm adopted.'

"My dear boy, God has allowed us to keep you for eleven wonderful years. You have been a most special blessing to our lives since we've had you. Remember the Christmas story about the birth of our Lord and Savior, Jesus Christ? Mary was Jesus' mother, God was his holy father, and Joseph was his earthly father. Joseph brought Jesus up just like he was his own son, along with Jesus' other brothers and sisters. That's kind of like our relationship. Did you know that you also have another brother?"

Kyzer looked at John intently, somewhat puzzled, but interested now in what he was saying.

"Elizabeth, your mother, had a baby son named Michael. Michael was born too early and he died. He is buried in Jonesboro. When we go back there sometime, I can show you his grave if you want. We were so sad to lose our little boy. Then, three days later, I hear a baby crying out on our front porch. When I opened the door, there you were, cold and crying in your little blanket. Now, we know that God sent you to us. We searched all around the town, but we never could find your mother and your father. Two weeks later, we moved here to Kellwood, and I just gave up trying to find them. So, you see, that is why we wanted to keep you, to love you, and to rear you along with Susannah and Rob. Kyzer, it is true that you are adopted, but I am telling you that you are loved equally along with our natural children. When you get older, you will understand. We are truly sorry for not telling you ourselves. I intended to tell you a while back, but I got so busy that I didn't. I only ask you to forgive all of us. We all love you so much."

Kyzer rolled off the bed into John's arms. "You never found my mother and father?" he asked.

"Why no, son, we never did."

"Then, you are both my father and mother. I'll just have to forgive Susannah and Rob, won't I?"

"Yes, son, me too. Let's go downstairs. I believe someone's waiting to apologize. You want to hug your mother? She's waiting for you."

CHAPTER 6

Elizabeth headed toward the back porch where she knew she would usually find her husband smoking his pipe in the late afternoon. "Henry is in the parlor waiting to see you," she said from the doorway.

"Tell him, I'll be there shortly. I have a good idea what he wants with me. We'll let him simmer just a bit."

John Kelsey had known Henry's parents, Samuel and Ruth Hollis, for several years. His brother, Charles, now lived in Richmond. Both boys were well educated and didn't seem to mind working at one time or another in the family's hardware business. Henry, the youngest son, was the best looking by far and John Kelsey knew he loved his daughter, Susannah.

Henry Hollis waited nervously in the parlor. The door opened, then closed. John Kelsey walked to his chair near the fireplace and took a seat. "Good afternoon, my boy. You wanted to see me?"

"Yes, sir. How are you, sir?"

"I'm fine. You're looking well, Henry."

"Thank you, sir. Nice weather we're having."

"I can't complain."

"Do you think it might rain, sir?"

"It's possible. Boy, is there something you wanted to ask me?"

"Yes sir, I do. I mean, uh, I want to … . I would like to marry your daughter, sir. I love Susannah. Would you please, sir, give us your blessing?"

"So, that's it. Well, Henry, this is all so sudden. I probably need to think about it for a while."

"Dr. Kelsey, sir, I'd take real good care of her."

"What if I said 'no'?"

"Sir, you just couldn't."

"You're not having to get married, are you? My daughter's not pregnant, is she?"

"Oh, no sir, I would never do anything like that. You know, I'm working for my father down at Hastings Mercantile."

"Yes, I know. What does your father say?"

"It's all right with my folks. They're gonna let us have two rooms above the store where we will live."

"Well, let me see … …"

"Sir, I'll work really hard. Susannah will be well taken care of." Henry stood there anxiously awaiting what seemed to him such a long time. In less than a minute came the decision.

"Henry, in view that these wedding plans are in approval with your parents, and that Susannah is eighteen, I give you my blessing and permission to marry my daughter."

"Oh, thank you, thank you, sir."

"When do you plan for this wedding?"

"In six weeks, around the end of June. May I shake your hand, sir?"

"Why certainly, son. Welcome to the family."

Susannah burst into the room where she had been listening at the door. She landed on her father's lap, presenting him with a big hug and kiss. "Thank you, Daddy. I'm so happy. Come on, Henry, we've got to find Mama and tell her the news."

Three days later, Susannah was in her bedroom trying on her mother's wedding dress.

"I believe a couple of darts in the bodice will suffice, Susannah. The dress will definitely have to be hemmed," Elizabeth said.

"I'm so happy that you are letting me wear your wedding gown," Susannah said. "Will it be all right for us to be married at Kellwood?"

"That would be nice, Susannah. We have about five weeks to finish planning."

Henry Daniel Hollis married Susannah Lee Kelsey on June 30, 1852.

Susannah looked radiant as she descended the grand winding staircase into the great hallway. Her dark blond hair was piled up under a Juliet cap of Venetian lace adorned with gardenia blossoms. She carried a bouquet of white roses tied with a white satin ribbon. Her mother's gown fit Susannah perfectly as if it had been designed especially for the beautiful young bride. Long puffed sleeves fell slightly off the shoulder complimenting the sweetheart neckline above the tight-fitting bodice. Imported Belgian lace covered her long skirt of ivory satin. A single strand of pearls that had belonged to her grandmother, Sarah, encircled her tiny neck.

John Kelsey stood at the bottom of the staircase to receive his daughter and escort her into the parlor where the wedding would take place. When Aurelia opened the door, standing in front of the fireplace were the Reverend Will Jennings, who was to perform the ceremony, and the nervous groom, Henry Hollis. Henry's expression suddenly changed from somber to overjoyed when he saw her. A big grin lit up his face exposing a nearly perfect set of white gleaming teeth as he looked into the face of the lovely Susannah. Henry's coal black hair, beard, and dark brown eyes made him appear distinguished as he stood there in his black suit, white high collared shirt, and necktie.

The mantelpiece was decorated with vases of fresh flowers arranged on a bed of English ivy. Tall, lighted tapers were glowing from the two silver candlesticks. Susannah's alluring entrance was captured and reflected in the large gold leaf plate glass mirror hanging over the mantel as she entered the room. Elizabeth sat in a chair to the side as she witnessed her daughter's wedding. A reception for the new couple was held afterward in the dining room.

Henry and Susannah Hollis' wedding guests included the groom's parents, Samuel and Ruth Hollis, along with Henry's brother, Charles, from Richmond. Susannah's grandparents from Jonesboro, George and Mary McArdle, and Aunt Katharine and cousin, Walt Jackson, were also in attendance. As a surprise for Susannah, George and Mary had brought Vanie along with them. Vanie danced around with joy when she was presented to Miss Susannah. Also attending were Dr. and Mrs. Geoffrey Vincent and Richard and Anne Braxton with their daughter, Dellanna. Rob stayed at the reception for a while but ended up in the kitchen helping Aurelia and Jesse with the dishes.

"Why you must be Kyzer," Anne Braxton said.

"Yes, ma'am."

"This is my daughter, Dellanna."

"Yes'um, I know her. We're in school together."

"Say hello to Kyzer, Dellanna."

"Hello, Kyzer."

"Hello, Dellanna. You wanna go out back and shoot my slingshot?"

"May I, mother?"

"Oh no, dear, not right now, not in your new dress and everything. Maybe another time."

"Goodbye, Kyzer."

"Goodbye, Dellanna." Who wanted to play with a stupid redhead, freckle face girl anyway?

Upstairs, the newlyweds changed their wedding attire into more comfortable traveling clothes. Jesse helped Henry bring down the luggage to load onto the buggy waiting in front of the house. After their farewell to family and friends, Jesse drove Henry and Susannah to the railway station. Now, happily married, the young couple anticipated their honeymoon. Just a few more hours and they would be in Savannah.

◀▶ ◀▶

The summer of 1854, Rob had a major decision to make. He graduated in May, ranked second in his class. He applied for admission to Virginia Military Institute at Lexington, waiting on his letter of acceptance. In the meantime, he was offered an apprentice job at Papa Kelsey's former company, the Kelsey Tobacco Company of Virginia. The owner wanted him to start work immediately. What to do? After several lengthy discussions with his parents, John was allowing Rob to make the decision on his own. Rob needed that letter in a hurry. He studied at length all the history surrounding the geographical area of Lexington. This caused him more determination than ever to become a soldier, his ultimate goal in life. He felt he could always come back and work at the tobacco company if he didn't make cadet or soldier.

Rockbridge County, Virginia, was located in the midst of the picturesque Shenandoah Valley. Scotch-Irish and German immigrants moved south from Pennsylvania in the early 1730's and settled there. The Virginia Legislature in 1777 established Rockbridge County, naming it for the natural bridge located in its southern territory. The county seat was named Lexington, taking its name from the town in Massachusetts where the American Revolution began.

During this time, the population grew slowly; however,

many citizens supported a few small private schools. Liberty Hall Academy had its beginning in 1749, becoming later, Washington College after George Washington's generous endowment to the school. By 1839, the citizens of Lexington also convinced the state of Virginia to convert their local arsenal of rowdy and foolhardy soldiers into Virginia Military Institute. Construction began in 1851 on the barracks where the cadets would be housed, the same year Lt. Thomas Jonathan "Stonewall" Jackson arrived there to teach.

Two weeks later, Rob's prayer was answered. The letter finally came. He announced his intentions to his parents that evening at supper. He would be leaving home in the fall to pursue his dream at Virginia Military Institute.

◀▶◀▶

That same year, Jesse turned twenty-eight and married a girl from the Chandalar Plantation. Her name was Sally, and everyone knew she was five months pregnant. John Kelsey paid Richard Braxton eight hundred dollars for her when she came to live out back with Jesse and Aurelia.

CHAPTER 7

That summer following Kyzer's fourteenth birthday, he made a startling discovery about himself. He wouldn't dare tell anyone about it, and why should he? Rob knew, of course. He had seen him naked, but now, Rob was sworn to utter silence about the matter. Both boys made a pact, this would remain their secret, locked deep inside them.

Rob was home for a few weeks and was able to spend more time with his little brother. In fact, Rob rather enjoyed his time, especially now that Kyzer was more grown up. He had already noticed his brother's big feet and long lanky body. The boys pitched in and helped their father work around the house whenever he was home. They went hunting and fishing together, and Kyzer was amazed at how well Rob could shoot a rifle. He thought Rob was really a good marksman. Kyzer offered to let Rob ride his stallion anytime he wanted. It was Saturday afternoon, and it was hot.

"What say, you and I go down to Moss Rock Creek for a swim," Rob said.

"That sounds good," Kyzer said. "I'll go and tell Mama. She always likes to know when I go off anywhere."

As soon as the boys arrived at the creek, all their clothes came off and they hit the water with a big splash. After a while of trying to dunk each other and a few bouts of water wrestling, they raced to the other side. They were having so much fun. Rob and Kyzer ran out of the water and fell down on the creek bank. They lay there together looking up at the sky, watching the sun dart behind the clouds. Kyzer was the first to stand. He looked down at Rob's naked body glistening in the sun, and immediately looked down at himself. Something was different, very different. Kyzer wanted to hide himself, but it was too late. Rob had already stood up and faced Kyzer, both now standing across from each other, staring in unbelief.

"Look at me and look at you," Rob said.

"That's odd. Why am I different?" Kyzer said while he reached down with one hand, pointing to himself. For some unknown reason after seeing Rob, Kyzer couldn't explain it. Why was his groin hair just laying there thinly exposed in small wire-haired filaments, kinky ringlets resembling fuzzy black wool. Rob, totally different with much longer hair, thick and bushy. At that instant, without saying anything, Rob and Kyzer knew at once, they were somehow very different. Mystified at the moment, they decided not to tell anyone about their surprising revelation and discovery. They didn't know anything else to say to each other, and they certainly had no solution concerning what could be done to change anything. This would have to be their secret for a long time. They dressed hurriedly, without looking at each other, and headed home in silence.

Kyzer spent a lot more time with his horse since the day Rob had left Kellwood, returning to Lexington. How he missed his brother already. His brother? He wasn't his real brother, of course, but he was the only brother he had. How he still longed one day to be just like Rob. Maybe he would be a soldier, too, or work at the tobacco company. Now, he just felt so strange, like he really didn't belong here. With the secret he carried, along with Rob, he knew now that he was definitely unlike his brother. Maybe a ride in the countryside would clear his head.

He was nearing the end of his ride, headed toward home, when Kyzer stopped his horse on the edge of the clearing. He climbed down, and tied his mount to a nearby tree. Lots of times, he liked walking in the woods, spotting different types of birds and wildlife. Most of the time, it was very peaceful in the wooded areas; and he could reflect on the scriptures he learned about at church as he walked there. 'He makes me lie down in green pastures, He leads me beside the still waters, He restores my soul. He guides me in the paths of righteousness for His name's sake. Yea, though I walk through the valley of the shadow of death, I will fear no evil, for thou art with me, thy rod and thy staff, they comfort me.'

Pop! Silence. Another loud pop. The sound continued a few more times. What was that noise?

It was like a blast of rushing air whizzing through the trees, then silenced abruptly by its loud sudden pop. Kyzer fell to the ground in a slow crawl, the sound echoing in his head. Close by, he saw two horses tied together at a small tree. Then, another one in the distance that looked a lot like Daisy, wandering around loose. The sound of another pop sent the mare running through the woods.

As Kyzer quietly crept forward, he stumbled onto the sight revealing the source of the noise. He remained hidden behind a large bush while he crouched there peering through its thick foliage. A man he recognized as Mr. Nate Gilliam stood there with a heavy bull whip in his hand. He was Maggie's father. She was a fourteen year old girl that Kyzer knew from school. Another man, he didn't recognize, stood on the other side. The two men had a young black man positioned between them, ropes tied to each of his wrists, pulling tightly, stretching him between two tree trunks. He was facing with his back toward Kyzer, shirt torn off, with gashes cut into his bleeding back. Kyzer froze, biting his lip from the shock of the horrible scene playing out in front of him. He suddenly realized that he was now a witness and would have to remain there, not making a sound. He felt his life depended on it.

As the man's head would turn from side to side, blood spurted from his eyes, nose, and mouth where the men had already beaten him in the head. His face was unrecognizable while the blood flowed down and spotted the ground.

"You took my daughter's innocence! Boy, you just took her, and she didn't have a chance," Mr. Gilliam yelled. He flailed at the limp body three more times. "You're gonna pay for this, nigger. You're gonna pay."

Kyzer almost yelled out when he saw the flashing blade of the deer knife unsheathed.

"Get his pants down. That filthy nigger bastard! Get'um down," Gilliam instructed the other man. He quickly unbuttoned the belt, unbuttoned the fly, and pulled on the legs until the pants were dropped to the ground. The man's worn boot tips were barely visible.

Only a few moans were audible from the black man while Gilliam brought the knife down and castrated him. Now, the victim hung there limp, his knees buckled under him, his weight pulling against the tension of the tightening rope. Nate Gilliam strode over to untie his horse, coming within ten feet from where Kyzer lay flat against the ground. He held his breath, exhaling in relief, when he watched the man lead his horse away.

Gilliam took another rope, tied a noose into it, and after several tries, managed to throw it over the large tree branch above. He put the noose around the black man's neck and tied the end of the rope to his saddle horn. He led the horse away until the slack was out of the rope. This caused the helpless victim to be stretched while it pulled upward, stretching the arms still bound at the wrists. It sounded like an arm snapped from its socket as the rope came flying off on the left side, leaving the arm dangling across the chest. After a few minutes, Gilliam yelled to the other man to cut the other arm loose. Then, he led the horse a few feet further, guiding him around a small tree several times, thus securing the end of the rope while he released the end from the saddle. The black man gave out a final moan while he was hoisted upward. His body twitched three times and fell into rest. By the time it reached complete stillness, the two men saddled up and rode away.

Kyzer lay there until he felt that the men were completely gone. He raised himself slowly from the ground and walked around the bush. He stood there trembling while his eyes gazed upon the man hanging in the tree before him. He looked past the man's pants resting around his ankles, past his bleeding naked body, past the noose around his neck, to the rope suspended tightly over the branch that held his battered head. He could hardly take it all in. Then, he looked at the rope continuing to the small tree where it was tied off.

Looking up at this gruesome sight, Kyzer focused on the man's face. Although beaten severely, he looked vaguely familiar to him. Could it be? Maybe. 'Oh my God, it was Jesse!'

Kyzer turned and broke into a run. He was running as fast as he could through the woods. He had to get to his horse and ride into town to tell his father what he had just witnessed. Kyzer, nearly out of breath, burst through the front door of Collins Infirmary. He ran down the hallway in search of his father. Frantically, he looked into several rooms and then the office. Dr. John Kelsey was no where in sight. Turning down the last corridor, Kyzer spotted his father coming toward him.

"You've got to come quick!" Kyzer's heart pounding. "They've taken Jesse and hanged him in the woods. I saw it. I saw it all."

"Who took him?" John asked.

"It was Mr. Gilliam and another man. You've got to come with me right now."

"Where is he?"

"Out there in the woods. I'll show you," Kyzer said.

"First, I need to get the sheriff, and then we'll be on our way." John Kelsey jumped on Kyzer's horse, Captain Midnight and pulled Kyzer up behind him. The horse bolted into full stride, headed toward the sheriff's office. Father and son arrived there in a flash. Securing Midnight to the hitching post, they both rushed inside. "Joe, Kyzer's got something he needs to tell you about." Sheriff Carlson sat there listening to Kyzer's story about the hanging. When he was through, the sheriff rose from his seat. "Let me get hold of a wagon, and we'll ride out there together."

The wagon stopped as close as it could to the place in the woods. Sheriff Carlson, John, and Kyzer got down and walked the rest of the way.

"Good God, John, was this your man?"

"Yes, Jesse's been with our family all his life. He's Aurelia's boy, you know. Married, about two years, got a baby girl named Epsy."

"Damn it, I knew it. I thought one day I'd have trouble out of Gilliam. He's a hot headed son of a bitch," the sheriff said. "Well, we can't do anything else out here. Let's get him down and loaded into the wagon."

"Joe, is it all right if I take Jesse back to the infirmary and clean him up. Sally and Aurelia don't need to see him like this. I'll get Uriah to help me with him."

"Yeah, that'll be all right, John. The evidence is all I need. I've seen enough out here. We'll save the ropes and his clothes. Just get something else to put on him."

Kyzer sat between his father and Sheriff Joe while they drove back to town with Jesse's body.

"Based on what your boy has seen and what he's told me, I'll have to take Gilliam into custody for questioning. Do you understand if I get a confession and arrest Gilliam for murder, Kyzer here will have to testify in court against him?"

"Kyzer, you understand, son?" John asked.

"Yes, sir. I think I can."

"No thinking about it, boy," the sheriff said, "you will have to do it."

"I will," Kyzer said.

It was a sorrowful sight later that night when John Kelsey broke the news to Sally and Aurelia. Sally held her baby close, rocking her back and forth, tears running down her cheeks. Aurelia started screaming, tearing at her clothes while she began to weep and wail. Elizabeth finally got her to calm down enough to lie down on her bed. Both women didn't sleep that night. They would cry so much, dozing off only briefly. Elizabeth stayed the night with them and helped to care for Epsy.

By morning, the news of the lynching had spread through the town. Nate Gilliam had been taken to the jail for questioning. Slaves from surrounding plantations and in town were in an uproar, both angry and scared that something like this had happened. John Kelsey had provided the coffin for Jesse as he lay in the Saint Andrew's Church on the outskirts of town. The body was held out until the following Sunday afternoon, the day of the funeral. The little church was overflowing from the tremendous outpouring of the slaves in attendance. They all gathered to celebrate the life of Jesse, concluding with his burial in the adjoining cemetery. Things wouldn't be the same without Jesse around Kellwood. Aurelia knew in her heart that Jesse would never commit that act against Miss Maggie. Someone needed to come forward with the truth.

A week later, Sheriff Carlson had enough physical evidence gathered, along with a statement from the only eyewitness, to warrant the arrest of Nate Gilliam. After three days of hard questioning, Gilliam implicated his brother, Jake. He was arrested and placed in a separate cell in the Chesterfield County Jail. With their attorney, the men planned to enter a plea of not guilty. In the meantime, the brothers would remain locked up in county jail until the following month when a circuit court county judge would arrive and the trial could begin.

CHAPTER 8

It was the tenth of November, the first day of the trial of Nate Gilliam. The county courthouse was packed to the limit of overflowing. Negroes filled the balcony and hundreds stood outside on the lawn, talking among themselves and waiting. Shortly after nine o'clock, the wagon from the jail pulled to the side door of the courthouse. Sheriff Joe Carlson escorted Nate Gilliam, hands bound in irons, through the vast murmuring sea of black. Once Gilliam walked past and was inside, the crowd sat on the ground while the trial got underway.

With all the preliminaries out of the way, Circuit Court Judge Randolph Billingsley said, "Mr. Pennington, you may call your first witness."

"If it pleases the court, the defense calls Miss Maggie Gilliam to the stand," said Attorney Tyrone Pennington.

"Place your hand on the Bible. Do you swear to tell the truth, the whole truth, and nothing but the truth, so help you, God?" the bailiff asked.

"I do."

"Have a seat, ma'am."

"Miss, please state your name and age for the court," Pennington said.

"Maggie Gilliam, age fourteen."

"Now, Miss Gilliam, you are the daughter of the accused, Nate Gilliam?"

"Yes, sir."

"What is your relationship with your father?"

"Since my mother died, I help out around the house. I cook, do the wash, and I can sew, just a little. I go to school every day."

"Does your father make you do all those things?"

"Oh no, Mr. Pennington. Since Ma's been gone, there's no one else to do them. I feel I have to help my father, him being at work all day."

"Where does your father work?"

"He's worked as long as I can remember at the lumber mill."

"Miss Gilliam, are you acquainted with a black man named Jesse Washington?"

She looked down at the floor. "Yes, sir. I know Jesse."

"Tell us, how do you know Jesse?"

"Lots of times, Pa would get Jesse to help him. He paid him to help with the fence last year."

"So then, how did you come to know him?"

"I would take them water. Pa and Jesse, I mean. I'd carry them water. Sometimes, fried chicken. Jesse said he liked my fried chicken."

"Well, Miss Maggie, is that all? Did he ever try to touch you or put his hands on you in any way? Like, would he ever try to get you alone or anything?"

"Objection, your honor," said Mr. Henry St. Charles, State District Attorney, "counsel is leading the witness."

"Objection, sustained," Judge Billingsley said. "Counsel will rephrase the question."

"Miss Maggie, just tell us in your own words exactly what happened to you last summer."

"Well, sir, one day Pa's gone off, and I'm at the house all by myself. I see Jesse out there in the yard. He's bustin' up some firewood at the wood pile at the end of the back porch. He's got his shirt off, and he's just a sweatin'. I thought maybe Jesse would like a cup of cool water so I dipped a cup and took it out to the edge of the porch. 'Here Jesse, I brought you some nice cool water if you want it.' He stopped his chopping, put down the axe, and walked over towards me. 'Why thank you, Miss Maggie, you mighty nice'. When he reached for the cup, he grabbed me around the ankle and pulled me off the porch on top of him. The cup went flying and hit the ground while he wrapped his sweaty arms around me. Next thing I know, he's rubbing his body all over me and kissing me on my mouth. He put his hand over my mouth when I'm about to scream out and he says, 'Miss Maggie, don't scream. You gonna like what I have for you'.

She started crying and sniffling as Pennington passed his handkerchief to her. "You need a break, Miss Maggie?"

"No, sir. I think I can go on."

"Then, what happened?" The attorney began moving around the floor.

"Next thing, he sat me on the edge of the porch, holding me there, trying to unbutton his pants. He's saying all the while, 'Don't you wanna have a little fun with me? I'm gonna treat you real nice'. Well, he gets his pants about halfway down, and I can see his private part is really firm. So, I just raise my legs up and kick him there. I kick as hard as I can, and he falls down on the ground. He's moaning while I run in the house and lock the door. I'm screaming all the time, 'Get away from here! Get away from me! I'm gonna tell my Pa what you did. You hear me, Jesse Washington?' I'm standing at the window, just crying.

Then, Jesse pulled his pants back up, and he ran out of the yard. When my Pa got home, I told him what Jesse did to me."

"Is that all you have to say?"

"Yes sir, Mr. Pennington."

"Mr. St. Charles, you may cross-examine," the judge said.

"Miss Gilliam," said Henry St. Charles, "do you know a boy named Kyzer Kelsey?"

"Yes, sir. Kyzer's in my class at school."

"If it's all right with you, I'd like to hold my questioning of you until we hear from him. Is that all right? You wouldn't mind, would you?"

"No sir, I guess not."

"Then, you may stand down, Miss Gilliam," the judge said. "Mr. Pennington, any more witnesses?"

"No, Your Honor, we rest our case."

"This court will take a recess for lunch until one o'clock," Judge Billingsley said.

The courthouse yard resembled a gigantic barbeque. People were everywhere, sitting around, packed lunches being passed here and there. The whites were all sitting in a shaded section on the lawn, while the negro groups spread out all over the place. The talk in the yard was, 'Pennington couldn't afford to put Nate Gilliam on the stand in his own defense because the cross-examination would probably kill their chances'. The testimony of Maggie Gilliam was their best defense — if she really could convince Judge Billingsley. It was a few minutes after one when the court resumed.

" Mr. St. Charles, are you ready with your first witness?" the judge asked.

"I am, Your Honor. The State of Virginia calls Kyzer Kelsey."

Nate Gilliam grew a bit fidgety in his chair as he watched the young fourteen year old boy walk to the stand. After he was sworn in, District Attorney Henry St. Charles instructed Kyzer to begin to tell the court and the judge what he witnessed that day. His testimony lasted until half past four when court was adjourned for the day.

The next morning, court reconvened, and Kyzer was back on the stand. "Remember, you're still under oath, son," Mr. St. Charles said while Kyzer continued. It was then Kyzer began to recount all the gruesome details of the horrendous act he had witnessed several weeks ago in September.

"You are telling this court, that this man and his accomplice, did indeed, inflict all these things upon Jesse Washington. Is that correct?" A nod from Kyzer. "Speak up, boy," St. Charles said.

"Yes sir, that's the truth."

"Is that man in the courtroom today?"

"Yes, Mr. St. Charles."

"Would you point out the man, Kyzer?"

"Yes, sir. He's sitting right over there." Kyzer pointed to Nate Gilliam while they looked each other in the face.

"No more questions," said Mr. St. Charles.

"Your witness, Mr. Pennington," the judge said.

"I have no questions," he said.

"The witness will stand down," Judge Billingsley said, while he watched Kyzer walk back to his seat. "Mr. St. Charles, you may call your next witness."

"Your Honor, the prosecution would like to recall Miss Maggie Gilliam."

Maggie Gilliam was fighting back tears as she approached the witness stand. Her body was slightly trembling, and she fought hard to keep her composure while she sat down.

"Miss Gilliam, this is just a reminder that you, too, are still under oath. Now, Miss Gilliam, after hearing the testimony from your classmate, would you ever think your father was able to do all the things that you have just heard?"

"I don't know, sir."

"I mean, do you believe he would be capable of committing such an act?"

"It's possible. I guess so."

"You guess so, well, let me ask you this. Have you ever seen him really mad or in a rage?"

"A few times."

"Has he ever hit or whipped you severely?"

Hesitating, she answered, "I remember maybe a couple of times."

"Objection, Your Honor," Pennington said, "A parent has a right to discipline a child. This line of questioning is unnecessary."

"Overruled. Counsel may continue," the judge said.

"All right, let's move in another direction. Miss Gilliam, being alone so often, what do you like to do after your chores are done? Read, sew, make up stories?"

"Objection, Your Honor, counsel is badgering the witness," Pennington said.

Objection, overruled. Let's hear what she has to say," Judge Billingsley said. "Repeat the question, Mr. St. Charles."

"After your chores, what do you like to do, Miss Gilliam?"

"I sit out on the porch when I read, mostly. Sometimes, I like to think about my married sister in Richmond and her little boy."

"Like daydream, perhaps?"

"Maybe not, daydream, sir. I just wonder about when all that will happen to me some day."

"All right, my dear. That's all the questions I have. Wasn't so bad, was it? No more witnesses, Your Honor. The State will rest."

"Following a recess for lunch, I will hear closing arguments," Judge Billingsley said.

It was around two when the closing arguments began. Tyrone Pennington stood from his chair.

"Your Honor, my client, Mr. Nate Gilliam, has been accused of murder in the first degree, the premeditated murder of a black man. Mr. Gilliam has struggled immensely to provide for his young daughter ever since his wife died. He truly regrets that she was suddenly thrust into the role she's had to endure since that time. Because he loves his daughter so much, he simply became enraged at what young Jesse did to his girl. He is sorry that he let his temper get in the way. It was only meant to be punishment, a whipping, nothing more. Things just got out of control. If he could change things, he would. He never intended to harm Jesse Washington in the way it all ended. Your Honor, we ask that you would find the defendant not guilty." Tyrone Pennington sat down and wiped his brow.

"Mr. St. Charles, you may proceed."

"Before I begin, Your Honor," Henry St. Charles said, "I would like to present three people to the court, if you will allow them to come and stand before you while I deliver my summation."

With an affirmative nod from the judge, the back doors of the courtroom opened wide, while two black women and a baby stood there. Aurelia made her way slowly down the aisle with Sally at her side holding Epsy in her arms. Gasps erupted over the entire courtroom as they positioned themselves where Mr. St. Charles instructed them to stand.

"Your Honor, this is all that's left of Jesse Washington. His family, he loved his family, too. Just because any man is angered, that doesn't give him the right to judge, to pass sentence, and to punish any individual, white or black. For Nate Gilliam to inflict his own judgment and wrath by serving his kind of vigilante justice on the person of Jesse Washington should never be tolerated. Any dog would deserve better. Mr. Gilliam bases his actions totally upon the love for his daughter and her version of the story. This was all done out of love, he says. I submit that Miss Gilliam's testimony is a total fabrication of her imagination. That she concocted in her mind a story. A story to tell her father, knowing that he would eventually punish Jesse someway for his rejection of her advances. Am I close here, Miss Maggie?"

An interruption, an outburst immediately came from the front row where Maggie was sitting. She could contain herself no longer as she sprang from her seat while she began to sob, cupping her hands over her face.

"Yes, it's true, it's all true! I made it all up. I wanted Jesse to hold me, kiss me, and make love to me, but he never would. I'm so sorry. I didn't intend for all of this to happen. I'm really sorry, Pa."

By this time, the crowded courtroom was on its feet, moving about, talking and shouting in an uproar. Maggie's spontaneous admission surprised everyone.

"Order in the court. I'll have order," Judge Billingsley said. "I will see Miss Gilliam and both attorneys privately in my chamber, immediately." He hit the gavel three times. "Court will reconvene at nine o'clock in the morning when I will render my verdict. Court is adjourned."

Following a sleepless night at the jail for Nate Gilliam, he was returned to the courthouse for the third time. This time for the verdict. The courtroom was packed more than before, the judge ordering the dismissal of all who could not be seated, including the balcony. He did allow standing at the back of the room in one single row for those fortunate enough to gain access and find a place. Everyone outside was on their feet, waiting to hear the news of the verdict.

"Please, rise." Judge Billingsley came in and sat solemnly on the bench without expression. The people were peering and gazing all around to try to see if they could tell how the verdict was going to go.

Judge Randolph Billingsley cleared his throat. "Would the defendant please rise?" Nate Gilliam stood to his feet. "After careful consideration, hearing the testimonies brought about this court by its witnesses, and talking at length with your own daughter, I have made my decision." He paused, looking directly at the defendant. "Nate Gilliam, this court finds you guilty of murder in the first degree. You will be retained in county jail until the time your brother, Jake Gilliam, will be tried in this court for his part. His trial will begin three days from now. Sentencing will be passed at a later date. Court is hereby adjourned."

Nate Gilliam was immediately rushed from the courtroom and returned to county jail. He showed no emotion, speaking to no one, while he was led away. A thunderous ovation of yelling and shouting broke out everywhere as news of the verdict spread through the streets.

The next week, a guilty verdict was handed down to Jake Gilliam following his trial. He was found to be a conspirator in the assault and murder of Jesse, along with his brother, Nate. Judge Billingsley sentenced both men immediately to death. They were scheduled to be hanged on the first day of December. Maggie Gilliam was sent to live with her married sister in Richmond. She would have to live the rest of her life with the knowledge that she caused not only the death of Jesse but also that of her father and uncle as well. A tragic ending for a young girl, only fourteen.

Was there any justice for Jesse Washington?

Although the trial, conviction, and sentence of the men responsible was over, Aurelia knew that nothing would ever bring Jesse back. During these days, she thought about him often while she, Sally, and Epsy returned to Kellwood.

CHAPTER 9

Kyzer lay in his bed with both arms under the covers. His nightshirt raised, once again he would attempt the amazing feat of what Rob called 'choking the chicken'. This ritual rite of passage started with a slow, even rhythm, the tempo quickly accelerating into a much faster pace. A sudden stop, while he pulled his hand from underneath the bed sheet. Opening his palm, he looked at the results, now oozing between his fingers. At fifteen, he thought he had everything figured out. Only now, he had to get himself cleaned up and dressed for school.

He would be happy when he was finally out of school. He knew he was an average student, but he recognized the value of a good education. His best subjects were arithmetic and history. He could even name all of the fourteen presidents in order — 'George Washington, John Adams, Thomas Jefferson, James Madison, James Monroe, John Quincy Adams, Andrew Jackson, Martin Van Buren, William Henry Harrison, John

Tyler, James K. Polk, Zachary Taylor, Millard Fillmore, and Franklin Pierce'.

Many times, Kyzer thought he might work at the tobacco company. It was located near Kellwood, but he had two more years of school before having to make the final decision. Since Jesse was gone, he took care of Daisy, Captain Midnight, and the mules. A few weeks ago, his father had bought three new male slaves. The oldest, Benjamin, took care of the livestock while Lemuel and Josiah, did the gardening. Josiah, merely a boy himself, and Kyzer became friends. They liked to fish together as well as hunt squirrels and rabbits with their slingshots. Kyzer felt comfortable around the negroes. They were part of the family, and each one knew his place. Kyzer was the happiest during the times that Rob came back home. He took time to be with him and taught him how to shoot Papa Kelsey's old rifle. He felt like he was ready to give up his slingshot.

Kyzer started noticing Dellanna Braxton. Lots of times at school, she was especially nice to him. At least, he tolerated being around her more. The day he asked her if she wanted to sit together while they took their lunch, she continued to do so from then on. How could he tell her that she didn't have to do it everyday? 'She kinda grows on you', he confessed to Josiah one day. Of course, Kyzer never liked to be reminded of the time last February when his teacher had the class put on a play about the life of George Washington, and he played George while Dellanna was Martha. Neither did he like, at the insistence of his mother, when he had to attend her thirteenth birthday party over at the Chandalar Plantation.

That year in 1857, James Buchanan was elected as the fifteenth President of the United States. Soon, there was talk in the North about the abolishment of slavery, mainly which territories and states could have slaves and which could not. The Kelsey's newly acquired slaves, along with Aurelia and Sally, helped to relieve a number of tasks presently handled by John and Elizabeth. Things continued to go well at Kellwood.

John and Elizabeth Kelsey were most happy about their wonderful children. Rob graduated from Virginia Military Institute as a second lieutenant and held a post with the Regular Army in Richmond. Susannah and Henry Hollis moved last year, also to Richmond, where Henry went into the hardware business with his brother, Charles. Susannah and Rob were able to see each other from time to time. Kyzer turned seventeen in April, and started his last year in school in the Fall. He and Dellanna remained just good friends at school. He much preferred the company of Josiah.

One day, after reading the scriptures in Exodus about all the commandments, 'Thou shalt not kill, Thou shalt not steal or bear false witness, Honor thy father and thy mother', Kyzer had a chance to be alone with his father. "Do you think my real father and mother are dead?"

"I don't know, son, perhaps. We will probably never know," John said. "Why do you ask?"

"I was wondering," he said. "I thought maybe if I could find them, I could honor them, too, like it says to do in the Bible."

"Kyzer, as I have told you before, we never found them. I'm sorry."

"That's all right. Guess what? I'm thinking about going to work at the Kelsey Tobacco Company when I finish school."

"Well, son, if that's what you want to do, I'm sure it will be all right with your mother and me."

"I've thought about it a great deal, even prayed about it," Kyzer said. "I feel that it's the direction I need to go right now."

"That would work out well, son, and you could plan to continue living here," John said.

"I've got this year to make up my mind so there's no rush," Kyzer said.

"We'll talk about it again whenever you want to discuss it. Want to go for a ride?" John asked.

Kyzer's final year in school flew by so quickly. He couldn't believe it. The eighteen year old was nervous for his first day at work, not knowing what was in store for him. Kyzer's first meeting with his foreman went well, he thought, especially when Mr. Caufield realized that his grandfather was Robert Thomas Kelsey, the original founder of the company.

"Well, Kyzer," Tom Caufield said, "We're going to start you in the curing barn, but before I take you out there, please allow me to tell you about the different kinds of tobacco. Please, have a seat."

"Thank you, sir."

"First, let me tell you, there are several factors involved to determine both the grade and the value of our smoking tobacco. This includes the size and shape of the leaves, the color, even the veins in the leaves themselves. This will all determine the actual burning quality of the tobacco. There are three basic types of manufactured tobacco, and we produce all three in the state of Virginia. The first is called flue cured or bright tobacco, which accounts for the majority of the crops. Second, the fire cured, which is not only a smoking tobacco but also a chewing tobacco mixture. Then, lastly, the air cured which is a gold colored tobacco noted for its burning quality. Any questions, so far?"

"No sir," Kyzer said.

"You can see some of the leaves displayed on the table. When you finish looking, we'll go out to the curing barns," Caufield said.

"How tall do the plants get?" Kyzer asked.

"About two to eight feet in height. The seeds are small and look like ground pepper. You can see for yourself how large some of the leaves are and notice they extend directly from the thick stalk."

"Yes, I can see," Kyzer said.

"Of course, curing is the drying process. You can see on some of the barns the fireplaces built under the lean-to sheds for the flue and fire cured method. In fire curing, a very slow burning hardwood fire is maintained. The vapor from the wood adds to the flavor, and this type curing takes from one to three weeks. Our air cured tobacco is dried out in the sun and then is hung in well ventilated barns. Kyzer, this is what your job will be starting out. You will actually be taking loads of tobacco from outside and carrying them into a curing barn to hang. You think you can do that?"

"Yes, sir."

"I will put you with another man for a while. Then you will work on your own. If you have any questions, ask him or come find me," the foreman said.

Kyzer finished his first day at work by late evening. He was tired, but he knew he would grow stronger each day. The job was so physical that it would really help him stay in good shape. He felt so grown. He would be earning his own money and living at home so it would be a good opportunity to begin saving for the future. He could even ride Captain Midnight to and from work every day. He knew he was going to like working at the Kelsey Tobacco Company of Virginia.

◀▶◀▶

The main issue of slavery, rising from extreme racial tension and spreading throughout the country, made American citizens suddenly aware of the ongoing situation. The upcoming election of a new President would prove to be critically important to the nation.

During the remaining days of 1860, a majority in the North didn't believe the Union stood on the brink of dissolution. The South made threats to secede so often most northerners considered it just another bluff. However, this time for the state of South Carolina, the bluff was about to become real. Major Robert Anderson of Kentucky, who was loyal to the Union, made the decision to move his garrison from Fort Moultrie in Charleston Harbor to a better site of fortification. Even though Fort Sumter was unfinished at the time, the current fort presented itself too accessible by land. The new location would be better for Anderson's men who occupied the harbor location for five weeks. The morning following December 26, a Union flag was spotted flying over Fort Sumter by the people of Charleston. This would be the final act, angering them to the extent of finally driving the state of South Carolina to secede from the Union.

Following South Carolina, six more states seceded. Delegates from these states met in February in the city of Montgomery, Alabama, to form a provisional government for the new Confederate States of America. Soon after, the Confederate Congress chose Jefferson Davis as President of the Confederacy and Alexander Stephens, Vice-President. The men served in this capacity until the new southern government would be permanently established.

On March 4, 1861, Abraham Lincoln took office as the sixteenth President of the United States. The newly inaugurated President made his plea for reconciliation between the North and the South. The people of South Carolina, adamant in their decision to break away from the Union, were determined that Fort Sumter should pass from Union occupation to the Confederacy. Pressed for time, President Lincoln made a decision between abandonment and relief. He would send the necessary provisions to sustain the troops, but there were to be no more troops for Major Anderson.

After a rather hurried cabinet meeting, the Confederate Secretary of War ordered General P.G.T. Beauregard, Commander at Charleston, to demand an immediate evacuation of Fort Sumter. If this order was refused, then the fort was to be taken by force. General Beauregard sent the demand for surrender to Major Anderson on April 11. Anderson refused, citing that he would be forced to give up the fort in another few days due to lack of necessary provisions. The unsatisfactory reply was unacceptable to Beauregard. On April 12 at 3:30 a.m., the General sent a final notice to Anderson that he would open fire in one hour. Being true to his word, a mortar fired the first shot at 4:30 a.m.

Dr. John Kelsey was working at his desk at the infirmary when Dr. Vincent suddenly rushed in. Brandishing a copy of the morning headlines, the doctor dropped the newspaper in front of John.

"Look here! My God, John, would you look at this?"

John glanced down at the bold, black print in all caps — **APRIL 12, 1861 WAR BEGINS! FIRST MORTAR HITS FORT SUMTER.** "We all knew it was coming, didn't we?" John said.

"My brother is in the militia in Pennsylvania. He'll most likely get called up," Dr. Vincent said.

"Yes, as you know, our son is in the Regular Army in Richmond. He is sure to go," John said. "Elizabeth is not going to like that, I'm afraid."

In the days that followed, in response to the Confederate challenge, President Abraham Lincoln issued a series of three proclamations. The first called up the militia from several states. The second proclamation announced that all southern ports would be blockaded. Two weeks later, the President called for three year volunteers for the Regular Army. By early summer, North and South had raised enough troops to begin their war.

With the letter in her hand, Elizabeth walked out onto the veranda and sat in her rocking chair, waiting for John to come home. She had been crying for so long inside the house, she thought it would help to sit outside, to take in a little fresh air. Aurelia, Sally, and Epsy were around back doing the wash, and Kyzer was at work.

Finally, he was home. John pulled the buggy in front of the house and stopped by the steps. He saw Elizabeth crying as he hurried up to her. "What's the matter, darling? Are you all right?" He was looking at her arm, extended to him, offering what appeared to be a folded letter.

"It's from Rob," she said. "You'll want to sit down to read it."

"He's all right, isn't he?"

"I'm praying he is," she answered. She watched John unfold the letter.

John sat beside her while he began to read. Elizabeth started rocking in her chair, staring straight ahead across the lawn at the beautiful mountains in the distance.

◀▶◀▶

May 30, 1861

Dear Folks,

I pray that you both, along with my brother, Kyzer, are doing well. I am fine. I was able to see Susannah and Henry this past Sunday, and they are both very well indeed. Susannah tells me that I should write this letter to you concerning the news I have already told to her.

By the time you will get my letter, I should be in Washington City. From there, I do not know where I will be. I have to tell you that I have resigned my post here in Richmond and have joined the Union Army.

I hope that you both will not think of me as a disappointment, a traitor to the South, but as a man who stands for what he believes. You have taught me this principle for as long as I can remember. I am truly and deeply grateful for that and also for you both. I feel our nation stands at a great crossroad today, and I must act accordingly to do what I feel in my heart I must do. This has been the hardest decision I have ever had to make in my life so far. I trust you will understand.

Please, do not be angry at me for my decision. I only ask that you continue to pray for me, as I know you always do. I do not know when I will get to write or see you again. I will always love you.

Your loving son,

Rob

1st Lt. Robert Zachary Kelsey

John looked up from the letter with tears in his eyes.

"God, help us all. It's out of our hands. We'll just have to give him up to the Lord. He's the only one who can help us now."

CHAPTER 10

Just five miles from Kellwood, across the James River, majestically stood the Chandalar Plantation. Rising aloft from the hillside, the opulent Greek manor house was situated overlooking several hundred acres of tobacco. This plantation alone supplied one quarter of the tobacco processed at the Kelsey Tobacco Company in Hastings. Over one hundred slaves and field hands were charged with its daily maintenance and operation at Chandalar.

The name for Chandalar Plantation was a derivative from the original family name of Chandler. Following the death of John Jacob Chandler, his only daughter, Elise, inherited the plantation. She chose to name it Chandalar in memory of her late father. The unmarried Elise, at twenty-three, eventually met and married a young banker, Paul Richard Braxton from Savannah, Georgia.

After two unfortunate miscarriages early in the marriage, she finally had a baby boy who she named Richard. When

Richard was nine years old, Paul Braxton had a fatal heart attack. Elise, still very young, had her hands full while continuing to run the plantation and in the upbringing of her young son. When Richard was twenty, his mother brought him into the family business until her death, seven years later. The year before she died, Richard Braxton gave up bachelorhood by marrying Anne Elizabeth Getty from Petersburg. In nine months, the spring of 1843, Anne gave birth to their only child, a beautiful baby girl named Dellanna.

Dellanna Braxton was reared in a strict but loving family. At a young age, Anne recognized the talent her daughter possessed in social dancing and in playing the harpsichord. By the time she was in her early teens, Dellanna played the pump organ at church. Her father bought her a grand piano for the music room at Chandalar where Dellanna often played for parties and other social gatherings. At fifteen, her father bought her a horse named Susie. In fact, there wasn't much he didn't buy for her. Her mother kept Dellanna dressed in the current fashion. She had so many dresses most had to be stored away in cedar lined trunks.

Dellanna felt she had come a long way since her school days. The days of sharing lunches with Kyzer Kelsey, even shooting slingshots with him on occasion, filled her mind with memories. She didn't see much of Ky these days. She discovered he was always working at the tobacco company or off hunting with Josiah. She remembered him as a close friend in school, and now she thought of him fondly from time to time. Of course, the one thing she always remembered was her first attraction to him. The eyes. She found his deep brown eyes the most captivating thing she had ever seen in her life. Despite all his admirable physical characteristics, the eyes won her over. Thinking of him, now more than ever, she just had to find a way for Kyzer to notice her.

At eighteen, Dellanna grew into a beautiful young girl. Her vibrant strawberry red hair was cut to fall shoulder length.

It was brushed straight, and many times she wore a bow or fresh flower in her hair. Her green eyes glowed from a pretty face. Whenever she pinched her cheeks and put rouge on her lips, she passed for a girl nearly twenty-five. Her slender body had blossomed into the shape of near perfection. Laced into a corset, her waist was pulled to 19 ½". Dellanna just enjoyed being a girl. She liked Dinah to help change her dresses and prepare her baths. Dinah had been Dellanna's mammy since the day of her birth. Those two spent more time together than Dellanna and her mother. After all, it was Dinah who nursed her through all her childhood illnesses, helped to bath and dress her, comforted her when she was sad, and always made her laugh. Dellanna and Dinah romped and played like school girls sometimes. They liked to play jokes on each other. Just like the time Dinah switched a pair of Dellanna's pantalettes with Mrs. Braxton's, trying to convince Dellanna how much weight she had lost. Then there was the time Dellanna sifted flour onto Dinah's pillow at night before bedtime. Howling with laughter the next morning, seeing her hair looking like one of those white powdered wigs worn in France, Dellanna had to confess her crime.

The news of war, as it spread through Chandalar, wasn't surprising to everyone. Of course, Dellanna was quite taken with it and upset. She never experienced anything so dreadful as hearing about a war or even a rumor about it. Not at her age, anyhow, and why couldn't folks be satisfied with everything the way it was? A large number of slaves that worked the plantation really didn't know how it was going to affect them. What would happen to them if suddenly they were freed? Where would they go? What would they do? A lot of questions came to many minds but not many answers. What about the state of Virginia? They felt caught in the crossfire.

The third of July had been a busy day at Chandalar for the past several years. In preparation for the events of the Braxton's annual fourth of July celebration, the entire plantation was excited, caught up in the busy activities of early morning. With the exception of Easter, Christmas, and every Sunday, tomorrow was another special day when all work and labor ceased. In celebrating the nation's independence day, it was a day of fun, feasting, frolicking, and fireworks. Practically everything in and around Hastings came to a halt.

Plans for the day at Chandalar began at noon, where invited guests enjoyed a delicious barbeque. From the wee hours of the morning on July third until noon on the fourth, three pigs were killed, gutted, and roasted on spits over open fires there on the grounds. Two long tables were pulled from storage and set directly in front of the house. Covered with white linen tablecloths, one table held a stack of pie tins to be used for plates, along with large pots containing ears of boiled corn. The other table held pitchers of ale, water, lemonade, and various pies and cakes. Activities in the afternoon included games of relay races, sack races, tug of war, pitching horseshoes, and apple bobbing. Guitar playing and banjo picking at varied locations on the grounds provided entertainment during the course of the afternoon. When night settled in, the guests moved inside the house to the music and ballroom for an evening of dancing and social chatter. The night concluded around nine o'clock as remaining guests gathered on the front lawn to view the fireworks display. With so many plans and arrangements completed already, invitations sent and received, the third of July was over. Dellanna prayed that it wouldn't rain tomorrow.

The fourth of July began cloudy and overcast, but by late morning, the sun was out. Just before noon, Richard and Anne Braxton stood on the veranda, greeting the guests upon their arrival. Everyone was graciously received by the hosts as they invited everyone to join in and help themselves to the barbeque.

Dellanna had not yet made her appearance. She stood at

an upstairs window, trying to conceal herself in the portieres while she peered out onto the front lawn.

"There you are, Miss Dellanna. What you doing hiding? Why, child, you not even dressed." Dinah said.

"I'm not going!"

"Why, my sweet? They's a lot of folks out there just waiting to see you. Several unattached young men just hovering around."

"I'm still not going."

"Now, Miss Dellanna, you haven't missed a barbeque since Master Richard's been having them. What's wrong, child?"

"I don't feel well."

"You don't feel well 'cause you haven't seen Mr. Kyzer yet, I know."

"He's not out there. Why, I wasn't even looking for him. It doesn't matter to me if he comes here or not."

"Well, if it doesn't matter, why don't my sweet get her dress on?"

"He doesn't even know I exist," Dellanna said.

"You just think that boy don't know. I've seen him here before looking for you."

She perked up. "When was he here? Tell me, Dinah."

"Couple weeks ago, I reckon. He come around when you gone to town with Mrs. Anne. He asked to see Master Richard. Nobody home, I tell him to come back later."

"Wonder what he wanted with him. Did he ask about me?"

"Oh, he just say that, asking to see Master Richard and everything. I know who he really wanted to see," Dinah said.

"Well, he never came back, did he?"

"Come on, child, don't fret about nothing. Let me help you get your dress on. What dress my sweet gonna wear?"

"I think the red one."

"Oh no, uh huh, you can't eat barbeque in a dress like that. My sweet wear the pretty blue one."

"I won't. I won't. That dress makes me look like an old lady."

In half an hour, Nathaniel, Dinah's son, opened the front door while Dellanna walked onto the veranda. She stood there in her hoop skirted, red taffeta dress with bodice overlay in fine red lace. The front featured a plunging neckline with large puffed sleeves off the shoulders. On her feet were black patent slippers. She wore pearl drop earrings and a cameo pendant on a black velvet ribbon tied around her neck. Several people stopped just to look at her. If it was one thing she could do well, Dellanna knew how to make an entrance. Nathaniel offered his hand to her as he escorted her down the stairs. When she reached the bottom, she gave a slight nod to him and made her way over to the table to have some lemonade. Two gulps and she set the glass on the edge of the table. She thought she saw him near the grape arbor while she made her way across the crowded lawn.

Dellanna glided nonchalantly through the guests, stopping within earshot of him. She pretended she didn't notice Kyzer standing there talking to the little tramp, she thought. Making a quick turn, a sudden swish of her dress, and Dellanna spun around, nearly colliding with the girl. "Why, Stella Gilroy, don't you look absolutely divine."

"What a beautiful dress you have on, Dellanna."

"This old thing. It was all I could find this morning. Who's your friend?"

"You know it's Kyzer," Stella said.

"Hello, Dellanna. I was just asking Stella if she had seen you."

"Well now, here I am," Dellanna said glaring a bit at Stella.

"Would you ladies care for a glass of lemonade?"

"Why yes, Ky. My throat is about as dry as a pan of parched peanuts," Dellanna answered.

"Nothing for me, thank you," Stella said.

"I'll be back in a flash," Kyzer said.

Stella and Dellanna stood watching his backside until he disappeared into the crowd. Moments later, he returned with a glass in each hand. "Where's Stella?"

"I wouldn't know. She just left suddenly," Dellanna said.

"Care for a lemonade?"

"Thank you, Ky."

"Would you care to take a walk, Dellanna?"

"That would be nice," she said. "How's your family?"

"My folks are well. They're actually here somewhere at the barbeque. You knew Susannah and Henry moved to Richmond, didn't you? I'm worried about my brother, Rob. We all are. With the war and everything, he's waiting on his orders."

"I'm sorry to hear that. War! War! War! That's all anybody ever talks about," Dellanna said.

"Well, Dellanna, what have you been doing lately?"

"I play my piano and take care of my horse, Susie. I love to go horseback riding," she said.

"You do? So, do I. We'll have to ride together some time."

"That would be nice. Come by, anytime. By the way, Dinah told me you were here a couple of weeks ago to see my father," she said.

"Yes, I believe I was. I was going to tell him that I have been working at Kelsey Tobacco for a while now."

"I knew that. Sorry, I already told him the news," she said.

"That's all right. Doesn't really matter anyway," he said.

"Why sure it does. You have a good job with a fine company. I'm impressed."

"Dellanna, I've been wanting to ask you for quite some time. I mean, I've been thinking about, uh, would you like to go and eat some barbeque with me?"

"Sure, I'd like that," she said. "I declare, I'm just about to starve to death."

"Then, maybe tonight, I want to ask you to go to the dance," he said.

"I would love to go with you, Ky."

When they finished eating, Kyzer and Dellanna strolled down to the edge of the tobacco field. He told her about the things he had learned about tobacco while she pretended to be interested. Walking over to a big oak tree, they sat for a while facing each other. Dellanna found it difficult not to keep staring into those penetrating dark brown eyes.

Suddenly, a strong gust of wind passed along the trail before them, lifting the dirt into small, cone-shaped spirals, spreading fiercely in all directions. Kyzer pulled Dellanna toward him as he stood with her, holding her close against his chest. He turned his body to shield her from the blowing dust storm. He tried to cover her head from the dirt now blasting them. They could feel the electricity in the air as the thunder began to clap while the lightning flashed the sky. Then, the heavy rain came in large drops pelting them while they broke into a run for the house. When they got to the edge of the lawn, it was vacated. Everyone was sheltered underneath the large front portico while many had gone into the hallway of the house. Soaked through to the skin, Kyzer and Dellanna dashed up the steps onto the veranda, holding each other and laughing hysterically. They stood there among a hundred guests, beads of water dripping from the ends of their hair while wet clothing lay plastered against their skin.

"You're beautiful," he said looking down at her dainty body.

"Thank you. You're handsome, too." She reached on tiptoe to kiss his cheek.

Plans for the afternoon were cancelled because of the severe thunderstorm. Most of the guests left Chandalar soon after the rain let up, planning to return at night for the dance. Several friends stayed to help Richard and Anne Braxton clean up from the barbeque and help get things set up for the evening. Kyzer rode his horse back to Kellwood to change his clothes. Tonight, he planned to meet Dellanna out by the grape arbor.

A stringed ensemble was set in the corner of the ballroom by the grand piano. Violins began to play, signaling the start of the dance. Guests were returning, dressed in more formal attire. Many of the ladies were redressed into their ball gowns, while the men donned coats and ties. The music and dances of the evening consisted mainly of the Virginia Reel and the beautiful waltzes. Guests were scattered all through the rooms of the main floor, everyone talking, laughing, drinking, and dancing. It was a wonderful evening of enjoyment for everyone.

In the grape arbor stood Kyzer and Dellanna as they held each other in a deep embrace. She felt her body almost go limp as he drew her tightly once again to him, caressing her softly in his arms. He kissed her neck, moving around until he stood behind her, arms cradled around, hands upon her breasts. She turned in his arms to receive his passionate kiss on the mouth. Their breathing grew heavy and labored while their bodies pressed together, thrusting almost uncontrollable urges through both of them. She broke away from his tender touch, falling back into the grapevines, trying to catch her breath. "We'd better stop. I'm sorry, I can't. Ky, please understand." Her breathing slowed a bit.

"I thought it's what you wanted," he said.

"Oh, I do. I really do, but not now. Not this way," she said.

"Dellanna, you know I would never force myself on you."

"Yes, I know. I'm sorry if I led you on. Don't be angry at me," she said.

"Whew! You really had me going there. I'm all right now, but I could use a drink," he said.

"We'd better get back to the dance before we're missed. I have to play the piano at eight o'clock," she said while they walked to the house.

Near the end of the evening, Kyzer got up the courage to

ask Dellanna to dance. He had been sitting by himself all night watching everyone. After stumbling around and stepping on her toes so many times, Dellanna determined that Kyzer was much better dancing the Virginia Reel instead of the waltz. Anyway, the evening wasn't a total disaster. Kyzer enjoyed dancing with Dellanna and holding her outside in the dark that night while watching the fireworks. It suddenly dawned upon him, this was that same redhead, freckle face girl he had known when he was eleven.

CHAPTER 11

The campaign of war began as Virginia was soon drawn in as part of the vast battlefield. The first serious conflict was fought July 21, 1861, at Manassas near Bull Run, a small creek in northeastern Virginia. Both the Union and Confederate armies were made up of poorly trained volunteers. The battle at Bull Run stopped the Union from its plans to march on Richmond and take it for the North. Union forces, also called the Army of the Potomac, began training and turning its raw volunteers into an army. The North realized they were in for a long fight as they prepared for the second battle of Bull Run. The Confederates destroyed the Union supplies at Manassas and Bristow.

After General Robert E. Lee was defeated at Antietam, he returned south to a high bluff overlooking Fredericksburg, Virginia, on the south side of the Rappahannock River. The little town was overflowing with soldiers from the Union Army of the Potomac, while First Lieutenant Rob Kelsey found himself preparing for battle. This was his first deployment to active duty, following his previous responsibility for training new recruits in Washington for the northern forces. At age twenty-six, for the first time, he was gearing up for his initial experience as a Union officer and soldier. He placed his faith in God as he prayed his years of military training would sustain him during this upcoming conflict.

General Lee had strengthened his Army of Northern Virginia to the point of anticipating an attack by the Union Army of the Potomac. Almost six hundred yards of open field lay between his lofty position on Maryes' Heights to the town of Fredericksburg. The Confederate First Corps artillery held their position on the Heights and on a twelve hundred foot long stone retaining wall built down below. The original stone wall, sunken and cut away, was built to run beside the main road leading to the city of Richmond. The wall itself, standing in most places shoulder high, was ideal for the Confederate defense.

Around noon on December 13, 1862, the first brigade of Union soldiers left Fredericksburg and formed their ranks on the edge of the field. As they charged the stone wall, they were cut down by the Confederate artillery. Throughout the rest of the afternoon, Union General Ambrose Burnside sent a total of seven divisions in fourteen charges against the wall. The futile attempts of attack brought only slaughter to the union troops. In the end, no Union soldier ever reached the stone wall. Resulting from his disastrous defeat, General Ambrose Burnside was removed from the command of the Army of the Potomac.

Fortunately for Rob, his brigade led the final charge of the assault which was soon ordered into retreat. His life was spared to fight again another day. Because of his deployment further north, following the battle at Fredericksburg, Rob missed seeing action relatively nearby at the town of Chancellorsville, Virginia.

Each day became more difficult for the delivery of the

mail. Sometimes, a letter took several weeks or even months to receive. Rob Kelsey felt relieved to finally receive a reply from his father. It was an answer in regard to the letter he had mailed his folks when he left Richmond. It felt good to know at last, that regardless of the present situation, they would always stand by him.

He had tried several times to get letters to them, letting them know of his whereabouts, but he never received an answer. Rob felt that he had to get this letter out because it might be the last opportunity to write for a while. He wanted to tell his folks that he had just received his orders to go to a little town in Pennsylvania around the first of July. This little town was called Gettysburg.

◀▶◀▶

Kyzer and Dellanna sat close by the edge of Moss Rock Creek. The level of the water had risen slightly, due to the amount of heavy rains of the past few days. The water gently splashed over the rocks, cascading into swirling ripples as it made its way downstream.

Dellanna spread a red checkered tablecloth on the ground while she opened the basket. She knew that Dinah had packed the lunch for her so she was anxious to see what it contained. Very nice, she thought, as she unwrapped fried chicken and biscuits on bone china plates from the linen cloths.

"Have something to eat," she said while she discovered the apple fritters.

"This tastes good," he said, biting into a chicken leg. "You didn't cook this, did you?"

"I'm afraid not, Ky. That's Dinah's delicious chicken."

"How's her son these days?" he asked.

"Nathaniel is doing well. He helps his mama around the house. It's just a shame for him to have the mind of a child in a grown man's body."

"Well, at least Dinah still has her boy. That's more than what Aurelia has left," Kyzer said.

"How is Aurelia?" Dellanna asked.

"Maybe a little better, I guess. She'll probably never be the same again. Seems like all the joy of life was just sucked out of her the day Jesse died."

"I feel so sorry for her," she said. "What about Sally?"

"She has Epsy to think about now. I'll always remember Sally that day in the courtroom, when the sheriff led Nate Gilliam out past her. She spit right in his face," Kyzer said.

"Good for her," Dellanna said.

"That Epsy, she's a sight. Sometimes, she doesn't want to mind so she gets switched by her mama. 'Course, Epsy won't ever remember her daddy. Maybe one day, I can tell her how courageously he went to his death," Kyzer said.

"I'm glad I didn't have to see that," she said.

"I heard a while back that Maggie Gilliam had to be taken from her sister's house and put into the insane asylum. They said she just went crazy," Kyzer said.

"And just to think, you both are the same age," she said. Dellanna reached over to touch his hand.

Kyzer leaned toward her, pulling her down, and they both fell back onto the grass. They lay there side by side, looking at the clear blue sky. "I think about Rob all the time. Ever since the battle of Gettysburg, we haven't heard anything from him," he said.

"We'll just have to pray that he's all right," Dellanna said as she rolled to his side and kissed him.

"That's what Mama said." He put his arms around her, and drew her close while he continued kissing her until she broke away.

Several weeks went by, and Kyzer knew he had to see Dellanna. He enjoyed her company, their companionable horseback riding, attending church together, and talking with her. He felt she was a good listener and encourager to him.

Enamored by her strong personal convictions and her true beauty, both inward and outward, he was fast falling in love with her. Then something else came over him. He was suddenly torn over a decision he knew he was going to have to make. Would he ask Dellanna to marry him or enlist in the army? With battles closing in from all directions, he wanted to do something, but everything seemed beyond his control. What could he do? At twenty-two, he knew he was able to be man enough to make the decision, but what about Dellanna? He would just have to talk to her. She could help him decide what to do.

It was a moonlit night, quiet and still, until the sound of crickets chirping erupted out across the front lawn. Kyzer sat with Dellanna on the settee by the edge of the veranda at Chandalar. He placed his arms around her as she laid her head upon his chest. When she looked up into his eyes, he lowered his chin to kiss her softly on the mouth. He squeezed her tightly as he held her there, waiting for the courage to say to her what was on his mind.

"Dellanna, we've known each other for quite a while. During that time, I have come to know you in a way that I find hard to put into words. I enjoy being with you so much to the point of having you always in my life," he said.

"I, too, love being with you, Ky."

"I wanted to ask you to marry me, but something else is troubling me," he said.

"What's that, my love?"

"It's the war," he said.

"The war. What's the war got to do with anything, with us?" she asked.

"I'm thinking seriously about enlisting very soon," he said.

"And, you want to marry me?"

"Why yes, Dellanna, I really do want to marry you."

"But, you'd rather go off now and fight in the war," she said.

"That's why I wanted to talk with you. I knew you could help me decide," he said.

"Ky, I can't help you decide that. I won't help you. That's something only you can decide," Dellanna said. "I wouldn't want to marry you and then have you suddenly off to who knows where. Can you begin to understand how I feel?"

"I suppose in a way I do," he said.

"You suppose? You don't know how I feel." Dellanna rushed from the veranda, down the steps, and across the lawn to the grape arbor. Kyzer following close behind. He grabbed her, spinning her around and locking her in his arms.

" I'm sorry, my darling Dellanna, I didn't mean to upset you. I love you so much," he said, kissing her passionately.

She tried to break away from him, but he continued holding her so tightly that she couldn't pull away. Suddenly, her body pressed into his while she allowed his caresses to begin to fulfill her desire. He pulled her down onto the grass, his body rolling over her while they struggled to loosen their clothing. Kyzer and Dellanna soon found true love as they lay together on that moonlit night in the grape arbor.

Three months later, and it was time to say goodbye. Kyzer had enlisted with a group of local volunteers and had been training with them for the past several weeks. Now, it was time for them to leave home for Richmond to be filtered into other units readying for battle. It had not been an easy decision, but Kyzer and Dellanna finally decided what would be best for them. Sharing in Rob's faith of the Union Army, Kyzer would join him in this fight and return one day to marry Dellanna.

Kyzer sat in the parlor at Kellwood with John and Elizabeth. With Dellanna by his side, Elizabeth stood to offer a prayer for her son.

"Father, God, I pray you would look down from your mighty throne in Heaven upon your humble servants here. Father, you know our hearts are heavy with despair and saddened to give another son to this war. I pray you watch over, not only our sons but also all the boys and men, some even brother against brother, who stand together now on this great battlefield. Grant them, I pray, safety and protection from all harm; and if it be your will, allow them to return to us when this war is finally over. I pray this in the name of the Father, the Son, and the Holy Spirit. Amen."

"Thank you, Mama," Kyzer said. "I'm going to find Rob out there, and we'll be back as soon as we can." Kyzer walked across to his father. "Well, sir, this is about it. Thank you for all you've ever done for me. I hope to make you proud of me as God knows I'm going to try my best. No need of you and Mama going to the station. Dellanna is going with me," he said.

"I've always been proud of you, son. If I lived another lifetime all over again, I could never be prouder of you than I am right now. Take care of yourself. We will pray for you." John sat back into his chair. "Goodbye, my son." He couldn't say anything more.

After one last kiss, Kyzer left Dellanna standing in the crowd on the platform as he boarded the train. Quickly running to his seat, he threw open the window, hoping to catch a final glimpse of her. Kyzer hung from the opening of the railway car for as long as he could, keeping Dellanna in his sight. He wanted to remember her standing there in her red taffeta dress, smiling and waving to him.

As the end of the train pulled out of her sight, Dellanna regretted not telling Kyzer that he was going to be a father.

CHAPTER 12

General Robert E. Lee was well aware of the Federal advance at Cold Harbor, Virginia on June 3, 1864. General Ulysses S. Grant strategically mobilized his army to Petersburg where he would attempt to capture the city. With the siege of Petersburg, a successful campaign there would give the Union a needed foothold and, hopefully, drive Lee out of Richmond only twenty-one miles away.

Long before daybreak, Kyzer's unit was already involved with the task that lay before them. He was working with a group of men ordered to rig an explosive charge to be set off near the outskirts of the city. His old job of carrying loads of tobacco to hang in the curing barns had paid off for him by helping to keep him in shape. Only now, he was carrying kegs of dynamite instead of tobacco.

A small wagon containing the dynamite was positioned as closely as possible to the center of the detonation area. It was Kyzer's job to help carry the kegs to the designated locations.

He helped the sergeant with the unrolling of the wire, but a specialist in explosives was responsible for the actual wiring and detonation of the charge. Kyzer also served as lookout as the small unit had to work together quickly and quietly.

"You all set there?" Kyzer asked the sergeant.

"Almost finished," he said. "Pass me the last roll of wire. Patrick has one more connection and we're ready."

Kyzer squinted his eyes, trying to focus his vision. "I see a Reb stirring over there."

"Hold on, son, we're almost ... ." A single shot in the dark sent the projectile, a musket ball directly into the forehead of the sergeant.

"Get out, boy! Get out of here," Patrick yelled.

Kyzer began to running like a swarm of bees was after him. Another shot rang out. Pow! This one caught Kyzer in the leg, tearing flesh, as he fell forward into the dirt. With the wiring complete, Patrick pulled Kyzer to his feet to help carry him. They had to make it to the control box and set off the charge. A shot in the back, Patrick fell dead as Kyzer hit the ground. He knew he had to make it to the box. With all the strength he had left, Kyzer fell onto the plunger, setting off the charge that shook the earth. The ground broke open, sending dirt and debris hundreds of feet into the air. While the dust settled from the aftermath, a huge crater was left in the earth. Before the smoke cleared, the Union line charged through the rough terrain as they pushed onward. To their surprise, they were trapped in the crater itself, running dead on into the wall of the deep ravine. The Union Army had run itself man upon man to the point of many being crushed. Many that died never fell because they were pressed body upon body. "It's like shooting fish in a barrel," one Reb yelled as he fired into the crater. Hundreds joined in the melee as the Confederates stood on the edge and opened fire upon their trapped victims.

Kyzer didn't know how long he lay there unconscious. He breathed shallowly to avoid choking on the dust thick on the ground upon which he lay. The pain in his leg grew more intense now that he lay pressed shoulder to shoulder with what must be a hundred men lying all around him. He wondered if his Confederate captors would shoot him if he moved to ease the pressure on the wound in his leg. Even as he wondered, he heard a movement, a shot. Through the ranks of captive Union soldiers lying on the ground, a whispered rustle passed. "Kid just asked to relieve himself, and they shot him in the head!" Kyzer shut his eyes and thought of Dellanna and his folks back home. He guessed he could put up with a little pain if it meant he'd get to where he was going in one piece. They'd expect him to do what he could to get back to them alive if it meant surviving and enduring the pain of his bullet wound until he could tend to it.

"Hey, soldier," he whispered. "When we board the train, I'll take a look at your leg. You're shot up pretty bad."

"Thanks," Kyzer said to the young private beside him.

"I'm Seth Devane from Pennsylvania. My folks live in Philadelphia."

"Good to meet you, Seth. I'm Kyzer Kelsey from Hastings. You can call me Ky."

"What have you heard about Andersonville?" Seth asked.

"Nothin' good," Kyzer said.

"Then, I guess we'll both be finding out real soon," Seth said.

Kyzer turned his head for a closer look at him. He guessed Seth to be about his age, slightly taller. He had a medium build and extra large hands that Kyzer noticed while Seth repositioned himself on the ground. He wore a thin mustache, goatee, and short brown hair. Just above his right eye was the wound he suffered where a bullet had grazed his head.

In the distance, the distinct sound of the approaching locomotive grew louder while the prison train thundered past and came abruptly to a halt. Soon after, the armed guards of the Confederacy had the men gathered into smaller groups while

Union officers were separated from their troops. The loading procedure commenced during the cover of darkness. Reflecting in Seth's bright blue eyes, lanterns and torches alongside the tracks provided the only source of light. Placing Kyzer's arm around his shoulder, Seth grabbed hold while he pulled his arm around Kyzer for support. It was all Kyzer could do to stand to his feet while one of the Rebs yelled at them. "Git yore damn Yankee asses up and loaded, you sons of bitches."

When the last car was locked down, the signal was given to start the train on its continued journey southward. After leaving the firelight of Petersburg Station, complete darkness fell. With the moonlight creeping through the cracks of the wooden slats of the box cars, Kyzer would have to wait until dawn for any kind of relief. It was just too dark. It would be a long night for all the men while they listened to the sound of clanking wheels vibrating on the tracks and lulling them to sleep.

With the first light of day, Seth awoke to find Kyzer already awakened. "Well, Ky, are you ready?"

He nodded.

"Let's have a look then," Seth said as he unwrapped the saturated handkerchief. He took out his pocket knife and slit Kyzer's pant leg upward, just past the knee. The cloth was stuck hard to the nasty wound, and the dried blood erupted once again while the trouser was pulled open by Seth with one quick jerk. Kyzer yelled while his body flinched in response.

"Sorry," Seth said. "Does anybody have any whiskey? I need some whiskey."

"Over here," yelled a voice from across the car.

While Kyzer took a few sips, Seth removed his own leather belt, wrapping it tightly above Kyzer's left knee. He pulled Kyzer's belt from around him and put the end into his mouth.

"Ky, bite down on this," Seth instructed. "I need a couple of you to hold him down while I try to get the bullet out."

Seth poured a splash of whiskey onto his knife while he directed the blade toward the oozing wound. Muffled sounds came from Kyzer in brief agony while he fell into unconsciousness. Seth made contact on his initial probe. Moments later, there lay the extracted fragment alongside the bloody knife in the straw on the floor. Rummaging through his own haversack, Seth took a scarf his mother had made for him, removed the belt, and bandaged Kyzer's leg. Close to noon, Kyzer came around while the train had stopped for the prisoners to be fed pieces of hardtack bread and water.

It took nearly two days for the journey. Conditions were horrible as prisoners had been herded into box cars like cattle. Food and water had been very limited, but it was some relief at last to reach this destination. Kyzer lay motionless in the straw while the train stopped. When the doors were pulled opened, the fresh air suddenly revived him. Those who could, stood to their feet while the order was given to exit the car and remain there together. Small groups were formed and marched to the North gate of the stockade by the armed guards. Kyzer, who had been separated from Seth, was loaded onto one of the wagons for those who weren't able to walk.

Thus began the two mile journey toward the main gate. Kyzer rode in the second wagon of the small caravan. Daily trips from the train depot looked as though it formed a natural road to the prison site. One turn off the main road in town led through the winding trail of tree stumps. Once, this had to have been a dense pine forest, trees now cut for the stockade. When the wagons crossed the bridge over the dry creek bed, Kyzer saw about twenty bodies lying on the ground in rows side by side. They were all barefooted and appeared to have tags fastened on their toes. Just beyond that place was a fenced area and barn where he saw wagons and horses. On the right side of the road stood two rows of stocks. Several, presently occupied, looked as though the prisoners they contained were almost dead. Kyzer saw a few men shackled together at the legs with a heavy cast iron ball and chains. The driver of the wagon yelled out, "That's Captain Henry Wirz's punishment for those caught trying to escape. The poor bastards, ones lucky enough to live after being tracked down in the swamp by the dogs, and there's lots of dogs."

The entourage stopped at the North gate. A smaller gate within the larger one opened while the wagons unloaded and the men were ordered inside. The panoramic view looking into the stockade was overwhelming. Kyzer could hardly believe his eyes as he stood there gazing across the sea of a multitude of thousands. As far as he could see, left, right, and beyond, the view was utterly devastating. He saw the sentry boxes perched high along the walls seemingly twenty feet high. He noted the vast distance between the north and south gates, completely amazed. Kyzer was at a loss. He couldn't believe he was actually here in this godforsaken place. It seemed to be the depths of hell.

"Welcome to Andersonville. Look here fellas, we've got us some fresh fish," yelled William Collins. "Where you all from?"

"Petersburg," several answered from the group.

"Hell, after the Yanks finish up there, it ought to be enough to send Bobby Lee packin' on down to Savannah. You boys hungry? Come with me and we'll get you somethin' to eat," Collins said. "I can show you where to camp. You need to stay this side of the creek where it don't smell so bad."

Kyzer and the men with him didn't really know what to do next or even what to expect. While the new "fish" began to move out, they noticed a group of men, looking wild and forceful, now encircling them. They kept moving toward the vast crowd that lay ahead.

"Get'um, boys," Collins yelled as the sticks and clubs became visible while the mob commenced hitting and bashing them in the surprise ambush, stripping them of their possessions. Kyzer fought back with all his might until a blow to the side of his head by a large stick put him out. A raider snatched his haversack and disappeared into the crowd.

After a while, Kyzer slowly opened his eyes. His head was reeling while dried blood was crusted down the side of his head. Attacked and ambushed, he knew that he would always have to remain alert and on guard; and, most definitely, he had to find out who he could trust.

"Here are some clean rags for your head," he said. "Looks like the bleeding's about stopped."

"Where am I?" Kyzer asked the stranger.

"Got most of your group separated from the Raiders. They left after taking all the goods. You're in the eastern section of the stockade. I'm Corporal Elias Caudel of the Pennsylvania Infantry."

"Thank you and your men for coming to our aid. We certainly weren't expecting that kind of welcome. My name is Kyzer Kelsey from Hastings, Virginia. What's with the Raiders?"

"That's William Collins and his men. There's about six leaders and a couple of hundred of the bastards who prey on the new arrivals every day. You have to watch your back. They're out to get anybody caught off guard anytime and anywhere. Collins is a real low life."

"They've got to be stopped," Kyzer said.

"There's just too many of them, and they're in cahoots with the guards. They look the other way," Caudel said.

"Still, we've got to band together somehow and beat them at their own game," Kyzer said.

"That's a lot easier said than done," Caudel said. "You men are welcome to camp with us if you want. We've got room for six more bodies."

"Don't know where else to go. We'll stay here, I guess," Kyzer said.

"This here's Private Erich Shikle. We're both from Harrisburg, been together since Gettysburg," Elias said. "Over there's Joe, Matthew, Josh, and Orry."

"I was with a private from the Pennsylvania Infantry, said

he was captured at Cold Harbor. We rode on the train from Petersburg together. He got the bullet out of my leg. Name's Seth Devane," Kyzer said.

"Don't know him," said Erich Shikle, "Maybe he's in artillery."

"We got separated. I had to ride the wagon into this place. I'm looking for him," Kyzer said.

"Elias, you were captured at Gettysburg?"

"Yeah, that's right. Got by with just a few mild scratches."

"I have a brother, First Lieutenant Rob Kelsey in the Regular Army in Washington. The last my family heard, he was headed to Gettysburg," Kyzer said.

"Well, about all you can do is just hope he survived. So many casualties there. I feel lucky myself. We lost a lot of men," said the corporal. "Erich, why don't you tell Kyzer here about the deadline?"

"You see that empty space over there by the wall? It goes out about twenty feet from the wall to the yard itself around the entire stockade. That's called the deadline. Anyone crossing it for any reason will be shot," Shikle said.

"Shot?" Kyzer said.

"Yeah, that's right, shot dead. Saw a man last week step over the line trying to get a letter out to a guard. He killed him," Erich said.

"Damn," Kyzer said. "I've seen a few of the guards already. They look like children."

"They are," Elias said. "The Reb's got these thirteen and fourteen year old boys and use them as guards to fill in, relieving the regular ones."

"What can I do to help out around here?" Kyzer asked.

"Well, first we all have to band together against the Raiders. Remember, don't go many places here by yourself unless you're sure you can make it back. We buy, sell, and trade in here to survive. We get a few rations sometimes but not every day," Erich said.

"So we share food, shelter, things like that," Kyzer said.

"If there's enough to go around. Sometimes, it's only enough for one," Elias said.

"Then, there's the dead. You may happen upon a chance to get something off a body," Erich said.

"Yeah, I got these boots three days ago from a young boy from Massachusetts. You just have to keep in mind that they won't be needing anything anymore," Orry said.

"Kyzer, I've got a piece of canvas over here. We can go find some sticks, and I'll help you fix yourself a shebang for shelter," Matthew said. "It'll help a bit from the hot sun and then the rain."

"Matt, I saw a few sticks piled near the stream this morning," Elias said. "Why don't you take Kyzer there to see of they're still there and show him where we wash, bathe, and use the latrine. Joe, you'd better go with them."

Kyzer left with Matthew and Joe while they headed through the throngs of men of the mass encampment on their way toward the little stream. Kyzer took it all in as he hobbled along on his bad leg, trying to keep up with Matt and Joe. He saw men lying on the ground napping, others maybe dying. Flies and gnats were working on open wounds and sores of skeletal bodies. Men were playing cards and showing their yellow rotted teeth as they laughed and talked. Men were sharpening knives on rocks and trying to shave and cut their hair with a pocket knife. A young boy was trying to play a banjo with a couple of broken strings. One boy was sitting there just crying. Two men were carrying a dead body away.

Kyzer caught up to the side of Matt. "Erich mentioned about buying, selling, and trading. How can I do that? I only have what's on me," Kyzer said.

"Check your pockets," Matthew said. "Greenbacks, buttons, thread, tobacco, a watch, almost anything can be used as a trade."

"I have a few greenbacks, a pipe in my back pocket, and the buttons on my shirt," Kyzer said.

"That's a start," Matt said. "I believe I see those sticks over there. You're in luck, my friend."

On their way back, a noise arose from the North gate signaling the entry of more new fish. The Raiders were at it again. "We gotta stop that gang somehow," Kyzer said.

A few weeks and Kyzer had settled into the routine of the stockade. No more encounters with the Raiders since the first day. He thought Fort Sumter or Andersonville, as it was more commonly called, was truly a living hell. By the time the summer arrived, it was almost unbearable. Food and water rations were scarce. The July heat erupted over the stockade while the hot, humid breeze stirred the stench from the creek. Kyzer's leg wound was almost healed, leaving him with a limp whenever he walked. He wiped the sweat from his head while he made his way through the crowded camp toward the creek.

Kyzer knelt by the edge while he unbuttoned and removed his soiled shirt. Submerging it into the muddy water, he kneaded the shirt like biscuit dough with his hands in a feeble attempt to wash it. He looked up and down the creek bank to see other men washing clothes and bathing. Men were scattered everywhere attending to their needs. Some were standing naked, some kneeling, some sitting, even a few urinating in the water.

"Mind if I join you? I need to bathe," he said.

"Sure. Do what you need to do, friend. Name's Ky."

"Dylan Barclay, Twenty-eighth Massachusetts." The soldier sat while he removed his worn boots and socks. Standing, he took off his shirt and dropped it to his bare feet.

Kyzer looked over at the young corporal with the dark brown hair and eyes. He turned away when the six foot, one hundred eighty pound Dylan unfastened his britches, letting them drop to his ankles. After he pulled his underwear off, he bent down to retrieve his shirt from the ground. He stood there naked while he lifted the bundle and held the dirty clothing against his broad hairy chest. Stepping into the creek, Dylan squat with legs spread while his manhood disappeared into the mirky water.

Kyzer rolled his wet shirt, compressed it between his fingers and squeezed the water from it. He held it by the collar while he shook the shirt as it fluttered before him like a wet flag. He put the shirt on again while his body heat and the hot sun above started the drying process.

"Where are you from?" Dylan asked.

"Home is Hastings, Virginia. I was captured at Petersburg in June. Did you say you're from the Twenty-eighth Massachusetts?" Kyzer asked.

"Yeah, I was captured at the Battle of Fredericksburg in December of '62. They sent a bunch of us here from Belle Isle in Richmond when this place opened in February. Things were better at first."

"I have a brother who was at Gettysburg. I took a bullet at Petersburg, ending up here. You got family, Dylan?"

"I have two married sisters in Boston. Our parents are dead," he said.

"You married?" Kyzer asked.

"I am. Wife named Rebecca. We've got five children, three boys and two girls. What about you?"

"Single. Got a girl back home. We plan to get married. Her name's Dellanna."

Dylan stood and placed his wet clothes on the creek bank. While he pulled his britches from the pile, with a bit of a struggle, he managed to get his wet pants back on. He sat to put on his boots.

"I guess I will take these wet clothes back to my camp and hang them to dry. I'll see you around."

Kyzer watched while Dylan soon disappeared into the thousands. Maybe he would see him again.

A few days later, the Raiders stood ready at the North gate to converge upon the new prisoners coming through the gate.

Seth Devane stood to his feet in the western section of the stockade.

"Who's with me?" he yelled out. "I cannot tolerate anymore aggravated assaults by the raiders. Come on men, who's with me? We've got to put an end to their reign of terror. Men, we need to become the regulators. By God, I'm going if I have to go it alone."

Seth Devane picked up a large stick and headed toward the gate. One by one, men everywhere were grabbing anything they could use for a makeshift weapon, following the leader. By this time, many in the eastern section had seen all of the men on the move far across the prison yard as they drew weapons, moving out to join them in the fight. The guards up in the pigeon holes were astounded at the activity below them, while hundreds of men joined together to attack the Raiders by the main gate. Kyzer saw his friend, Seth Devane, leading the way as he came across the yard swinging his club. Immediately, he joined the fight, mingling in with those in his section who were giving their support to him. Blows to the head, back, and legs commenced in a fracas, putting both sides into ultimate pain and suffering. Several men were beaten or knifed to death as a result, but in the end, the six ring leaders of the Raiders were captured and bound.

After the fighting had ended, Kyzer found Seth as he ran to him, causing them both to stumble and fall to the ground. "Seth, you've just done for us what I've wanted to see done for a long time. Bless you, brother," Kyzer said as they stood to their feet.

"Now, what are we going to do with them?" Seth asked.

"Well, we can't just leave them tied up here. Someone will kill them. I know. Ask Wirz for a trial," Kyzer said, wiping the blood from the cut on his arm.

"A trial," Seth said.

"Yes, a group of us can go before Captain Wirz and ask him. We'll demand a trial," Kyzer said.

That's exactly what happened that very afternoon. Captain Heinrich Hartmann Wirz, seemingly amazed after the conclusion of the near riot situation at his post, was very much interested in hearing from the small delegation who now petitioned him. Kyzer, along with Seth Devane, Erich Shikle, and Elias Caudel, stood before the desk of Captain Wirz, the Commandant at Andersonville. Henry Wirz was a tall man, slim, having normal facial features with the exception of an aquiline nose. He dressed neatly in a Confederate uniform with his distinguished presence enhanced by black hair, beard, and well trimmed mustache.

"Captain, Sir, I am Private Seth Devane of the Pennsylvania Infantry. This is Privates Kelsey, Shikle, and Corporal Caudel. We wish to submit a petition for your consideration."

Captain Henry Wirz, standing, began to speak in English with his broken German accent while his secretary aide sat recording the minutes by the side of the desk. "You have secured as prisoner, leader of the Raiders, eh?"

"Yes sir, we have," Private Devane said. "We ask for a trial to be held among the prison body to judge these men for crimes they have committed against their fellow prisoners."

Wirz turned to his secretary. "You have seen such crimes? What crimes?"

"Yes, my Captain. They rob, steal, beat, and sometimes kill other prisoners, just for their personal property," the secretary said.

"Tell me, Private Devane, how will you conduct this trial? Will you have a jury?" Wirz asked.

"Yes, Captain," Devane answered. "We will have a judge, lawyers, and witnesses like in a regular court. The jury will be made up of twelve men selected at random from new arrivals, those who do not know what has happened in here. We only ask that you hold these men under guard outside the stockade until we are ready for trial."

"This request is highly unusual. I have never experienced

anything like this in my entire career; however, I see nothing wrong in the way you are presenting it." Wirz asked again another question to his secretary. "With the Raiders subdued, having lost their control, do you think we have a better relation among all prisoners?"

"Most definitely, sir." The secretary agreed as he continued recording the minutes of the meeting.

"Then, I will give my books of law to you for reference, and you will have your trial. I will hold the men outside under guard until the day of the trial. You will be charged with the set up of the court on the prison yard. If a guilty verdict is rendered, you will construct the gallows, and I will order the execution. A not guilty verdict will release the men back into the general population. Agreed?" Wirz asked.

"Yes sir. Thank you, sir," Seth said.

"Dismissed. Go, have your trial."

On July 10, 1864, within the walls of the stockade, the six ring leaders were tried: A. Munn and William Rickson, two sailors in the U.S. Navy, John Sarsfield of New York, Charles Curtis of Rhode Island, Patrick Delany and William Collins of Pennsylvania. They were found guilty and sentenced to hang. Seventeen other men were sentenced to floggings as they were made to run the gauntlet among the prisoners. With execution set for the following day, an order was given by Wirz to have the needed lumber and building supplies brought in quickly. The gallows had to be hastily built by a volunteer group of inmate carpenters.

A Catholic chaplain, Father Peter Whelan, administered the last rites, and afterward, the Raiders were hanged by fellow inmates. As the men dropped, Willie Collins' feet hit the ground with a thud as the old rope snapped. The rope broke and Collins had to be hanged a second time. In an instant, Munn and Delany were without motion, dangling there revolving in a slow rotation. Curtis, Rickson, and Sarsfield's necks did not snap. They died of strangulation as their legs continued to jerk and twitch. Sarfield's knees came up almost touching his chin, while his legs jerked downward until they finally stilled. It was over. The Raiders were taken down and buried dishonorably in a separate plot in the prison cemetery. A somewhat restored peace soon flowed over the camp as the brutality was put to an end.

CHAPTER 13

Kyzer pulled a piece of hardtack from his pocket as he sat down to eat by the creek.

"Been looking for you," Seth said while he sat beside him. "I want you to come over to our side, boys got a tunnel started there."

"A tunnel?" Kyzer asked.

"Yeah. We've been digging for three weeks, but you dare not tell anybody."

"How do you dispose of all that dirt, Seth?"

"We've got a tent set up, and we dig at night. You tie your britches leg around your boot, fill the leg with the dirt, then walk to the edge of the creek, and squat down to untie the cord. Standing, you walk around until you drop the dirt before you return to camp. What do you think?"

"Sounds a bit risky to me," Kyzer said.

"Oh, it is, no doubt about it, but the darkness helps. It could result in being put into the stocks or the ball and chains. That's the risk we're taking. Join us."

"I don't know. What would I tell Elias and the boys, Matt, Joe, and Orry?"

"Just make up something or even tell the truth. Tell them you met me, and I asked you to come over to our camp for a while. Never mention the tunnel though," Seth said.

Kyzer thought for a few minutes. "All right. I'll do it."

That evening Kyzer met Seth at the creek. "Well, what did they say?" Seth asked.

"I just told them I was going to camp with you for a while since you helped save my leg and everything. Elias said I could come back anytime," Kyzer said. "I don't know if I could ever go underground to dig."

"That's all right. There's where our Pennsylvania miners come in. You can be a lookout or help carry the dirt," Seth assured him.

Kyzer was surprised to see Dylan Barclay sitting there as Seth introduced him to Billy Hopkins and Michael Lancaster. As Kyzer sat talking with Dylan, they began their watch at the tent entrance. Kyzer never noticed the man who lay asleep at the back of the tent. As they continued their talk, the sleeping man suddenly awoke with a jolt as if he recognized the familiar voice laughing and talking at the door. He leapt from his pallet, bolted across the tent, and threw himself onto Kyzer's shoulders. Kyzer threw up his arms in defense while he prepared to strike his attacker. With only the dim light from a single lantern, the men pushed back while they now looked into the face of each other. Kyzer pulled the man closer while wrapping his arms around him. Tears began to roll down the faces of both men as they hugged and embraced. The others didn't know what to think.

"My God, you're alive! I can't believe it's really you. Everybody, this is my brother, Rob."

Kyzer and Rob sat there together. "When have you heard from the folks, Ky?"

"I haven't. I doubt they know anything about me since Petersburg. I pray they're doing well."

"I got a letter off to them before I left for the Gettysburg campaign," Rob said. "I didn't expect an answer. What about your leg? Looks like you took a pretty good hit there."

"Yeah, I'm very lucky. My sergeant and a specialist were killed while we were trying to rig a dynamite charge. You heard about the big explosion at Petersburg?"

"I heard it blew a big crater into the ground," Rob said.

"Well, guess what? I was the one who pushed the plunger, setting it off."

"That's remarkable. You're a hero, Ky."

"Oh, I don't think so. I was just fortunate to be right there at that precise moment. Later, I heard we lost almost four thousand on account of that blast. I took a bullet trying to escape. Lucky for me, it was Seth who got it out for me on the way here. We rode the train together. Tell me about Gettysburg, brother."

"I got hit in the shoulder on the afternoon of July 3, following Pickett's charge. It was a surface wound, and I was able to scrape the fragments out of my skin. It took a while to get well, but it finally healed up all right. We took a formidable position for battle. The Rebs were positioned along the tree line on Seminary Ridge. Our brigade faced them a mile away on Cemetery Ridge just south of Gettysburg. Major General George Pickett advanced his assault toward us, but our powerful artillery blew gaps into their lines. They kept advancing, and the Union artillery changed from shells to canister. With those tin cans packed with iron balls, it made our cannons become like giant shotguns, mowing down their ranks. While the Confederates continued to close and regroup, the Union infantry sent volleys of minnie balls into them. The Rebs charged our lines, and hand to hand fighting broke out. Since there weren't enough Confederates left to hold the line, their only choice was to surrender or go back across the mile of open ground. That's when I got hit and captured in pursuit of a small band of Rebs."

The brothers spent the rest of the night talking about Gettysburg and Petersburg while Dylan crawled into the tunnel to dig. The tunneling continued routinely for the next few weeks until the middle of August when heavy rains set in for several days. The digging was forced to stop for fear of a cave-in, while the water pounded the earth. Near panic struck as part of the western wall near the creek washed away during the storm. Brigadier General John H. Winder ordered guards to man the gap until the wall could be reconstructed, preventing the now 33,000 inmates from escaping. Winder, at once, telegraphed Adjutant General Samuel Cooper not to send anymore prisoners from Richmond to Andersonville.

On August 13, near the hundred foot washed away portion of the wall, a miracle happened. Gushing there from the ground sprung a new source of fresh water for the prisoners. It was believed by many to be an act of Divine Providence because of the hundreds of lives it probably helped to save. The inmates who first witnessed this mighty act called the place Providence Spring.

Providence Spring was the place Kyzer liked to go when he wanted to be alone, among the thousands all around. If he closed his eyes for a few minutes, he could pretend that he was alone. He sat at the mouth of the spring watching the clear water gush like an eternal fountain.

"Dear Father in Heaven, I know I don't speak to you as often as I should. I'm hoping you'll be forgiving me for that. I'm just thanking you today for the spring of living water rising up from this well and flowing across this ground. You have promised us the living water that if we believe on your son that we will never thirst again. I thank you for that promise and this, the physical water you have provided for our need. Thank you for sparing my brother and allowing me to find him here. I pray you will keep us safe as well as all who dwell within these prison walls. Return us to our homes and our loved ones if it be your will. Please watch over Dellanna for me. I pray this prayer in the holy name of Jesus. Amen."

"I thought I might find you here," Rob said. "What are you doing?"

"Just thinking," he said, "thinking about Dellanna and the folks."

"Seth tells me the tunnel should be finished in a few more days," Rob said.

"I've got a bad feeling about this tunnel," Kyzer said. "You know, sometimes the best laid plans don't always work out."

"It's a chance for escape. You just have to decide if you want to take that chance," Rob said.

And, take that chance he would. Two weeks later, the men sat huddled inside the tent waiting for Seth to emerge from the tunnel.

"I've been almost to the end," Seth said, pulling himself out of the hole. "I'm guessing it's five, maybe six more feet to the end. We can all go tonight, if you want."

"Yes, let's do it. It's what we've been working for." They all agreed. Tonight, they would make their escape.

"I'll go first," Seth said. "Dylan next, he'll help me with the digging. Give us three hours then send in Michael. If he doesn't come back, you'll know the three of us made it."

Seth and Dylan worked hard together as they each took turns chipping away at the Georgia red clay while using a small cast iron skillet as a shovel. Nearing the top, they discovered the earth wasn't as hard while the excavation became much easier. Five more scoops, Seth Devane was breathing the refreshing air of freedom. He could see the stars as he looked through fragments of loose blades of grass. He quietly continued pulling away at the dirt, sending it down to Dylan who pressed hard, packing it into the sides of the small cavern.

'I can see the tree line about fifty yards from here. Pass the word to Lancaster. When he sees we've made it into the woods, he's next," Seth said. "Then, it's every man for himself. Hope to see you on the outside. I'm gone."

The other three men waited and worried, crouching there together. Billy Hopkins started shaking as his body trembled with emotion. Kyzer knew he was scared. However, they sensed no sign of a returning Michael.

"They made it," Kyzer said. "Rob, you go next. Billy and I will be right behind you."

'Just a few more feet to freedom' was all Rob Kelsey could think about as he slid on his belly, elbowing his way along the dirt floor in the dark. Reaching the opening, with one deep breath, he pulled himself up and out of the hole. In a crouching position, he began a slow paced walk, and then broke into a run as he reached the edge of the woods. The snap of a broken twig was the only sound heard in the still of the night.

A guard suddenly aroused from his nap in the nearby pigeon roost. He aimed his rifle into the darkness as he stood peering from atop the wall. He waited.

"Kyzer, you go next, after your brother," Billy said.

"No, you go. I won't leave you. I'll be last. Just go, damn it!" Kyzer said.

Moments later, Billy's head emerged, kepi pushed down tightly against his forehead. Arms extended up while he pulled his shaking body halfway out.

"Halt! Who goes there? Stop, or I'll shoot," a voice yelled.

Billy froze. Then, in an instant, he was running across the field. A single shot rang out from the carbine into the back of Billy Hopkins' head.

Kyzer panicked. He knew now he couldn't go. He could only hope and pray that Rob and the others made it. Kyzer fell back against the wall as he turned in the other direction, crawling back toward the entrance as fast as he could. He was out of breath as he came up inside the tent. He couldn't stay here. Grabbing the lantern and a few things he could carry, he opened the tent flap and started a brisk walk across the prison yard toward the camp of Elias Caudel.

A wagon load of guards and dogs were out the rest of the night in search of the escapees. By early dawn, Dylan Barclay, Michael Lancaster, and Rob Kelsey were captured. Lancaster's right foot had nearly been chewed off by the dogs before the guards finally got to him. Shackled in irons, the three men were taken before Captain Wirz who demanded they should also confess any others who were involved in this escape attempt. Unable to get a confession, Wirz put the prisoners into the stocks for two weeks. Seth Devane was never found.

A sudden thunderstorm erupted. The intense rainfall poured down upon Michael Lancaster, Dylan Barclay, and Rob Kelsey, drenching their near naked skin. The men hung side by side, fastened securely in the stocks, their bodies racked in excruciating pain. Their pants were left on, but shirts had been torn off and boots removed. The rain continued to pound the backs of their heads and hands as they protruded from the crossbar of the stock. At least, the soaking rain had helped to cleanse the strong odor in their pants where they had messed and relieved themselves. Lancaster's foot had been dressed and bandaged, but now the blood flowed again, mingling with the muddy rain water standing around the base of his stocks.

"I'm dying, oh God! Look at my foot, and these damn bastards don't even give a shit," he moaned.

"Hey, you goddamn Rebs, we've got a man out here that needs some medical attention. He's bleeding to death. How's about showin' a little mercy and compassion?" Dylan yelled out.

No response.

"That's all right. It'll soon be over for me, anyway," Michael said. "Dylan, you and Rob keep yourselves strong and make it out of here."

"We're all going to make it out," Rob said.

After a while, the rain stopped as the sun came out spreading its warm rays onto their raw skin. It was agonizing for the three men. With their parched throats, they could no longer speak. The guards would come around three times a day to give them water and something to eat. By the third morning, Michael Lancaster was gone. He was left hanging there all day, baking in the sun. Swarms of buzzing horseflies lit on his bowed head while the flies ravished at his face, eyes, ears, nose, and open mouth. At times, a couple of buzzards would swoop down upon him where they began to peck on the back on his head. Dylan and Rob would yell out at them; but after a while, it didn't do any good. They just kept coming back. In late afternoon, the wagon stopped to load and take Lancaster to the dead house. By this time, the buzzards had eaten away the flesh from the top of his head, exposing the skull. One even sat perched upon his bare shoulder as it pecked out his eyes.

Rob closed his eyes in escape of this horrible sight. All he could think about now was Kyzer. Did he make it out of the tunnel or was the shot he heard the one that killed his brother?

Toward the end of the second week, Dylan Barclay and Rob Kelsey barely clung to life as they hung motionless in the stocks. Rob and Dylan's legs had given out as the pressure on their necks and backs took the brunt of their body weight. A numbness in the lower back gave way to spasms while they floated in and out of consciousness. The Captain and two guards approached and stood before the stocks.

"I see you men are still alive. It is not intended for you to die. This is only punishment for your escape attempt. I tell you that your tunnel is no more. It is destroyed, sealed up. You want to try escape again? You will get four weeks in the stocks, do you hear? I give you both mercy. You will now spend the next two weeks together in the ball and chains."

Captain Henry Wirz turned and walked away while the guards unlocked the stocks, releasing the prisoners. The next day, Dylan and Rob awoke to find themselves shackled together and alive.

◆▶◀▶

At fifty-six, Doctor John Kelsey could only feel the effects of the war as he saw it in the lives of the people of Hastings, most of them barely able to get by. The life that he had known was gone. He knew things would never be the same again. The economy was gone. It was hard just to have food. John didn't go to the hospital every day so he tried to keep a small garden, and it had been rapidly stripped away. Most of the time, he thought about his boys. The last word he had known about them was that Rob was going to Gettysburg, and Kyzer was leaving for Petersburg. He knew Elizabeth prayed for them every day. How he longed for the war to end and the boys to come back home.

With battles all over places in Virginia raging close to Hastings, it was fortunate that Kellwood and the Chandalar Plantation remained untouched by the war. However, the big houses were falling into decay. Without money for repairs, and practically all the slaves gone, there was nothing left for the upkeep. When told by the Kelseys that she had been freed by the Emancipation Proclamation by President Lincoln, Aurelia chose to remain at Kellwood, the only life she had ever known. Whenever he was able to pay, John Kelsey promised her wages. Sally took Epsy and left with an adventurous young black man headed to New York.

Dinah and Nathaniel remained in service to the Braxtons at Chandalar, but all the plantation slaves were gone, many to the North. Chandalar, the tobacco plantation, was devastated by the effects of the war, while it now lay in shambles. The rich tobacco fields once filled with tall leafy stalks, wasted away, resembling a horrific drought. The barren fields were stripped while the early stages of erosion were setting in.

Elizabeth spent much of her time rocking on the veranda. She wrote an occasional letter to Susannah. At times, she would go to the kitchen to help Aurelia prepare something to eat. On some days, she walked out to the little cemetery and pulled the weeds growing there.

In December, a few days before Christmas, a tiny bastard baby was born at Chandalar. Dinah delivered the child, a girl that Dellanna named Lydia. She chose the name of the rich lady from the Bible, Lydia, a seller of purple. The baby had bright red hair like her mother, but it was too early to determine if she resembled her father.

Dellanna's father kept her locked away in her room upstairs since first learning of his daughter's condition. Richard Braxton was tempted to put her out of the house by sending her to Anne's relatives in Richmond. With the war going on everywhere, at his wife's insistence, he agreed she should remain there in seclusion, mainly in her room. Dellanna was free to move about the house, but under no condition could she venture outside or be seen in public. Whenever company or guests came calling, she remained in her room. This also meant no attendance at church services or social events, the price she paid for her sin and the shameful disgrace she brought upon her family. Dellanna assured her father that she would marry Kyzer when he returned. She hoped her father would allow her to resume a normal lifestyle with her daughter. In the meantime, Dinah and Nathaniel helped to take care of both of them inside the house.

As Lydia grew, each day Dellanna thought about Kyzer. Where was he? What was he doing? When would he be home?

CHAPTER 14

Rob Kelsey was never the same after the day he was released from the stocks and coupled together with Dylan Barclay in the ball and chains. First, he didn't know if his brother had been killed by the shot he heard that night or by some miracle he had gotten away after all. Now, his eyes were beginning to sink back into his head, and his teeth were rotting away. Rob soon found difficulty in pulling his own weight whenever he had to go anywhere attached to his chain mate. Even Dylan, with so much weight loss, found it difficult to get around.

In two weeks, when they were released and put back into the prison yard, it surprised Rob to find Kyzer sitting near Providence Spring. "I thought you were dead," Rob cried.

"Wasn't me. They got poor Billy Hopkins instead." Kyzer jumped up to hug him. "Lucky for me, we switched places at the last minute."

"Barclay, Lancaster, and I hid out in the woods all night.

They brought in the dogs and caught us by early morning. Lancaster's dead. He died in the stocks."

"I was hoping you got away, Rob; but at least you're alive."

"Dylan and I have been chained together for the past two weeks. He's lost a hell of a lot of body weight, and I don't feel very well myself."

"Yeah, I can really see it in your face."

"Wirz kept on us, pressing for a confession; but we kept insisting it was just the three of us. Seth got away, I guess. We never saw him again, Ky."

Over the next few months, Rob's condition of diarrhea, chronic cough, and weight loss reduced his body dramatically, leaving him looking much like a living skeleton. Most of his teeth were gone, and now he couldn't walk. The scurvy had just about eaten him up. Kyzer took care of his brother by feeding him and helping him with his personal needs as Rob lay there on his pallet.

The siege of Petersburg lasted seven more months while General Grant sent Sheridan to destroy the railroad which allowed supplies to be carried into Richmond. Lee sent forces to retaliate, but the struggle ended in defeat of the Confederates at the battle of Five Forks on April 1. The next day, Grant attacked Petersburg, driving Lee into hopeless retreat. Federal troops secured the city and marched into Richmond. On April 9, 1865, Grant and Lee met at Appomattox, Virginia. The final terms for surrender were signed by the two generals in the parlor of the McLean house. The South had lost. The war was over. The news spread through Andersonville like wildfire.

Kyzer could tell immediately that his brother's life was slowly drifting away. Since the first day of May, Rob just lay there motionless on a pallet underneath his shebang with Kyzer at his side. The only response Kyzer could get from him was the look through his staring eyes. Sometimes, he noticed a twitch in Rob's fingers as he tried to move his hand. When Kyzer held his hand, he detected only a slight response.

"Don't guess you feel much like talking today, brother, so I'll just talk to you. The big news around here is that Lee surrendered to Grant a couple of weeks back, and this war is finally over. The little battle that supposedly would be over in a few days lasted almost five years. The good news now is that very soon we will probably be leaving this place. Can you imagine that? What about that? Rob, do you understand what I'm saying? Look at me. Squeeze my hand, brother. The bad news is that following the surrender, this actor, fellow by the name of John Wilkes Booth, up and shot the President in Washington. He and Mrs. Lincoln were attending a play at Ford's Theatre when the assassin entered the presidential box and shot Mr. Lincoln in the head with a small derringer, they say. He died the next morning on April 15. Now, the entire country has been thrown into a state of national mourning and turmoil. There's still talk, though, about the prisoner exchange that Wirz has been telling us about. So far, there hasn't been much news about that. Here, I'm going to give you a little water. Just think, maybe in a few days, you and me will both be walking out of this godforsaken place. If the hell mentioned in the Good Book is worse than this place, I can't even begin to imagine what that would be like, can you? Now, what do you want to talk about, Rob?"

Kyzer poured some water onto a rag and gently wiped what was left of Rob's face. It was full of sores, some oozing, some scabs. His darkened eyes lay sunk into their blood-circled sockets. His jaw slightly dropped in attempts to draw in a breath. When his mouth opened, a watery blood secretion flowed from the cavities where teeth had been. It was almost unbearable for Kyzer to see Rob like this, but he continued to try to take care of him. He prayed that it would soon be over while he lay the wet rag across Rob's forehead. With no detected movement or response from his brother, Kyzer tried to pass the time as he continued to talk to him.

"I always wanted to ask you why you never married, course

that's really none of my business anyway. I just wanted you to know that I thought you would make a great father someday. You have been my greatest inspiration. Would you believe that I've always wanted to be just like you? You will always be my hero, Rob. Guess what? I'm going to marry Dellanna. You remember her, don't you? I promised her we'd get married when I came back home. Yes sir, we're gonna get married and have ourselves a houseful of young'uns. I hope I can be a good father some day. Hey, remember that time when you beat me up for telling the folks that I saw you smoking rabbit tobacco? It was only because you wouldn't let me smoke, too. And, all those times when you thought I was asleep in bed, and I'd hear you moan and rustle around under the covers, I thought something awful must be wrong with you. I felt you jerk and twitch, and all the while, you were just chokin' the chicken. Do you think our father ever did that? Of course, he's your father, not mine. Susannah made damn sure to let me know that I was the little bastard that was adopted. But, you know, from that time until now, I've never felt any difference. I'll always remember John and Elizabeth, how they never showed any partiality between us. We've got ourselves a set of loving, Christian parents, don't we? About me, your little orphan brother, once there was talk that Uncle Will was my real father and his Atlanta mistress was my mother. He always denied that story. I even asked him once long ago and he told me that he wasn't. I never believed he was, anyway. I don't look anything at all like him. Will and Katharine's boy, Walt, must be about twenty-three years old now. Do you think he could possibly be off in this war somewhere? Even in here? God forbid. I can't remember when it was the last time I saw him. He was always a scraggy looking kid. You and I will have to look him up sometime after we get home and settled. It'll be good to see the folks before long, won't it? You know, Mama's going to be surprised to see her two boys, Rob ... .Rob?"

Rob was gone. He was finally at peace and rest. It was

probably better this way. Kyzer knew this. He knew John and Elizabeth would be spared of having to see their son suffer as he had these past few months. Kyzer sat there for a while. He didn't know where Elias and the others were. He was thankful to have had this past hour alone with his brother.

Kyzer reached down and picked Rob up in his arms. Rob felt as though he didn't even weigh a hundred pounds. Kyzer moved along slowly as he carried his brother past hundreds who would look up and then back down as he limped toward the gate. Dead bodies were usually placed here to be picked up by the wagon and taken to the dead house. Kyzer sat down by his brother, Rob, as he waited there for the wagon to come.

Two days had passed since Rob had died when the North gate swung open and Captain Henry Wirz entered the yard. This one time, the gate remained opened as the wagon pulled to a stop, surrounded by a team of guards. Wirz stood there smiling as he began to call out to the prisoners.

"You men, gather around. I have good news for you. Come closer. A prisoner exchange has been granted, and the gate is open for you to walk out. You see, I tell you that the exchange is coming. I do not lie; I speak truth. I always come before you unarmed and trusting. Now, you walk to the depot where the train is waiting."

Wirz turned the wagon around and left through the open gate. Soon, the mass exodus began as thousands stood to their feet, starting their journey through the gate of freedom.

"You coming with us, Kyzer?" asked Elias.

"Naw, you go on ahead. I'll be along later," Kyzer said.

"Well, I guess this is goodbye then. Me and the boys are headed out."

"I hope everything goes well with you. Thanks for all you've done for me. I'll never forget it. It was good to know you," Kyzer said.

"Same here. Good luck to you. Sorry 'bout your brother. Goodbye, my friend." Elias wanted to say much more to him but the words wouldn't come. How he wanted to throw his arms around Kyzer but he dare not. He had to hide his emotions quickly as he forced himself to turn and leave.

Kyzer sat there while he watched Elias Caudel walk away. After a while, he decided to go down to the dead house. He saw a young Reb standing there near the table.

"Hey soldier, I'm looking for my brother. He died two days ago, and I was wondering where he might be," Kyzer said.

"What's his name?"

"Kelsey. First Lieutenant Rob Kelsey."

"I'll have to check the roster to find the name and assignment number. Each soldier is given a number. Kelsey. Here it is, 1st Lt. Rob Kelsey #12889. He was put into the ground yesterday."

"Could you tell me where the grave is located?"

"That road over there leads into the cemetery," he said pointing the direction. "Just follow it in. You'll see the trenches along the back. He should be in that section. Just look for the number."

"Thank you." He turned and limped toward the road. As Kyzer walked into the cemetery, he was overwhelmed with what he saw. It was unbelievable, almost like the first sight of the view into the prison months ago. Only this time it was thousands of wooden markers stretched out row after row. What a sight to behold. He was awestruck.

It took a while to get there, but Kyzer could see the section that the Reb told him about. He looked down at the markers numbered 12887, 12888, 12889, Rob's grave. He fell to the ground and wept. After a while there, Kyzer walked back to the North gate. Thousands were in the process of leaving while hundreds still remained in camp. It was an eery feeling for him to be in a prison yard with the gate standing wide open, and he couldn't even leave. Kyzer thought about their futile attempt to dig out by tunneling. It would seem now to have been easier to leave that way rather than walk out of the main gate. Where could he go? To the Andersonville Depot, or pick a direction and start walking. Kyzer knew he couldn't walk far on his bad leg, let alone the distance from south Georgia to Virginia. He would have to wait on a train headed north.

"There you are Kyzer," he said. "I was hoping to find you." The haggard man stood before him in his ragged clothing and worn boots. His frail body was propped on a handmade crutch.

"Hello, Dylan. You heading out?"

"Yes, I am anxious to get home to Boston. Sure hope I can get on the train today."

"Good luck. I'm in no hurry right now," Kyzer said.

"Kyzer, I'm really sorry about Rob. I know you will certainly miss him. He told me so much about your family while we were in the chains."

"Yeah, I'm really missing him now. He was my hero, you know. At least, his folks won't have to see him like you and I. I've just come from his grave. I know where it is located. One day, after all this war is over, I'd like to come back here," Kyzer said.

"Not me. I don't guess I'll ever come back. It's going to be hard to try to forget all the death and disease in this pitiful place," Dylan said.

"Look at us, though. We survived. I will go home to marry Dellanna. You will go home to your wife and children. Just think, thousands of men will remain here in the ground. They will never get to do that. We are so blessed," Kyzer said.

Dylan put his arm around Kyzer's shoulder, offering a brief hug. "I guess this is goodbye, my friend. We've been through so much together. It is truly a blessing for me to have known you and your courageous brother, Rob. May God be with you always."

"And you, the same. Goodbye, Dylan Barclay," Kyzer said as he watched him walk out of his life.

When Kyzer got to the depot, men were camped out on both sides as near to the tracks as possible. In one part of town, a ladies' auxiliary had set up tables offering cornbread and soup. Kyzer couldn't remember the last time he ate so he headed over to the lines around the tables. He heard one of the women say that they had run out of soup, but pieces of cornbread were left. Kyzer was finally able to work his way forward to grab one of the last pieces. His mouth was so dry, he couldn't eat. Suddenly, he became very ill and weak, his eyes rolled back, and he collapsed onto the street. The Confederate lady standing nearby was moved with compassion.

The restless crowd began to stand as the whistle announced the arrival of another train. As it came to a halt, hundreds of the more able-bodied pushed and shoved their way on board.

Dylan Barclay, at last, took his seat on the train. Goodbye to Andersonville.

◆▶ ◀◆

"Where am I?" Kyzer asked as he opened his eyes.

"Good morning, son. You're in my house in Andersonville. I am Mrs. Percy Sturdivant. Please, call me Abigail."

"How did I come to be here?"

"My boy, you've been really sick. Do you remember being at the train depot?"

"Why yes, I do. I remember."

"That was three weeks ago. You were burning up with a fever. I had my husband carry you here and we've been taking care of you since then."

"Bless you, ma'am. I'm very grateful to you and your husband."

"Your fever finally broke yesterday and I feel you are doing much better now. I told my husband, Percy, that I believe our boy is going to make it."

"Why did you take me in?"

"We lost our boy at Gettysburg. I've often thought many times if our Carl ever needed help, maybe some nice northern lady would be there to comfort him. I felt it was my Christian duty to help you. What is your name, young man?"

"Kelsey, ma'am. Kyzer Kelsey from Hastings, Virginia. My father's a doctor there. How can I ever repay you?"

"You just rest now. I'll be back in a while with some food for you. Would you care for a drink of water?"

As Kyzer sat up in the bed, he looked around the room. A gentle breeze flowed through the open window, white ruffled curtains moving in rhythm while the warm sunshine peeked through the window panes. Dressed in a white cotton nightshirt, and propped on two large down filled pillows, the luxurious feather bed felt very comfortable to Kyzer. A multicolored quilt covered the four poster knotty pine bed. He saw a stack of clothing located on the chest, butternut trousers, blue plaid shirt, a leather belt, socks, and a pair of drawers. Setting on the floor were a pair of brown boots. Mrs. Abigail had everything arranged very nicely.

Kyzer slid from the mattress, grabbing for the nearby bedpost. He felt the weakness in his knees as he reached down for the chamber pot. He pulled his nightshirt up while he positioned himself. It felt almost human again to be able to pee into a chamber pot inside a bedroom.

"Oh Kyzer, I'm sorry. Please, excuse me," Mrs. Abigail said as she walked in, surprising him.

"It's all right. Don't go, Mrs. Sturdivant. I'm sure I don't have anything you haven't seen before," he said as he let his nightshirt fall.

"I should have knocked," she said.

"If you don't mind, I am finished with this. If these clothes are for me, I appreciate them, ma'am."

"The clothes are for you. You look about the same size as Carl. I know he would want you to have them," she said as she held the drawers before him.

Kyzer stepped into the drawers, pulling them up as he tied the drawstring. He pulled the nightshirt over his head and lay it across the end of the bed. With his back toward her, Mrs. Abigail couldn't help notice his broad shoulders and muscular arms despite his present weakened condition.

"If you'll sit back on the bed, I've brought a pan of warm water for you to bathe," she said. "I'm heating some vegetable soup for you. It should be ready by the time you are bathed and dressed. Here is a bar of soap and a towel. Do you need help with your bath?"

"No ma'am, I believe I will be able to take care of myself. Thank you."

"Kyzer, if you don't mind my asking about that place on your back. Were you shot there?"

"Why, no ma'am. That's a birthmark. I always joked with my mama saying that if anything ever happened to me, she could always tell it was me by looking for the little strawberry on my shoulder."

"I didn't mean to be so personal," Abigail said.

"No offense taken, I assure you. I forget it's there since I never see it. It is a reminder for me, though, about the night of my birth. You see, I'm adopted. I was abandoned by my mother. Let me get some clothes on, and I'll tell you about it. I hope one day to be able to find her."

"Very well, after you bathe, I will send Percy in to help you get dressed," Mrs. Abigail said.

"Hello there, Kyzer. I'm Percy Sturdivant. Abigail says I may need to help you."

"I could use some help with the socks and boots," he said, looking at the short little man with the bushy grey chin whiskers.

"How are you feeling, son?" he asked.

"I'm doing well, thanks to you and Mrs. Abigail. Your kind generosity is overwhelming."

"We can't begin to help everybody, but my dear wife told me that we needed to take care of you. You must know that you're lucky to be alive," Percy said.

"I certainly do. Mrs. Abigail is quite a remarkable woman. I'm very grateful to her for all she has done for me. And you too, sir."

"Kyzer, the Missus told me to ask you if you felt like walking to the kitchen to have some soup with us," Percy said.

"If you'll excuse me while I finish up, it will be a pleasure to join you both in a few minutes."

After Percy left the room, Kyzer stood in front of the mirror over the dressing table. He stared at the man looking back at him. His thoughts suddenly flashed back to Andersonville. Other than catching his reflection in the stream at Providence Spring a few times, he felt he no longer looked like the man he once knew. He ran his fingers through his long matted hair, the beard making him appear much older than his present twenty-four years. He unfolded the shirt, putting it on, buttoning the front, and tucking it into his pants. He reached for the belt, running it through the belt loops around his thin body as he fastened the buckle. Kyzer walked to the kitchen and stopped in the doorway. "This is about as good as I can look, I guess," he said.

"Why Kyzer, everything seems to fit perfectly, and you look really nice," Abigail said. "What about the boots?"

"They're fine. I was just thinking, maybe after we eat, I could use a shave and a haircut."

"If you can trust me, I'll be glad to do it. I have cut Carl's hair since he was a boy. Percy goes to a barber in town, says he wants to keep what little hair he has left," she laughed.

Abigail began clearing the dishes from the table following their meal together. "Percy, why don't you and Kyzer go sit on the back porch? When I finish in the kitchen, I'll come out there to wash and cut his hair."

"Would you care to join me on the porch, son?"

"Certainly, let's go," Kyzer said.

In a while, Abigail assembled everything she needed onto the small table. The water basin, soap, towels, comb, mirror, scissors, and straight razor were all laid out in a neat arrangement.

"I believe the last time I did this, Carl was only seventeen. Are you sure you're ready to give me another try at it, Kyzer?"

"I'm ready. Do I need to take off my shirt?"

"If you want. I'll just have to bear seeing you without it, won't I? Come over here, and we'll begin with a good head scrubbing." Abigail washed his hair until it began to shine in a luxuriant dark brown hue. After towel drying, she combed out the tangles. "How much do I need to cut?"

"I wear it about a medium length, but you cut it as short as you want. I really don't care. I'm more anxious to get this scraggly beard off," Kyzer said.

"All right, I'll do my best. Kyzer, you said you would tell about your adoption. Feel like talking about it?"

"I don't mind. I was born in 1841 in Jonesboro, Georgia, close to Atlanta, you know. My adoptive parents are Dr. John Kelsey and his wife, Elizabeth. They have a daughter, Susannah, born in 1834, and a son, Rob, born in 1836. Elizabeth miscarried a baby boy named Michael just three days before they found me on their front porch. I was eleven years old when I found out that I was adopted. At first, my folks said they searched everywhere for my real mother and father. The search ended when we moved to Hastings, Virginia, to live with John's mother after his father died. I don't know if my mother and father are still alive; but one day, I would like to find them. My brother, Rob, just died a few weeks ago at Andersonville. Susannah is married and lives in Richmond."

"That's an interesting story. I'm sure your folks can hardly wait to see you again. Do they know that you're here at Andersonville?" Abigail asked.

"I don't think so," Kyzer said. "Now, I have to go and tell them that their beloved son is dead."

"Kyzer, we want you to stay here with us until you are much stronger," Percy said. "Would you do that?"

"I will. Maybe there's something around here I can do to help you," he said.

"I'm a furniture maker," Percy said. "I could use an extra pair of hands in my wood shop."

Abigail finished cutting Kyzer's hair into a nice, medium length. "Now, let's work on that beard," she said, picking up the straight razor. "Do you want to leave a mustache?"

"No ma'am. Just shave it all off."

After his shave, Abigail held the hand mirror in front of Kyzer's face. "You look very nice," she said. "Gracious me, I've just noticed you have beautiful dark brown eyes."

"Thank you, Mrs. Abigail. My girl, Dellanna, tells me she loves my eyes. I plan to marry her when I get home."

Two weeks later, the day arrived when Kyzer felt well enough to begin his trip home.

"Mr. and Mrs. Sturdivant, I thank you from the bottom of my heart that you took me into your home and cared for me over these past few weeks. I could never begin to repay you for your kindness to me. I'm going to miss you," Kyzer said.

"We have enjoyed your company. You allowed us to care for you as if you were our own son," Percy said. "It has been our pleasure to have you stay with us."

"That's very true, Kyzer," Abigail said. "I know, as a mother, how much your folks must be feeling. They would be longing for your safe return home."

"Good luck, son," Percy said as he heartily shook Kyzer's hand.

Kyzer put his arm around Abigail as he walked her to the front porch. "Goodbye, Mrs. Abigail. I'll never forget you."

"May God bless and keep you always," she said. "You are welcome here if you should ever return, my boy."

With a sigh, Kyzer turned and stepped from the porch, walking with the limp from his left leg. He turned to wave back at Percy and Abigail standing there on the street. Mrs. Abigail waved to him.

Kyzer sat among the restless crowd at the Andersonville Depot, eagerly waiting. He was waiting on the train that would be there soon to take him home.

CHAPTER 15

The sun was shining brightly that morning in June when Kyzer stepped down from the train. The station was practically deserted as he walked through the front entrance and onto the street. He remembered that the town would be filled with people going routinely about their business by mid-morning. It was Saturday, but at the moment, nothing was stirring in Hastings. As Kyzer walked through the town, he noticed some of the businesses were boarded up and closed. There were just a few people, here and there, along the street. He didn't recognize anyone he knew, and he had only been gone just over a year. As he rounded the corner, he stopped by a lamp post to look down the street. At the end of the block stood the neglected old brick structure with the broken faded black shutters that was Collins Infirmary. Kyzer stood there for several minutes, realizing that through those doors, he would probably find his father.

"Dr. Vincent, it's Kyzer. Is my father here?"

The doctor stood from his desk, completely surprised to see the young man standing before him.

"My God, it really is you, Kyzer." Dr. Geoffrey Vincent rushed around the edge of the desk and locked his arms around Kyzer's broad shoulders. "Welcome home. How wonderful to see you."

"I was hoping to find the old man busy at work."

"Sorry, he's not here. John is coming in later this afternoon to help me inventory supplies. When did you get here?"

"I just now arrived after a very long train ride. I'm really tired."

"I'll tell you what. If you can wait until I can gather a few things, I'm headed out past your place. You're welcome to ride with me."

"I can wait. Take your time," Kyzer said.

Within the hour, Doctor Vincent had Kyzer in the buggy headed toward Kellwood. "Now, don't be surprised at what you're going to see when we get there. Kellwood is probably not going to look the way you remember it. The times have changed things drastically."

Sure enough. The doctor was right as he stopped the buggy at the end of the drive while Kyzer climbed out. "Thank you for the ride home. I want to walk down along the drive to the house."

"Be sure and tell John that I said for him to take the afternoon off. I can manage the inventory by myself. I'll be glad to drive you to the front of the house, if you want."

"Naw, I really want to walk. I'll see you later, and thanks again for the ride."

Doctor Vincent pulled his buggy away, leaving Kyzer standing at the beginning of the once very beautiful landscape. The oak trees stood gnarled and ugly against the backdrop of dry barren fields. Looking toward the house from where he stood, Kyzer saw the once majestic white columned front portico now faded into its grey tint. Several of the drab green shutters were broken or missing altogether. Shrubs and flowers planted along the front of the veranda were no longer visible. Weeds were growing in bare places on the lawn and healthy green grass was gone. Plantation life as he remembered was gone.

Elizabeth was sitting in her rocking chair when John came from inside the house to join her on the veranda. "John, look yonder at the end of the drive. A few minutes ago, Dr. Geoff stopped his buggy to let a stranger out, and then he drove on down the road. The man is just standing there, looking all around. Now, he's heading this way, and he walks with a limp. Probably another beggar, don't you think?"

John held his gaze only for a moment toward the man when he reached over and grabbed Elizabeth's arm, pulling her from the chair. "My God, Elizabeth, that's no beggar. It's him. It's Kyzer!" John held to Elizabeth while they bolted down the steps, screaming and shouting with jubilation. Running as fast as they could toward him, they met under the big oaks. Kyzer lifted Elizabeth off her feet as he held her up, spinning her around a few times. He hugged and kissed her as he put her down. Then, he grabbed John in a bear hug while John threw his arms around the boy.

"It's so good to see you and have you home. Our prayers are answered," John said.

"I have longed for this moment for so long. Kyzer, I can hardly believe that you're really here. Praise be to God, He has brought you home to us," Elizabeth said.

"You both look wonderful to me," Kyzer said. "How's Dellanna?"

"Oh, uh, she's doing well. We see her from time to time. I guess you'll be wanting to see her before long," John said.

"Oh yes, I can hardly wait," Kyzer said. "How's Captain Midnight?"

"He's good, probably in the pen out by the barn," John said. "You want to see him?"

"Yes, might as well walk on out there while we're heading in that direction," he said.

"I'm going to let you both do that, Kyzer, while I find Aurelia and let her know you're home," Elizabeth said. "We'll prepare you a special supper tonight to celebrate your homecoming. Kyzer, you've been shot. What happened to your leg?"

"Got that at Petersburg. I guess my limp gave it away, didn't it? Why don't I plan to tell you both about everything after supper. After I see Midnight, I would love to take a nap. I'm really tired. Maybe, you could invite Dellanna over for supper tonight," Kyzer said.

"I don't know, we'll see," Elizabeth said while she veered toward the house.

John and Kyzer walked to the barn. Kyzer opened the gate to the pen as he walked in and called to his horse. "Midnight, it's me. Hey boy, remember me?" He walked over and patted him on the neck as the black stallion reared his head. "We'll go for a ride later. I'll see you in a while." Kyzer closed the gate and walked over to where John was waiting. "I have to tell you something before we go back to the house that is very difficult for me, but you have to know. I found Rob."

"You did. You found him? Where? Is he all right?"

"I am truly sorry to have to tell you this, but we were together at Andersonville, the prison in Georgia. I found him there where he has mercifully died on the second of May. I was with him there until the end. He took a hit in the shoulder at Gettysburg and survived that. It was the scurvy that got him. I'm sorry, sir."

John grabbed a fence post as his body slid to the ground. "Oh no, not Rob," he cried. "My boy can't be gone. He just can't."

"I saw him suffer so much during those last weeks. He couldn't get any better. He told me he was glad that you and his mama wouldn't have to see him like that. He's at peace now."

"Scurvy, you say?"

"Yes, sir. It was dreadful."

"We're just going to tell Elizabeth it was a fever, you hear? Rob got sick with a fever and died, that's what I'll tell her."

"Just so that you'll know it, I'm telling you now that I know where he is buried. I've been to his grave."

"Oh Kyzer, you were with him. I'm so glad. He wasn't alone. You were with your brother. I'm so happy you've come back. You're home with us now."

"Do you want to tell the news to Mama alone?"

"No, son, you go with me. I want you with me when I tell her," John said. The slow walk to the house seemed so long for John and Kyzer as they walked together trying to hold back the tears. When they entered the house, Aurelia was sweeping in the great hallway.

"Bless my soul, it's Mister Kyzer. We's so glad to have you home."

"I'm glad to be home. You're looking well, Aurelia," he said while he gave her a hug.

"Oh, but you so thin, just like a scarecrow. I's gonna have to feed you, and get some meat back on those bones," she laughed.

"Where's Elizabeth?" John asked Aurelia.

"Miss Elizabeth, she up in her room. I believe she puttin' on another dress for Mister Kyzer."

"Would you mind going upstairs and asking her to please join us in the parlor? Thank you, Aurelia."

Several minutes later, Elizabeth stood in the doorway. Her beautiful black hair was freshly brushed and pinned up, and she was wearing another dress.

"Come in, my dear. Please close the door," John said as he and Kyzer stood together in front of the fireplace.

"What's wrong?" Elizabeth asked, sensing something wrong as her body began to tremble. "It's Rob, isn't it?"

John looked directly into her eyes, and she knew. She began to cry. John walked over to his precious Elizabeth and put his arms around her. He held her close, her head resting upon his chest.

"Yes, darling, it's Rob. Our Rob is gone," he said while they both took a seat on the sofa, tears continuing to fall down their faces.

"Tell me, when did it all happen?" she asked.

"Kyzer, would you tell your mother what you told me, son?"

Kyzer fell to the floor at Elizabeth's feet, placing his large hands onto hers while he knelt there.

"Mama, we were both so very fortunate. Rob took a bullet to the shoulder at Gettysburg, and it healed. I survived the wound in my left leg. Then, I found Rob in the prison at Andersonville, the one in south Georgia. We were there for several months when Rob took a fever. He died a few weeks ago, just two days before we were all released from the stockade. I was with him when he died. He was a good soldier, brother, and such an inspiration to me. I grieve with you both in his passing."

The Kelsey family sat together for a long while in the parlor, reminiscing about the happier times they all shared with Rob.

"I'll have to write Susannah tomorrow," Elizabeth said. "She has to be told. I know it's not possible for us to go to her right now." She looked across the room where Kyzer sat in John's chair.

"Kyzer, we both thank God for your safe return."

"I know, Mama," he said, "I know."

"You go on upstairs and take your nap. Someone will come for you when supper's ready," she said. Kyzer kissed her on the cheek and left the room. "John, you've got to go and get Dellanna. Tell her to leave the baby with Dinah and come eat supper with us. Just don't tell her Kyzer is here."

◀▶◀▶

The deep blue sky spread its glorious color over the ashes

of Richmond. Susannah Hollis sat with her daughter on the bench outside the post office, the building itself only charred and smoke damaged from the great fire. She opened the letter marked *Special Delivery*, happy now to hear again from her mother. Hurriedly, she began to read about the exciting news of Kyzer's return home until she reached the paragraph that told about her brother's death. Her expression rapidly changed as the letter dropped onto her lap while the ray of happiness she felt turned to grief.

"What's the matter, Mama?" asked ten year old Mary Ruth.

"Oh my darling, your Uncle Rob has passed away, and Grandmother wants me to come home."

"May I go with you?"

"Why yes, Mary. I'll have to talk with your father to decide when we can make the trip. Guess what? Uncle Kyzer has just returned home from the war," she said.

"I'm glad," Mary said, pulling Susannah by the hand. "Come on, let's go find Daddy right now."

While she dried her tears, Susannah and Mary walked down the street toward the store. Hollis Hardware sustained minor damage, considering all the rubble and debris still visible in the streets after the burning of Richmond. It was hard to believe that this former stronghold capitol of the Confederacy, for the most part, now lay burnt to the ground. Reconstruction was going to be slow, but Charles and Henry Hollis kept busy trying to supply all the necessary building materials and hardware to demanding customers in the city. The doors were propped open by two small kegs as Susannah and her daughter entered the store.

"Charles, have you seen Henry?" Susannah asked as she approached the counter where he was weighing nails and bagging them.

"I believe he's out back. Susannah, have you been crying?"

"Yes, I'm afraid it's bad news for my family. Kyzer has just returned home with a leg wound he received during the siege of Petersburg. He and Rob had been imprisoned at Andersonville in Georgia where Rob took ill with a fever and died. My folks want me to come home if I can."

"Susannah, I am so sorry about Rob but glad to hear of Kyzer's safe return."

"Thank you, Charles. Mary, you stay here while I go talk to your father."

"Mary, would you like to help me bag some nails?"

"Sure, Uncle Charles," she said.

"Henry, I need to talk to you right away if you can stop work for a few minutes," Susannah said.

Henry climbed down from the stockroom ladder as he went over to Susannah and kissed her.

"What are you doing here? What's the matter, darling?"

"I've just come from the post office. I got a letter from Mama. She wants me to come home right away. Kyzer has come home, but Rob … .Rob is dead," she cried as Henry cradled her in his arms.

"Oh, honey, I'm so sorry. What happened?" he asked.

"Kyzer was shot in the leg, but he's all right. They both were in prison at Andersonville where Rob got sick with a fever and died. The letter said that was around the first of May. They buried him there," she said.

"What do you want to do?" he asked as she sat on a wooden crate.

"Henry, I know that you and Charles are so busy with all the business you are getting now. I thought I would take Mary and go to Mama's for a while. Is that all right with you? I can go now to the station and find out when we can take the train," she said.

"That's fine with me. I would like to go with you, but I really think I need to stay here with Charles. I'm sure your folks will understand. Let me get you some money, and you can go ahead and purchase your tickets," he said.

Susannah put the money into her purse as they walked over to Mary who was now sitting alone on the counter. "Hello, Daddy," she said.

"Hey there, my darling girl. Mary, how would you like to take a train ride and go visit your grandmother in Hastings?"

"Oh Daddy, could I? When can we go?"

"Well, Daddy's got to stay here, but you can go with your mother as soon as we can get the train tickets," he said.

"Hooray," Mary shouted. "Let's go right away."

"I guess that settles it then. We're off to the depot," Susannah said. "Darling, I'll see you tonight. Thank you for letting us go." She kissed Henry goodbye while she took Mary's hand and walked out the door.

All the way to the depot, Susannah recalled her childhood memories with Rob and Kyzer at Kellwood. Growing up there with the boys had been a pleasant experience for her. However, she would always remember the early years in Jonesboro, the town house, Vanie, Aunt Katharine, Uncle Will, and her grandparents. Then later on, life at Kellwood had been different and wonderful for her. Susannah felt free to roam in the nearby woods, go horseback riding, and swim down at Moss Rock Creek. She would play with her dolls, but the most fun was playing hide and seek and other games outside with Rob and Kyzer. That is, whenever they wanted to play with her. Sometimes, she felt excluded when Rob chose to be with his friends whenever they came around.

She remembered the time her friend Hortense McCafferty was visiting, and they secretly followed Rob and his older friend Billy Martin down to the creek. The boys were already in swimming when they stumbled upon their clothes piled beside the creek bank. The girls decided to hide the clothes and then watch what would happen. Hortense suggested that they scatter them in several different places nearby. The boys would surely know that someone had been there so the girls hurried to find themselves a good spot to hide and watch the action.

It wasn't long until the boys made their startling discovery. Standing on the creek bank, they were surprised to find their clothes missing and scattered everywhere among the bushes and rocks. Susannah would always remember the expression of total amazement and shock on Hortense's face that day. They not only saw her brother Rob naked, but the well endowed Billy Martin. They watched the boys running around in a panic, naked as jay birds, gathering up their clothes while looking for the culprit who had taken them. The snickering girls thought this was the funniest sight ever, especially getting to see Billy Martin without his clothes. So, this is what boys looked like. She recalled the little rhyme she and Hortense made up later on to taunt them sometimes when the boys would aggravate or tease them. "Violets are blue, and red is the rose; I've seen Rob and Billy without any clothes." The boys would turn red and grit their teeth with embarrassment.

Her biggest regret came on the day of Kyzer's eleventh birthday. The day she had the argument with him and told Kyzer that he was adopted. She was relieved after he eventually forgave her for the outburst. From then on, she felt he would always be her little brother, and she would love him just like Rob.

Now, Kyzer was shot in the leg, Rob was dead, and she was going home to Kellwood. Susannah and Mary stood at the window of the ticket agent in the depot.

"When is the next train leaving for Hastings? Please sir, I need a ticket for one child and one adult."

CHAPTER 16

At Chandalar, Dinah opened the door to reveal the weary looking doctor standing there on the veranda. "Good afternoon, Dr. Kelsey," she said.

"Hello, Dinah. Is Mr. Richard at home?"

"No sir. Mr. and Mrs. Braxton left about an hour ago. They's gone into town," Dinah said.

"Where is Dellanna?"

"Miss Dellanna upstairs with the baby. Is there anything wrong, sir?"

"Dinah, Kyzer is home, arrived today. He's asking for Dellanna to come for supper tonight at Kellwood. Would you ask her to come down, and please don't mention anything about Kyzer. It will be a surprise for her," he said.

"I'll go right up and tell her you're here," Dinah said. "She is going to be so happy. Come on in, and have a seat in the parlor."

In a few minutes, Dellanna entered the room. John Kelsey stood from his chair.

"Sit down," she said as Dellanna sat on the sofa. "Hello, Dr. Kelsey. I apologize for the way I look. Lydia and I have been taking our nap this afternoon. Dinah tells me my folks have gone into Hastings. Is there anything that I can do for you?"

"Well, actually Dellanna, it is you that I intended to speak with in the first place. Elizabeth and I have just received the sad news today that Rob is dead."

"Oh no, Dr. Kelsey, not Rob," she cried.

"I'm sorry, there is no easy way to talk about it. Elizabeth and I are both just devastated. I thought maybe you might come for supper tonight and stay a while," he said. "I think it would help Elizabeth's feelings."

"I would be glad to do that. I'll just need to get a few things to take for Lydia," she said.

"I was thinking, would it be possible for Dinah to keep her while you're gone?" he asked.

"Well, I suppose that would be all right. I could feed her just before I left, but I would need to get back home before very long," she said.

"If you don't mind, I believe things would be better tonight without the baby. Please, just for tonight. You know that you are always welcome to come anytime and bring her with you," he said.

"It is about time for Lydia to be waking up. She's been asleep for almost three hours," Dellanna said. "I'll want to go upstairs and change my dress. After I feed her, I'll be ready to go."

"I will wait for you on the veranda, and we'll ride together. I will drive you back whenever it comes time for you to leave," John said.

"Again, I'm so sorry about Rob. We can talk more on our drive to Kellwood," she said. "I shouldn't be too long. I'll have Dinah bring you something to drink."

After an hour, Dellanna appeared on the veranda in a beautiful pale green dress of silk brocade. She knew her waist would never again be nineteen and one half inches since the birth of her baby, but laced into her corset, she could still fit into most of her dresses. The green dress was probably the last new dress she had bought since the war, and she only wore it for special occasions. For some unknown reason, she felt like wearing it tonight. Dellanna looked very pretty with a dab of rouge on her cheeks and lips, and her vibrant red hair turned under accented by an emerald green velvet ribbon headband.

"I guess I'm ready, Dr. Kelsey."

"Why Dellanna, how nice you look this evening. You didn't have to go through all the trouble of getting dressed up," he said.

"There aren't many occasions around here anymore to actually dress up so I don't mind. I thought if I didn't drag this old thing out, before long it would just get moth eaten," she said.

"Now, remember, I'll have you back here as soon as you need to get back," he said.

"I've already given my instructions to Dinah. She is going to inform my folks where I am. Father still doesn't like me going out socially, but I don't feel that this is a social visit. Besides, he isn't here to stop me," Dellanna said.

It was almost a five mile trip from Chandalar to Kellwood. The buggy ride was a pleasant one while Dellanna and the doctor shared their thoughts as they remembered Rob. There was only one brief mention of Kyzer when Dellanna said she hoped Kyzer was doing all right wherever he was. Dr. John stopped the buggy close to the steps as he helped Dellanna down onto the drive. He offered his extended arm as Dellanna took hold while he escorted her onto the veranda.

"Would you mind waiting here for just a moment? Please, have a seat on the settee," he said to her. "I'll be right back."

John walked into the great hallway, making his way toward

the parlor. He found Elizabeth and Kyzer sitting there talking together. "Kyzer, you're up, son. How was your afternoon nap?"

"Really nice. I'm trying to get used to sleeping in a bed again," he laughed.

"Elizabeth, may I see you a moment? Kyzer, please keep your seat. We'll be right back," he said as he closed the parlor door. "Wait here," he said to Elizabeth as he had her to stand behind the opened front door. John went onto the veranda to retrieve the awaiting guest. "Dellanna, I'm trying to find Elizabeth. I'm sorry, but would you please go into the parlor? We'll join you there," he said.

Dellanna opened the door, walked into the room, and closed the door behind her. A sudden shriek! John and Elizabeth stood silently together in the hallway while they listened to the cries of joy and happiness erupting on the other side of the parlor door.

Dellanna couldn't believe that Kyzer was sitting there. "Oh, my darling, I'm so glad you're back. It's a dream come true," she said.

"I have waited for this day for so long. Dellanna, you look so beautiful," he said while he took her into his arms and kissed her passionately.

"When did you get home?"

"Just this morning. Oh my darling, how I have missed you."

"And, I have longed for you," Dellanna said. "Tell me, where you've been?"

"I was captured at the siege of Petersburg after taking a bullet in my left leg," he said.

"What, your leg? Oh, darling, I've been so worried about you."

"It's all right. See here," he said, pulling up his pant leg. "Now, I just walk with a limp, that's all."

Dellanna reached to put her hand on the unsightly scar

on his leg. "What a terrible gash. I'm so sorry, darling. Was it painful?"

"Oh yes, but I owe my life to a young private from Pennsylvania named Devane. It was Seth who got the bullet out and bandaged my leg. We were on the prison train together that day, the train taking us to Andersonville in Georgia."

"You were in prison?"

"For several months, we were held there in the most horrible conditions. That's where Rob died. I'm sure John must have already told you about him. Let's not talk about it now," he said. "Tell me, what have you been doing this past year while I've been away?"

"Oh Kyzer, darling," she began to weep.

"What's wrong, Dellanna?"

"I wanted to tell you, oh how I wanted to, but I just couldn't. I didn't want you to worry."

"Worry? What do you mean?" He looked somewhat puzzled as he offered his handkerchief to dry her eyes. She paused as she looked into his dark mesmerizing eyes.

"Kyzer, darling … ., I have a baby. We have a baby. You are the father of a beautiful baby daughter. She was born on the twenty-third of December. Now, she's six months old. Her name is Lydia Dyan. Please forgive me. I really wanted to tell you on the day you left," Dellanna said.

Kyzer sat there staring across the room, feeling stunned and surprised. "You knew, you already knew before I left, and you didn't tell me?"

"Please, don't be angry with me. Wait until you see her. She's beautiful."

"I guess you'll want me to marry you now, really soon," he said.

"I want to marry you. I do, but there's no rush. Kyzer, you don't have to marry me. I can take care of my baby," she said.

Kyzer sat there in his chair while he thought for a moment. "I'll marry you. I want to marry you, Dellanna."

"We'll talk about it later, darling. Let's go find your folks. Surely, they must be wondering about what's going on in here," Dellanna said.

Dellanna walked with Kyzer out to the veranda where they found John and Elizabeth. "What a marvelous surprise," Dellanna said. "Isn't it wonderful to have Kyzer home?"

"I just got a big surprise myself," Kyzer said as he began to smile, it breaking into a big grin. "I'm a father!"

"Yes, we know, son," John said. "We love whenever we get to see Lydia."

"Dellanna and I are going to be married before long," Kyzer said.

"That's wonderful news," Elizabeth said. "We need a little excitement around here. A wedding would be really nice."

"Is supper about ready? We need to eat real soon so I can take Dellanna home and see my baby girl," Kyzer said.

"Let me check with Aurelia, and I believe that can be arranged. I'm sure you're really anxious to see her," Elizabeth said.

After a hurried supper together with John and Elizabeth, Kyzer excused himself and Dellanna as he prepared to drive them to Chandalar. When they arrived, Dellanna led Kyzer directly into the parlor where she was certain to find her folks.

"Good evening, sir," Kyzer said as he extended a handshake to Richard Braxton. "Mrs. Braxton, I trust you are doing well."

"I'm doing well now that you've made me a grandmother," she said.

"Don't mind Anne. Have a seat, boy," Richard said. "It's just that we were totally surprised when we found out about the baby. Dellanna tells me that you have honorable intentions and that you will be married soon. Is that right, Kyzer?"

"Yes sir, Dellanna and I will be discussing that before long," he said.

"Very well. Welcome home. It's good to have you back in one piece. I see from the looks of things, your leg is messed up pretty bad."

"Richard!" Anne exclaimed. "Don't get so personal."

"Father, Kyzer was wounded at Petersburg, and he and Rob were prisoners at Andersonville. Rob is dead. He died there in May," Dellanna said.

"Oh, I'm sorry, son. I didn't know. Kyzer, how are Elizabeth and John?" Richard asked.

"Sir, I just told them the news this morning. The thoughts concerning Rob's death, I'm almost sure they are just now realizing it. They were devastated at the news."

"Dellanna, I'm sure Kyzer is wanting to see his baby," Anne said.

"Well, Ky, are you ready?" Dellanna asked.

He nodded.

"Follow me upstairs," she said. Dellanna opened the door to her bedroom. Dinah was seated in the rocker near the crib.

"Hello, Mr. Kyzer. Good to have you home. You have a beautiful daughter," Dinah said.

"I'm glad to be home. Thank you, Dinah."

"The baby is about to wake up, Miss Dellanna. I'll excuse myself where you two can be alone."

"Good night, Dinah," he said as she left the room.

"Well, darling, here she is," Dellanna said, pulling back the light coverlet for him to see the small red headed bundle just about to wake.

"Hello, Lydia. It's your Father! Your Father is here to see you at last."

"You can pick her up. It's all right, she won't break," Dellanna said.

Kyzer's big hands gently slid under her while he lifted and cradled his daughter in his arms. "She's so little," he said. "She is beautiful, just like you."

Dellanna stood by his side, smiling at her future husband

holding their daughter. "Well, all I can say is that she doesn't have your eyes."

Kyzer stayed in the room with Dellanna while they sat together and talked. He held Lydia for a while until time for her feeding when he left for Kellwood. It had been an eventful day, but now he was tired. During the drive home, he thought about getting married and the responsibility he would soon face as a husband and father. Maybe he could find work again at the tobacco company. He could offer to help John around Kellwood in return for allowing him to continue living there with his wife and daughter. He couldn't believe he had held his own daughter in his arms this very night. Kyzer's last thoughts were of Dellanna in the pale green dress as he drifted into sleep.

◀▶◀▶

John, Elizabeth, and Kyzer stood there anxiously awaiting the arrival of the train from Richmond. Running almost an hour late with its bell loudly clanging, the puffing steam engine pulled the train to a halt in the station. There she was at last, emerging from the rear of the rapidly departing crowd, a very stylish Susannah walking toward them. At her side, the petite Mary Ruth, holding fast to the hand of her mother.

Dressed in a long full skirt of dark blue gaberdine, Susannah wore the matching long length jacket belted tightly at the waist. It opened in the front, revealing a white ruffled silk blouse underneath. A large sparkling diamond and pearl brooch mounted in silver was fastened to her jacket lapel. In her left white gloved hand, she carried a small blue handbag and parasol. On her head, she wore a wide brimmed dark blue hat attached with a large pearl hat pin. Her long hair was pinned and put up, and delicate pearl drop earrings hung daintily from her small ears. At first glimpse, Kyzer thought she looked like what he imagined as the Belle of Richmond, elegantly dressed in her fine Parisian couture. Certainly, this couldn't be the same tomboy sister he had known growing up on the plantation.

Hurriedly, Kyzer rushed to Susannah as his arms encircled her in a welcoming embrace while she let go of Mary Ruth. "Hello, Sis, you look very nice. I'm glad to see you. And, Mary, what a pretty girl you are becoming."

"Oh Kyzer, I'm happy that you're home and all right," Susannah said, turning now toward her folks. "Mama, you look wonderful. How are you, Daddy?"

"We're good," John said.

"I'm glad you were able to come, dear" Elizabeth said.

"Henry sends his regrets. He would have loved to come with me, but he and Charles are so busy at the store," Susannah said. "Mary could hardly wait to get here."

"Mary, we're so happy that you were able to come with your mother," Elizabeth said.

"Me, too, Grandmother," Mary said. "I love coming to Kellwood."

"Let's collect your luggage, Susannah, and we'll be ready to leave for home," John said. "This is a wonderful homecoming. All we're missing is Rob."

"I'm so sorry, Daddy," Susannah said as she caught up to the side of her father while she put her arm around his back. "We all know that he's not suffering anymore. I believe an even more joyous homecoming will be one day in Heaven when we will all see each other again."

"Susannah, how long are you going to be able to stay?" Kyzer asked.

"A while, I guess. Henry is quite busy with his work, and Mary is out of school for the summer," Susannah said.

"Then, could you stay here until Dellanna and I are married?"

"Perhaps, I suppose," she said. "When is the wedding?"

"Now, that you are here, I'll talk with Dellanna. Maybe she will agree to have the wedding soon."

"I should be able to stay for a couple of weeks," Susannah said.

"I'll ask her tonight when I see her," Kyzer said.

A week had passed and the wedding was set for Saturday evening at Chandalar. On August 15, 1865, the two families were gathered in the foyer just before five o'clock, the time when the ceremony was to begin. Reverend Will Jennings walked into the parlor, turned, and stood to the left of the mantel. The mantelpiece held a beautiful three armed silver candelabra in the center, flanked on either side by porcelain vases of multicolored fresh flowers.

Richard Braxton escorted his wife, Anne, to the mantel where she lit the candle on the left. She sat in her chair as Richard turned and walked out to the foyer. John Kelsey entered with Elizabeth, followed by Mary Ruth. Elizabeth lit the candle on the right and was seated on the sofa with Mary. John remained standing to the right while Kyzer walked in and stood at John's right hand as he turned to face the doorway. With all the weight he had lost, Kyzer fit perfectly into a suit he had worn as a young man. It was black linen with a matching vest. While Reverend Jennings moved toward the center, Susannah entered and stood at the place he had just vacated. As the grandfather clock in the foyer struck five, the radiant bride stood at the top of the stairs.

Dellanna descended the staircase holding Lydia in her arms. When she reached the bottom, she paused briefly while Dinah took the baby from her. From a nearby table, Dellanna picked up her bridal bouquet of white roses while she walked toward her father. Richard Braxton escorted his daughter into the parlor for the wedding. Dellanna had a band of gardenia blossoms crowning her shoulder length shining red hair. She wore her beautiful dress of pale green silk brocade. Dinah walked in with Lydia and stood holding her at the back of the room. Nathaniel wandered in, peering at the doorway while

Dinah motioned him to come stand by her. The reverend began the ceremony.

"Dearly beloved, we are gathered here this evening to unite Kyzer John Kelsey and Dellanna Elise Braxton in the bonds of holy matrimony. If there is anyone present, who by any just cause shows reason why they may not be lawfully joined together, let him speak now or forever hold his peace." He paused. "Who gives this woman to be married to this man?"

"Her mother and I," Richard Braxton said, kissing Dellanna's cheek, and then walking over to stand beside Anne's chair.

"Kyzer and Dellanna have chosen to recite their own wedding vows. Please face each other, joining hands, and repeat your vows. Kyzer will begin," Reverend Will Jennings said.

Susannah took the bouquet from Dellanna as she turned and placed her hands into Kyzer's.

"I, Kyzer, take you Dellanna to be my wife. I promise to be faithful to you, keeping myself only unto you alone. I will love, cherish, protect, and honor you in all things. I give you all my worldly goods, whether we attain riches or naught. I will remain at your side in sickness and in health. I love you, Dellanna, with all my heart and for as long as I live, death only being which will ever separate us. I promise to be the best husband and father I can be. I am thankful for our beautiful daughter, Lydia. I will love you both forever." He smiled, looking down at her while she gazed into his alluring eyes.

"I, Dellanna, take you Kyzer to be my husband. From this day forward, I pledge my love and devotion to you. I promise to be faithful in all things, wherever we shall be and wherever we shall go. I give you all my worldly possessions as I give myself in sickness and in health, wealth or poverty. I promise to be faithful and keep myself only for you. I will love only you for as long as I live until the day that death separates us."

"Kyzer, is there a ring?" Reverend Will said.

"I offer now the wedding band of my Grandmother Sarah until the time I will be able to purchase a ring," Kyzer said.

"Kyzer, do you give this ring as a token of your love for Dellanna?"

"I do," he said.

"Dellanna, will you receive and wear this ring as a token of your love for Kyzer?"

"I will," she said.

"Kyzer, place the ring on Dellanna's finger, and repeat after me. With this ring, I thee wed, in the name of the Father, the Son, and the Holy Spirit." Kyzer repeated the vow as the Reverend Will Jennings concluded the ceremony.

"Seeing that Kyzer and Dellanna have both pledged their love and vows to each other; and Dellanna has received the ring, I pray that God will continue to bless this union with happiness and with many children. As an ordained minister of the Gospel, in the presence of these witnesses, by the laws of Chesterfield County and the State of Virginia, I pronounce that you are both husband and wife. What God has joined together, may man put not asunder. Kyzer, you may kiss your bride."

While the reverend stood to the side, Kyzer and Dellanna each took a candle from the candelabra. Together, they lit the center candle, blowing out the one they held, as they returned them to the holder. This act signified their unity as they now became one. Their parents stood hugging them, offering their words of congratulation while Anne motioned the wedding party toward the dining room to begin their reception.

John Kelsey pulled Kyzer aside while pressing some money into his palm. "Here, son, take this. I don't have much cash on hand to give you, but I believe this is enough to provide you and Dellanna with a night's lodging at the Hastings Hotel for your wedding night."

"Thank you, sir. We appreciate it," Kyzer said. "What a wonderful surprise and gift."

"By the way, I've already talked with Dinah; and she has secured a nurse for the baby. They will keep Lydia for you tonight," John said.

"Oh, thank you so much. I've got to find Dellanna and tell her the news," Kyzer said.

Dellanna's eyes opened while she lay there gazing at the large crack running across the plastered ceiling in the hotel room. Morning sunlight breaking around the edges of the closed draperies, her body suddenly jolted at the thought 'where's Lydia?' Her heart rushed a beat until she remembered that Lydia was with Dinah at Chandalar. Her mouth broke into a smile as her entire being still tingled with thoughts of the previous night of lovemaking. She could hardly believe it was real. Kyzer was now her husband. She turned her head as she looked at him while he slept. Rolling to her side, she propped onto her pillow while she began to study every inch of his face. How peaceful he looked sleeping and how different he looked with his beautiful dark brown eyes sealed shut.

Dellanna pulled the covers down to his waist and watched for a moment while his broad chest rose and fell in a completely relaxed rhythm. Now then, did she dare? This would be her first chance to know as she continued to inch the cover downward to try to satisfy her curiosity. She discovered very quickly that Kyzer was definitely circumcised, but she found it a bit odd to see all the tiny ringlets of wool filling his private area. He looked like Nathaniel, she thought. Once she had walked in when Dinah was helping Nathaniel from his bath. A strange coincidence? Perhaps, they could talk later. Nothing really to be worried about now. Kyzer began to stir a bit. With one strong and gentle swoop, he pulled her on top of him. Moments later, they shared love and sheer romance as they found themselves locked within the confines of their most intimate embrace. How they both had longed for this very moment, and now, it had happened. Together at last for the rest of their lives. Exhausted, they lay there on the large four poster bed, laughing with joyous ecstacy.

"Would you look at that crack in the ceiling?" Kyzer said as he quickly dove underneath the covers. "I bet you're ticklish!"

In a few days, Susannah and Mary Ruth boarded the train to return to Richmond. With Susannah gone, Kyzer moved Dellanna and Lydia from Chandalar to Kellwood. Dellanna found it hard to say goodbye to Dinah, but she was married now so her place was with her husband. They had talked about a town house of their own; but, for now, Kyzer needed to find work really fast. Now, he had not only himself to think about, but also his beautiful wife and baby.

CHAPTER 17

Katharine reached to free her blue gingham dress, now caught on the step as she climbed into the buggy. She was pleased to find her parents doing well when she left their home after a nice visit. George and Mary McArdle had been blessed with good health all these years, and Katharine was thankful for that.

It was a hot but beautiful summer day in Jonesboro. The sky was bright blue without a cloud to be seen. Since it had been a while, Katharine decided to drive out by the cemetery before she started home. Walt was at work down at the lumber mill so it would be several more hours until he would be home. She could hardly believe that her son had just turned twenty-three, and she had reared him by herself since he was four. She felt fortunate to have him home from the war and all in one piece. Walt had survived Gettysburg. Now, he was back at his old job and able to help her with the chores at home. Katharine knew it wouldn't be much longer until he would probably find the right girl, settle down, and get married.

Katharine stooped to brush away the dirt and a few dead leaves from his headstone. *William Jacob Jackson 1805-1846.* Her husband was dead at forty-one years old. Katharine tried only to think about all the good years she had shared with Will, but the bad memories always crept back to haunt her. Would she ever be able to find peace and forget those final days leading to his death? Sometimes, it was just like a hellish nightmare. She sat alone underneath the shade of the elm tree as those thoughts returned once again.

◀▶◀

Crackle! Pop! Pop! Pop! A flash of light. The strong smell of burning tar flowed through the open bedroom window. Firelight seemed to be coming from the front of the house out in the yard. Awakened abruptly in the dead of night, Will and Katharine's first thoughts were to get to the baby and get out of the house. While Will pulled his pants on, Katharine ran to baby Walt's room and snatched him from the crib. Will looked out the front window to discover a smoking cauldron of what he believed to be tar in the midst of a blazing fire. He could see the outline of six or eight men assembled around the fire, several brandishing rifles and shotguns. They were talking together, but Will couldn't make out what they were saying.

"Stay in the house," Will said as he picked up his loaded shotgun. Opening the door, he stepped onto the porch. "What's going on here? What do you men want?"

"Are you William Jackson?" a voice in the crowd yelled.

"I am. Who calls me out in the middle of the night?"

The voices hush as a tall man stepped forward. "Meet me in front of the fire," he said.

"Sir, state your business here or get off my land," Will said.

"I don't think so. You'll know who I am before this night is over," the man said.

Barefoot, Will walked to the bottom of the porch steps while he turned and motioned for Katharine to remain in the house. With quickened speed, another man leapt from the porch roof onto Will's back, knocking him to the ground. Catching Will off guard, the man wrestled the shotgun free from Will's grasp while he leveled a strategic blow to the side of his head in the struggle. Pressing Will's head to the ground, the assailant momentarily released his hold while he put a knee onto his back, pulling Will's arms behind to bind him. Two other men sprang from the group and ran toward Will as they grabbed his arms and brought him to stand before the tall stranger.

"Go inside and fetch the wife. Put her into the chair on the porch. I want her to have a real good view," the ring leader said to Tom who stood nearby.

Tom walked onto the porch and found the front door locked. "Open the door, or I'll break it down," he yelled out to Katharine. In a moment, the door opened.

"Please, don't hurt my boy," she said as Tom put her into the chair. Katharine sat there in her nightgown as she began to shake with fear while she held her baby tightly.

"Don't you dare move. I'm telling you. Do not attempt to get up," Tom said.

Will kept staring across at his captor unable to recognize him while the men held him firmly between them. It all seemed like a bad dream at first, but this was really happening.

"So, you're Will Jackson, eh? I don't believe I've had the pleasure of making your acquaintance, Mr. Jackson," the man said. "That must be your wife and little boy sitting up there on the porch. What a nice little family you have there. And your wife, a pretty thing, I do declare. What is her name, if you don't mind my asking?"

Will mumbled under his breath, almost in a whisper, "Katharine."

"Speak up. Man, you act like you're ashamed of her."

"Katharine. It's Katharine," Will answered.

"May I call you Will? You see, Will, my name is Devon McGuire. I live in one of the biggest houses on Peachtree Street in Atlanta. I believe you already know where my house is located, don't you, boy? I understand that you have made several trips there as the delivery man for the lumber I purchased from the Jonesboro Mill. Perhaps, you know my beautiful wife." He paused, turning to look over his shoulder into the darkness. "Sabra, why don't you climb down out of that buggy and come say hello to Will?" He motioned for the man called Wilcox to go get her.

"You drunken fool. What are you trying to prove?" Sabra McGuire asked her husband. "Untie my hands at once, and let's be on our way home."

"Not a chance, you bitch," Devon said. "You're both gonna pay. I've been watching you for some time now, and this is the day of reckoning."

"Come on, Devon. Let's go in the house and we'll talk," Will pleaded.

"How dare you call me Devon. You don't know me from Adam."

"I apologize. Please, let me explain," Will said.

"The talking part is over. Wilcox, bring her over here to me and hold her. I'm going to fix her so that no man will ever want her again," Devon said.

Devon McGuire pulled his straight razor from his back pocket and flipped it open. Wilcox stood behind Sabra as he held her around the shoulders. In one swipe, Devon cut a plug of hair and threw it on the ground. Another swipe, then another, as he continued shaving her head, the hair falling down at her feet. When he was finished with her hair, he made a slash with the razor to her right cheek and then to her left, while the blood flowed down her neck. Sabra screamed out in pain as Devon tore off her dress, ripping at her underclothes until she stood completely naked before him. Blood was dripping down her body from the cuts on her face. "You still think she's beautiful?" he taunted.

Will struggled to free himself while the two men held him fast. "You bastard! Punish me, if you will, but leave her alone," Will cried.

On the porch, Katharine shielded the eyes of her four year old while tears fell down her face.

"Please stop, Mr. McGuire. God, have mercy," she pleaded. "Try to think about what you're doing."

"You haven't seen nothing yet," he said.

Devon McGuire picked up the large wooden paddle lying on the ground near the fire. He dipped it into the hot tar and brought it down first across her breasts. Sabra screamed out in excruciating pain as he continued dipping and coating her body. Wilcox let her fall to the ground as she lay there screaming. Once again, McGuire picked up the razor, this time cutting open a pillow. Holding it over her writhing body, he sifted the feathers all over her until the case was empty. Sabra moaned for several minutes until her shocked body fell into unconsciousness. "How do you like your mistress now, Will? She's a sight to behold, isn't she?"

"You're a sorry son of a bitch! A poor excuse for a man, you dirty rotten coward. Sabra never deserved the likes of you. You go to hell!" Will shouted.

"I'll see you there, son. Guess what? I reckon it's your turn now," McGuire said. "Wilcox, bring young Will over here and remove his pants and drawers."

The two men dragged their victim closer while Wilcox stripped Will naked before Devon McGuire. "So, this is what my wife wanted to leave me for. Ha!" McGuire looked at Will in rage. "You know, Will, I cannot blame you entirely for your part of this affair, but what I do now will be a reminder for you both. This is how I will repay a wrong done unto me," he said. "Get down on your knees, boy. This will be over quickly."

In a few minutes, McGuire handed down his instructions.

One man took a pole and ran it through the handle of the pot, passing it to the other man. This endeavor took two more men as they lifted the pot from the fire and carried it behind where Will was kneeling. While they held it directly above him, Devon placed the paddle into the pot, and using it as a lever, he pulled downward, splattering the hot molten tar upon Will's head, body, and extremities. Will yelled out in anguish as the tar ran down, scalding and burning him with unbearable pain. Devon stood over him scattering a bag of feathers onto his back and front. With his foot, McGuire kicked him in the chest, sending Will toppling over, rolling on the ground trying to find relief.

"Come on men. Let's go. I've had about enough excitement for one night," Devon said as the men gathered where their horses were tied. They mounted up, and by the time the last man had his foot in the stirrup, they rode away at the first light of day. Devon McGuire never looked back as he climbed into his rig, picked up the reins, and headed north to Atlanta.

Katharine rushed inside the house with Walt and put him back into his bed. "Go back to sleep, son, while I go see about your daddy and the lady," she said. "I'll be back in a few minutes." Katharine turned to go, not sure if she would find them dead or alive. She ran down the steps across the yard where Will was lying, screaming in his agony. "Will, what can I do?"

"Help us," he moaned. "Go, get Doc." The sun was coming up.

Her heart was racing as Katharine ran back inside the house for young Walt. She dressed quickly and headed to the barn to saddle a horse for the ride into Jonesboro. She put Walt up into the saddle while she swung herself behind him as they rode away. Hopefully, she could find Doc Harlan at home before he left for the hospital.

The sun was fully up by the time Doc and Katharine arrived back at the Jackson place. Katharine held Walt as she climbed down from Doc's buggy, her mare tied to the back. She walked past the smoldering fire, a few dying embers still glowing in the sunlight. Will had crawled over to where Sabra was lying, where he now lay beside her.

"Walt, son, you go up there and sit on the porch. I need to help Doc, all right?"

"Okay, Mama."

"What do you need me to do, Thomas?"

"Katharine, do you have an old quilt or blanket? We could use something like that to transport them to the side of the house out of the sunshine," Doc said.

"We have a horse blanket out in the barn," she said.

"That might work. Hurry, and bring it here," The doctor knelt by Will's side. "Will, can you talk?"

"It hurts," he said. "I want you to see about Sabra."

"Ma'am, can you hear me?"

"Yes," she answered in a whisper.

"We're going to get a blanket and move you closer to the house out of the sun. I'm a doctor. I'm going to take care of you."

Katharine was back with the horse blanket. Doc motioned for her to place it by the woman. She worked fast unfolding the thick woolen fabric as she spread it next to Sabra McGuire.

"Are you able to roll onto the blanket?" the doctor asked.

"I'll try," Sabra said as Doc Harlan helped to position her. "Katharine, grab hold of the corner and I believe we'll be able to pull her to the side of the house." Upon reaching the shaded area, they were surprised to turn around and find that Will had followed them on foot. He promptly collapsed onto the blanket beside Sabra. Doc hastily opened his bag, removing astringents, bandages, and scissors as he began attending to the lacerations on Sabra's face. He turned her gently while he positioned her head.

"Katharine, start pulling the clumps of tar and feathers from Will's head and face until I can get to him. Be sure to clean around his eyes, nose, and mouth first, then his body,"

Doc said. "I will assist Mrs. McGuire. Would you get a bed sheet to put around her?"

Katharine and the doctor worked tirelessly all morning carefully removing the crusted tar and feathers, then using lye soap and warm water to cleanse the burned skin of Will and Sabra.

"We need to get them inside onto a bed," Doc said to Katharine. "Let's try and move her first. Mrs. McGuire, do you think you can stand?" Doc pulled her slowly to her feet while Katharine helped walk her into the house to the bed in the spare room. Quickly, they returned for Will, as they led him to his bedroom.

"We'll make a paste of baking soda and water to apply. That will help sooth the skin as we brush it on them," Doc said. "I'm going to the hospital to get some more things I need. I'll return shortly. In the meantime, keep bathing them with the soda and give them water to drink."

For the next two weeks, Doc Harlan came to the Jackson place every other day to provide treatment for Will and Sabra. All the while, Katharine constantly cared for her husband and the woman with her cooking, feeding, bathing, and emptying the chamber pots. She even took time to mend Sabra's ripped dress and stitch up her torn undergarments. Katharine had plenty of time to talk separately with both Will and Sabra. During that time, she tried in earnest to fully understand Will's involvement with the woman who now lay on the bed in her spare room. Sabra's ultimate confession of a lonely woman seeking the attention of a warm, caring man was heart-rending. It was hard to accept Sabra's apology, but alas, she had been horrifically punished by her own husband, along with Will. Maybe forgiveness was all that was left.

"Your face is healing nicely," Doc said as he removed the last bandage from Sabra's face. "I'm sorry, but you will always have the scars."

"A constant reminder, I'm afraid," Sabra said, "but I thank

you for caring for me. You, too, Katharine. I am eternally grateful for your kindness."

"Will you be returning to Atlanta?" Katharine asked.

"Heavens, no," she said. "I will go to my mother's in Savannah. I will divorce Devon McGuire."

The next day, Will, Katharine, and little Walt drove their wagon to take Sabra to the train station in Atlanta. Will paid for a one way ticket for her to Savannah.

"Sabra, I guess this is goodbye," Will said.

"Thank you both for every kindness you have shown me. Katharine, I am so deeply sorry for all the hurt I have caused you. It will never happen again. Will, take care of Katharine and little Walt. She loves you so. Don't worry about me. I'll be fine, especially after the divorce settlement I will seek," Sabra said.

When the train pulled away, that was the last time Will saw Sabra McGuire. Over the next few weeks, he was never the same. Physically, with his burnt body, it was difficult for him to return to work at the mill, even after trying it for a few days. Emotionally, he was angry and depressed. He had tremendous anger toward the man who had tortured both Sabra and him. He was saddened and disheartened for allowing himself to remain involved in his adulterous relationship. It was becoming more than he could handle. Katharine found him totally indifferent as he distanced himself seemingly from everyone, even little Walt. Then, there was those last two days when Will vanished from the house. He simply left without saying goodbye.

Katharine and Walt had been staying with her parents in Jonesboro during Will's absence. On the third day, she asked her mother to keep Walt while she drove back home to pick up a few things she needed. That's odd, she thought while she approached the barn. The side door is standing open, and it was always closed and latched. Katharine, in a hesitant manner, walked through the doorway and stood facing the stalls. Everything seemed to be all right, even all the tools were in their place. Walking across to the central area, Katharine turned in horror as she gazed upon the darkened figure suspended by the rope attached from the hayloft. Hanging there by the neck was Will Jackson, his mouth opened and eyes bulging out. It just couldn't be, not poor Will, a suicide. She fainted.

The next day, Katharine remembered awaking at her parent's, dazed and confused when her father read to her the headlines of the *Atlanta Journal* — **LOCAL BUSINESS TYCOON FOUND SHOT TO DEATH** — *"Yesterday morning, local businessman, Devon McGuire, was found fatally shot at his residence on Peachtree Street. Dead by a single shotgun blast to the face, the body was discovered by a business associate after Mr. McGuire failed to attend a scheduled ten o'clock meeting at his office. Mrs. Sabra McGuire has 'no comment' as she currently resides in Savannah, awaiting her upcoming divorce proceedings. A complete investigation is to be launched today. Currently, there is no evidence to the identity of the suspect or murder weapon. There was no forced entry at the mansion. Funeral arrangements are pending and incomplete at this time."*

"Mama, Granny said that I would find you here at the cemetery," Walt said. "I just got off work."

"Hello, darling. I'm ready to go home and start supper now. I imagine you're starved, Walt Jackson," she said.

While Walt walked his mother back to the buggy, Katharine knew she had truly loved Will with all her heart. What she didn't know was whatever happened to Sabra McGuire.

Sabra McGuire ended up with the mansion, twenty-five per cent stock in the company, and a divorce settlement amounting to a little over two million dollars. Sabra sent Dr. Thomas Harlan a very generous payment for his services. For over twenty years, she had supplied Katharine and Walt with a substantial annual allowance, although she never saw them again. Katharine always believed that the flowers she sometimes found on Will's grave were placed there by Sabra.

Incidentally, no suspect was ever found or tried for the murder of Devon McGuire.

Case closed.

CHAPTER 18

"I've talked with Tom Caufield at the tobacco company today," Kyzer announced as he took his place at the supper table. "Dellanna will be down in a few minutes."

"What did he have to say?" asked John Kelsey.

"Well, at first, I saw this sign on the door that read *NOT HIRING*; but after I got in to see him, Caufield asked me if I would be interested in a foreman job," Kyzer said.

"That sounds good," John said.

"He told me that they needed to fill the position for the evening shift, and since I was a previous employee, he saw no reason why he couldn't train me for the job. I'm to report on Monday afternoon at three o'clock."

"That's wonderful, dear," Elizabeth said.

"Dellanna's happy about it," he said. "Speaking of Dellanna, here's my beautiful wife, now. Would you look at that smile? A vision of loveliness."

"Good evening, everyone. Sorry I'm a little late to the table. Lydia, you know," she said.

"Only too well," Elizabeth said.

"What's for supper? I'm starved," Kyzer said.

"Kyzer, you mentioned a while back that you knew where Rob was buried," John said.

"Yes sir, I do. Number 12889, I'll never forget it," he said.

"I was thinking. Maybe before long, we could all take a trip to Andersonville. You know, when you get settled into your work and everything," John said.

"That would be good," Kyzer said.

"What about it, Elizabeth? Do you want to go?" John asked.

"Please excuse me, John," Elizabeth said, clearly shaken at the moment while she left the dining room and went to her room.

"We'll talk about it later," John said.

The summer ended as the warm climate began to cool down. The morning chill sent a slight ache into Kyzer's leg. By the time the dew was gone, the pain and stiffness he felt soon vanished. He liked working during the evenings because it gave him time to be with Dellanna. Lydia was growing so fast that he was amazed. He enjoyed getting to be with her, also. With her bright red hair, Kyzer thought she looked like Dellanna. He wanted to save to buy Dellanna a wedding ring. It would be a good surprise to have it for their anniversary or Christmas next year, he thought.

Many times after Kyzer left in the afternoon for work, Dellanna would take Lydia and go to Chandalar. Her folks were always glad to see her and the baby, and Dellanna loved her visits with Dinah and Nathaniel. She knew it had been difficult for Dinah to rear her son. Nathaniel was nearly twenty-six and mentally retarded, but he was always happy and smiling. Dinah refused to feel sorry for him, just like she refused to have him put away when he was a young child. He mumbled when he tried to talk, but his mother always understood him.

Dellanna played checkers with him, careful to allow him to win every time. As soon as one game was over, Nathaniel was eager for another to begin. Sometimes she distracted him, offering a peppermint stick to him, and he would forget about the checker game for the moment. If he ever got upset, Dellanna would read a story. Dinah would always sing to him. Dinah rarely let Nathaniel out of her sight since that night when he was seventeen. He wandered off by himself into the nearby woods and was lost for two days. Dinah feared the worst, but prayed that her only son would be found alive. At last, one of the plantation slaves found him asleep by the edge of Moss Rock Creek.

Dellanna sensed something strangely different about Nathaniel while they continued their game. She noticed he kept looking at her, just staring. Several times, she would have to point at the checker board to indicate to him that it was his turn to move. While they sat at the table in the kitchen, Dinah left the room to check on Lydia who was taking her afternoon nap. Suddenly, Nathaniel pounced across the checkerboard, putting his hands on Dellanna's shoulders. He pulled her toward him across the table while he kissed her on the mouth then released her as checkers fell onto the floor and scattered everywhere.

"Nathaniel, no!" she exclaimed, backing away from the table and screaming for Dinah.

"What's wrong, child?" Dinah burst into the kitchen.

"It's Nathaniel. He just kissed me," Dellanna said, "on my mouth."

"Nathaniel, I know you love Miss Dellanna, but you can't kiss her like that. No, son. Don't ever do that again," Dinah said. "Dellanna, I'm sorry. Please leave us while I talk to him. Are you all right?"

"I'm all right, just surprised, that's all," she said. "I'm going to get Lydia and go for now. See you in a few days."

"Nathaniel, look here. Don't do that again. Mama kisses you; and you kiss your Mama, that's all right. You can't kiss Miss Dellanna, and don't you ever touch her, you understand?"

He mumbled a few words before Dinah began singing to him. She held him close while he remained calm as if nothing happened. She hoped that he really understood. Later, when Dellanna told Kyzer about the incident, he warned her always to have Dinah present whenever she was in the company of Nathaniel.

By early spring, John Kelsey purchased the tickets for their trip. Beautiful, flowering trees adorned the streets in the town of Andersonville when the Kelsey family stepped from the train. John, Elizabeth, Dellanna, along with sixteen month old Lydia, stood on the porch while Kyzer knocked at the door of the little house. Abigail Sturdivant fell back in surprise when she opened the door and recognized who was standing there.

"Percy, come quickly. It's Kyzer," she yelled while she hugged him and invited them all into the house. Percy hurried from the kitchen into the sitting parlor.

"My stars, I can't believe it's you. Kyzer, you're looking so well," she said.

"Mr. and Mrs. Sturdivant, these are my folks, John and Elizabeth Kelsey. And, this is my wife, Dellanna, and our daughter, Lydia."

"So good to meet all of you. Please everyone, have a seat. Percy, bring in a chair from the kitchen and put on the tea kettle," Abigail said. "What a precious little girl."

"I hope you don't mind us all coming here without notice," Kyzer said.

"Why, certainly not. What a wonderful surprise. I have thought about you so many times, just wondering how you were doing," Abigail said.

"Our son has told us how you found him and cared for him all those weeks. We are so indebted to you," John said.

"Yes, we certainly are," Elizabeth added.

"Percy and I were privileged to do our best to attend to your son," she said. "And now, just look at the wonderful family he has."

"Thank you both so much," Dellanna said. "If it weren't for you, I might not have my Kyzer here today."

"I guess you must be wondering what we are all doing here," Kyzer said. "We're on our way to the cemetery at Andersonville. Remember, I told you that my brother is buried there."

"It's really nice and peaceful there," Abigail said. "Will you be going this afternoon?"

"No, we'll probably get rooms at the hotel and go to the cemetery in the morning," Kyzer said. "We're all very tired from the train ride."

"If you'll stay until evening, I can prepare supper for you," Abigail said.

"That won't be necessary. Thank you for your kind invitation, but we can have our meal at the hotel," John said.

"Mrs. Abigail, we didn't plan for a long visit. I wanted you and Mr. Percy to meet my family and spend time with you this afternoon," Kyzer said. "We'll need to go in just a while."

"What about allowing me to pick you up in our buggy in the morning and drive you out to Andersonville?" Percy asked.

"That would be good, thank you," Kyzer said. "We'll meet you in front of the hotel, say around ten o'clock."

The next morning, Kyzer and his family sat outside the Andersonville Hotel waiting on Percy Sturdivant to arrive. Within a few minutes of ten, Percy pulled to the front, everyone climbed into the buggy, and they commenced the two mile trip to the cemetery.

"Mr. Percy, would you drive to the prison site before we enter the cemetery?" Kyzer asked. "I want my family to see it."

John, Elizabeth, and Dellanna stood in awe as they tried to take it all in, even to imagine what this place must have looked like only a year ago. Kyzer filled them in with details as he recalled the various areas to their attention. Presently, the old stockade looked as a vast wasteland with piles of debris still visible. Many places known only to Kyzer were completely gone.

"Do you feel like taking a little walk down there?" Kyzer asked as he pointed across the former vacant encampment.

"I'll wait in the buggy with Lydia. You take your folks and go. I'll keep Mr. Percy company until you return," Dellanna said.

"Mama, you feel like walking?" She gave a nod. "Let's go. There's no hurry so just take your time." Kyzer led them to a certain spot at the base of a little plateau and stopped. "This is it," he said, "the place of our campsite, the place where Rob died."

Elizabeth cried as John put his arm around her in comfort. Kyzer came around to her side and tried to comfort her as well. The three stood there, reflecting in a moment of silence together.

Walking toward the east, Kyzer led them past a few sunken holes scattered in the nearby area, now overgrown in weeds. As he pointed them out, he shared with John and Elizabeth about the night of his aborted escape attempt through the tunnel. He couldn't bring himself to tell about the capture and how Rob was made to suffer in the stocks and the ball and chains. That would forever be known only to him.

"I want to show you the place where the water sprang up from the ground, and then we'll go," Kyzer said. "It's located at the bottom of this little hill, the place called Providence Spring."

"Look, it still flows here today," Elizabeth said.

"Yes, Mama, the spring probably helped to save many lives when we were all so desperate for water. It's name is credited by an unknown soldier who attributed the act as one by God's divine providence," Kyzer said as he looked in the direction of the buggy. "I guess we need to get back to Dellanna and Percy."

The sun was shining brightly against the clear blue sky while Percy drove the buggy into the cemetery. Kyzer motioned the direction as they rolled through the avenues of sectioned markers placed along the road on both sides, row after row. For almost as far as could be seen, a vast field of wooden markers stood silently in the sunlight. As the buggy grew closer, Kyzer had Percy to stop.

"We can walk the rest of the way," he said.

Kyzer helped Dellanna down with Lydia while John assisted Elizabeth. They walked together through a single row of graves, stopping along the way to read the names. Kyzer suddenly stopped and looked down. Before them lay Rob's grave — *Lt. Robert Kelsey — VA*.

Elizabeth immediately bent to touch the marker as she fell onto the grave and wept. John pulled her up as he held her close to him. Looking into the sky, an eagle soared above, spreading its wings as it gently glided away. A feeling of peace and tranquility came over the Kelsey family while they shared the afternoon together in the cemetery.

Tomorrow, they would have to leave for home.

CHAPTER 19

Christmas in 1866 was a jubilant time for the Kelsey family at Kellwood. Elizabeth's parents, along with her sister, Katharine, had made a trip there to visit during the holidays. Walt Jackson didn't get to come because he was working hard to save enough money to get married. In the spring, he would marry Miss Alexa Leigh Hamilton from Jonesboro. Lexie was the daughter of banker Quinton Hamilton and his wife Alexandra. After a week, the McArdles and Katharine left Kellwood to return home to Jonesboro.

On Christmas morning, Dellanna was surprised to open the small box containing her beautiful gold wedding band. Kyzer thought ahead to have it sized so the ring fit perfectly. Kyzer received a pocket watch from Dellanna. They were both very surprised and pleased with their gifts.

"Dinner is ready," Aurelia announced as she stood in the doorway of the parlor. John Kelsey brought out a bottle of wine that he had been saving for the occasion. Everyone enjoyed the wonderful meal together. Afterward, Dellanna and Kyzer left to spend Christmas with her parents at Chandalar.

That evening, they were alone in the music room. Dellanna sat at her piano while she played a medley of songs she knew from memory. Kyzer sat relaxed in his chair while he listened to the beautiful music. Suddenly, the music stopped. Dellanna walked over and sat on his lap.

"Kyzer, honey, remember when you left to go off to the war?"

"Yes, I remember; but, that seems so long ago."

"The moment I saw the train leave the station that day, I knew I should have told you about my condition. I always regretted not telling you about the baby."

"Don't feel badly about that now. It was probably for the best. I would have only worried that much more. Sometimes, things just seem to work out, especially those beyond our control."

"Well, I have a big surprise for you, the other part of your Christmas gift. I want to tell you now, I'm pregnant. By August, you should be a father again. Dinah says it's so."

"Oh, Dellanna. I can't believe it! What great news. That's wonderful. I'm so happy, darling. Course, it's gonna be a boy this time, you know."

"We shall see, I reckon. I believe I might have a boy."

"I'm so excited. How long have you known?"

"Dinah confirmed it last week. I've been anxious to tell the news but wanted to tell you first on Christmas Day. Merry Christmas, my darling."

"Dellanna, you have made me really happy. Does your mother and father know?"

"Not yet, I haven't told anyone. You never knew what all I went through when I was pregnant with Lydia, did you?"

"No, tell me about it."

"Daddy was so angry. I thought he was going to hit me, but he didn't. I kept it hidden for as long as I could. Mama found out eventually, and then together, we told Daddy. He was going to send me away to my aunt's. With the war and everything, at Mama's insistence, he agreed I should remain in seclusion here at Chandalar. I had to spend most of the time in my room. I couldn't go to church or see anyone socially. I promised him we were going to be married when you returned."

"Honey, do you think I'm going to be like him when I reach his age?"

"Let's hope not; however, Lydia is not sixteen or seventeen right now."

"Dellanna, I'm sorry I caused you so much trouble by getting you pregnant, but I didn't know. You never told me."

"Well, everything's all right now. Let's go find Mr. Richard Braxton and tell him he's going to be a grandfather again. He'll be much happier this time."

By the spring of 1867, Elizabeth Kelsey found herself tired all the time. She didn't let on to anyone about it, but each day she could tell something was wrong with her. It was getting more difficult to do her chores and walk through the many rooms of the house. When she climbed the main staircase to her bedroom, she would have to stop several times before she could reach the top. One night before bedtime, Elizabeth finally had to tell her husband.

"John, I don't know what's wrong with me exactly, but I'm having problems, especially walking up the stairs," she said.

"How long has this been going on?" he asked while he pulled on his nightshirt.

"For just a short while now, maybe a couple of weeks, but every day now grows more difficult. It's not so much in my breathing, just hard physically to walk," she said.

"No shortness of breath?"

"Not as bad as the difficulty in walking," she said.

"All right, I'll tell you what we're going to do. You get Kyzer to bring you to the infirmary in the morning. Looks like to me, we need to do some blood work."

"You're the doctor," she said.

The next week, John Kelsey sat in his office with Dr. Geoffrey Vincent. "Advanced stages of acute leukemia. How can I tell my Elizabeth she is dying?"

"Don't you think she probably already knows?" Doctor Vincent asked.

"I don't know. It's possible. I feel she would want to know. I believe I would," John said.

"Then, you're just going to have to tell her. There's not much else you can do for her now, John."

"Kyzer and Dellanna's baby is due in August. Let's hope and pray she can hold on until then," he said. "God help me to find the right words and right time to tell her."

The shadowy moonlight stole across the edge of the veranda the next evening while John sat with his beloved Elizabeth and shared the dreaded news.

"Oh darling, I already knew it. It's something I believe that God sometimes allows you to feel whenever He is ready to call His children home. I'm ready. My only regret in leaving now will be missing my family that I hold so dear and love with all my heart."

Three weeks later, at age fifty-three, Elizabeth died peacefully in her sleep. Her brief suffering had ended while John was heartbroken. He had wanted to tell her the complete truth about Kyzer but felt toward the end, it wasn't necessary. He would spare her that painful revelation. Now, he had to break the distressing news about Elizabeth to George and Mary McArdle, Katharine, and their own precious daughter, Susannah.

Plans for Elizabeth's funeral were finalized while John Kelsey struggled with his grief. Henry, Susannah, and Mary Ruth arrived from Richmond along with Mr. and Mrs. Hollis and Charles. Expected later in the afternoon from Jonesboro were Mr. and Mrs. George McArdle, Vanie, and Dr. Thomas Harlan. Katharine, her son and new daughter-in-law, Walt and

Lexie Jackson also arrived. Richard and Anne Braxton, Kyzer, Dellanna, and Lydia would attend, along with Aurelia, Dinah, and Nathaniel.

The service was set for Friday at eleven at the Episcopal Church of the Ascension in Hastings. Helpful direction was given by the undertaker Uriah Priester while the service was to be conducted by Reverend Will Jennings. Elizabeth looked as beautiful in death as she had been in life. She was laid to rest in her favorite Sunday dress, the sky blue linen with pearl buttons. Glowing white candles placed into stands surrounded Elizabeth's open coffin, illuminating the flower filled altar. Numerous friends and acquaintances filed down the center aisle to pay respect to her and the family seated on the pews of the front two rows. When it came time for each family member to take their final viewing, each individual took the snuffer and extinguished one of the candles. With only one remaining lit candle, John tried hard to steady his hand while he put it out. When the service was concluded, the burial followed at the Kelsey Family Cemetery at Kellwood.

Aurelia, Dinah, and Nathaniel were busy with all the food while Vanie pitched in to help. Members of the church congregation, as well as many friends and townspeople, made the provisions for a meal for the Kelsey family. Friends and relatives were finding their places all around Kellwood after they left the cemetery while they awaited the time for the meal to begin. Some were seated on the veranda and on the lawn while others were in the dining room, or scattered within the great hallway. John Kelsey sat in sorrow with the immediate family crowded in the parlor.

"The service was very nice, John," Mary McArdle said.

"I wish I could have told you sooner about your daughter's condition," he said. "She went so fast. I should have realized we didn't have much time."

"We know, son. I know that you did all you could for her," George McArdle said. "We all loved her so."

"Yes, John. I'll never forget all you and Elizabeth did for me, many times even before Will died," Katharine said. "Then, when I was left with little Walt, you sent money when I needed it. She was a dear sister to me."

"When is your baby due?" Susannah asked Dellanna and Kyzer who were seated close to her.

"In August," Dellanna said.

"At least, I know about this one," Kyzer laughed.

"I was never able to have any more children," Susannah said, "but I'm happy to have Mary Ruth."

"She's such a pretty little girl," Dellanna said.

"Thank you," Susannah said. "Your Lydia certainly looks a great deal like you, Dellanna."

"I guess it's the red hair, don't you think?"

"You want to get something to eat?" Kyzer asked John.

"No, son, you go ahead. I'm not very hungry," he said.

"Dellanna, would you fix me a plate? I want to talk to Papa John," Kyzer said while he patted John Kelsey on his knee. "I feel so fortunate to have had you and Mama adopt me. I hated the thought of it, at first. It's different, believe me, when you're just eleven and then later after you're grown."

"We always felt you came at just the right time, three days after Elizabeth lost Michael. Kyzer, you filled that void for her when she needed it the most," John said. "She loved you so much."

"I will always miss her kind, gentle ways and devotion to her family. She was never quite the same after losing Rob, was she? I'm sorry that she had to go through all that," he said. "Now, to think, they are together in Heaven."

"John, I have a previous appointment and need to excuse myself," Reverend Will Jennings said.

"The service was really nice. Thank you, Brother Will. Elizabeth would have approved, no doubt," John said, then turning to his daughter. "Susannah, you need to help me with the sleeping arrangements for everyone tonight."

"Daddy, now don't you worry about that. We have it all worked out," Susannah said.

"John, you take as many days off as you need," Dr. Vincent said. "Don't hesitate to let me know about anything else I can do for you or your family."

Vanie was overjoyed to see Susannah and her family. They had plenty to talk about all afternoon. Doc Harlan chatted over an hour catching John up on the latest happenings in Jonesboro. The rest of the afternoon was spent with the family, reminiscing as they all celebrated the life of Elizabeth. From the sad tears of sorrow to the joy of laughter, they shared the day together in love. Life goes on. That night, Dellanna smiled at Kyzer while she felt her baby suddenly move for the first time.

◄► ◄►

Jared Kyzer Kelsey arrived on the ninth of August on a dull misty morning at Hastings Infirmary. Dr. Geoffrey Vincent delivered the frail little boy while Kyzer waited in anticipation with Richard and Anne Braxton. Dinah and Nathaniel were on hand with them to tend to Lydia.

"A boy! I have a boy," Kyzer yelled. "How's Dellanna?"

"She's doing well," the doctor said. "You all may see her and the baby in just a few minutes."

When they entered Dellanna's room, Kyzer kissed her while she held her newborn son before his father. "He's so small," he said.

"Yes, and a little jaundiced right now. Doctor Vincent says to put him in indirect sunlight at varied intervals when we get home," she said. "He'll soon grow strong with proper nourishment."

◄► ◄►

Along with the October chill that year, a tall handsome stranger blew into town. Six foot two inches tall, weighing one hundred and ninety pounds, the man with the slim build and large hands walked into the general store.

"I'm looking for Kyzer Kelsey," said the man wearing the short brown haircut and thin mustache.

The clerk looked into his inquiring deep blue eyes, the small scar slightly visible above his right eye. "He lives out of town at the old Kellwood Plantation."

"And, how may I get there, sir, seeing I have no transportation? I have come this far from Pennsylvania by train," the stranger said.

"You can rent a horse and buggy at the livery stable just down the street," he said. "Follow the main road out of town. In three miles, you'll come to the beginning of the tobacco fields. Keep going until you pass the second turn to the right. You'll see the oak tree lined drive up to the house, a big white Greek Revival. That's Kellwood, sir, the Kelsey family home."

"Thank you for your time and trouble," the stranger said as he left and walked in the direction of the livery stable.

A loud knock brought Aurelia to the door as she opened it to reveal the man in the dark brown trousers and tan shirt now standing before her.

"I'm looking for Kyzer," he said.

"Mister Kyzer down yonder by the barn," Aurelia said.

"I thank you," he said while he walked away.

Kyzer stopped his work and put down his hammer as soon as he noticed the man walking toward him. In an instant, he was on his feet as Kyzer threw his arms around the shoulders of the man he now recognized. "Seth Devane, I can't believe it's really you!"

"It's me, all right," he said.

"What brings you here to Hastings on a Saturday afternoon?"

"A trip to Richmond. My business partner and I own the Grande Hotel in Philadelphia. We're looking at the prospect of building another one in Richmond," Seth said.

"That sounds like a wise idea, probably a very good decision. There's lots of construction going on in Richmond these days," Kyzer said.

"I've come south on the premise of acquiring and possibly purchasing a site for us. Decided since I was this close, I'd try to find you. I remembered you saying that you were from Hastings. Anyway, I never knew if you and the others made it out of Andersonville," he said.

"Seth, come on up to the house. We can sit and talk there. I want you to meet my Dellanna."

"Kyzer, do you have problems with your leg?"

"Well, thanks to you, I still have it. At least, I can limp like an old man and do pretty much what I want to do around here, most of the time. I work at the tobacco company my grandfather started near here, actually just down the road. Have a seat, Seth. It's so good to see you. How long has it been?"

"Over two years, I reckon. I met your house servant at the door," Seth said.

"Aurelia? She's no longer a servant though. She receives wages now. After the war, when the slaves all went free, she chose to remain here with us. My father pays her to work for us."

"Where is your father?" Seth asked.

"Dr. John Kelsey? He's always at the infirmary in Hastings. He spends quite a lot of time there since we lost Mama last year," Kyzer said.

"Oh, I'm sorry. Her name was … ."

"Elizabeth. She was a wonderful lady. The leukemia took her in about three weeks. And, you don't even know about poor Rob," Kyzer said.

"What happened to Rob?"

"I'll tell you about him in a few minutes. Here comes Dellanna and the baby," Kyzer said while Seth stood to his feet. "Seth, this is Dellanna and our son, Jared. Dellanna, this is Seth Devane."

"Pleased to know you, Seth. This is a surprise for Kyzer,

I'm sure. He has often talked about you as the only one who got away."

"The only ... ..." Seth looked puzzled as he gazed toward Kyzer. "You mean ... ."

"We'll talk about it later. Dellanna, where's Lydia? She's our daughter, Seth."

"She's out in the kitchen with Aurelia. Seth, we would be honored to have you stay for supper this evening. Could you?"

"Dellanna, it would be my pleasure. Thank you for your warm hospitality, " he said.

"Is there a Mrs. Devane?" she asked.

"Only my mother," he said. "I'm still single. I plan to settle down one of these days."

"Well, I'll let you two catch up a bit while I leave you alone. We'll have supper around six o'clock. Would you care for something to drink?"

"A glass of water would be nice, thank you," he said.

"Kyzer?"

"Nothing for me, honey," Kyzer said while he brought out his pipe and lit it.

"Seth, the night we planned our escape from Andersonville, we never knew you made it out until later on. Lancaster followed you immediately, then Dylan Barclay. Rob was next. Everyone, so far as we knew it, had cleared the tunnel. Then, I switched places with Billy. Billy Hopkins was shot in the back of the head while he panicked, just went crazy and ran. I knew my chance was forever gone," Kyzer said.

"Damn, I never knew it." Seth fell back against his chair.

"That's not all," Kyzer said. "Wirz sent the dogs out that night. Early the next morning, Lancaster, Barclay, and Rob were caught down by the swamp. The dogs had nearly chewed off one of Michael's feet by the time they were all captured. Seth, what happened to you during all this time?"

"Lucky for me, there was a hollow log partially submerged under the water in the creek. I hid there all night under that log.

I could hear the ferocious barking of the dogs in the distance while I prayed they wouldn't find my scent. Just before dawn, I was able to slip away in the fog. I hid in a box car headed north for days and just kept going north. I walked many a mile tired and weary, until I eventually made it home. Tell me, what happened to the boys?"

"Rob told me that they were taken before Captain Wirz who demanded they tell him of anyone else involved in the escape attempt. The three of them confessed nothing and were consequently put into the stocks for two weeks. After the first week, Michael Lancaster's foot became gangrenous while he literally bled to death in the stocks. Rob said the vultures came and pecked out his eyes and brain before they took his body down."

"My God, how awful," Seth said.

"Then, Dylan and Rob were fastened together in the ball and chains for another two weeks. They both nearly died after that but somehow survived. Dylan eventually grew stronger, much better than Rob, who never got over it. Rob lingered for weeks while the scurvy just ate him up. He died just two days before the prison closed and everyone was released. A sad day for me. He's buried in a peaceful plot, a beautiful place in the Andersonville National Cemetery. Last year, before Mama died, we were able to go there and visit his grave."

"So tragic," Seth said. "I can't imagine."

"I saw Dylan Barclay for the last time that day when the gates of hell at Andersonville were opened and the mass exodus began. You see, that's why I've always told Dellanna that you were the only one — the only one who survived. The rest of us all died there."

"I'm sorry, Kyzer. I really am, but we can keep their spirit alive every time they are brought to our minds and we remember them. We all stood and fought together with strength and valor in our common cause for the freedom of all men. They did not die in vain," Seth said.

That evening after supper, John Kelsey joined Kyzer and Seth, already seated on the veranda.

"A nice place you have here, sir. It's so calm and peaceful," Seth said.

"We like it here very much. Kellwood was originally built by my father before he was married in 1804. I was born here in an upstairs bedroom. My wife Elizabeth and I brought our family here from Jonesboro, Georgia, after my father died when the children were small. Kyzer, here, was just a baby. This is the only home he has ever known," John said.

"Well sir, it's a place to be appreciated, I must say," Seth said.

"You should have seen it in the glorious days before the war when Kellwood was the tobacco plantation. Hundreds of slaves working here and over at Chandalar. Dellanna's family owns that. You should really see that place. It's bigger than Kellwood," John said. "Kyzer tells me it was you, Seth, who took the bullet out of his leg following the siege of Petersburg."

"Yes sir, I tried to do the best I could," he said.

"Well, you did a pretty damn good job with it. I doubt I could have done much better," John said. "If you will excuse me, Seth, I have some paper work I need to finish. Do you need to stay here for the night?"

"Oh, no sir. I took a room in town before I left. I'll be leaving before dark."

"Your welcomed to stay. Visit as long as you want, and come back, anytime," John said as he walked into the house.

"You know, Seth, I've thought about this so many times. 'What if Rob had been the one to come back, and I didn't?' John and Elizabeth's lives would have been so different. Maybe she wouldn't have died."

"You can't really say or even think that, Kyzer. Anybody can say 'what if?' Of course, I never knew your adoptive mother, but John seems to me somewhat like your real father might be, I mean from what I've observed today."

"He's a good man. He's always been fair and honest with me," Kyzer said. "However, deep down in his soul, I'll always believe that he longs for Rob."

"I remember that night in the tent when Rob awoke at the sound of your voice and jumped on top of you. I didn't know what to think," Seth said.

"Yeah, that was quite a surprise for me," Kyzer said.

"At the time, I would have never guessed that you two weren't true blood brothers. Rob always had so much concern about you," Seth said.

"And for me, I always wanted to be just like him. Guess I would have to call him my hero."

"I liked Rob myself. He was a very smart and intelligent young man. He seemed to really like the military," Seth said.

"Do you ever think about Andersonville, Seth?"

"I used to think about it, a great deal. It bothered me for a long time until finally, I was able to let it go. Now, I don't have time to think about it. I have thought about you and Rob, though. Speaking about time, it's about time to leave. It will be dark soon."

"When are you going back, I mean to Philadelphia?"

"I have a meeting tomorrow back in Richmond, and my train leaves on Monday around noon."

"I will have to go to work at three on Monday afternoon. We probably won't be able to see each other again,' Kyzer said.

"Listen, if we end up in Richmond before long, I'll be back down this way. I'll come again to see you," Seth said.

"You might be married by then," Kyzer said.

"I'll have to meet someone first. Really, I just don't have time right now. There are many things I want to see and do before that happens. Well, goodbye my friend."

"Goodbye, Seth. Take care of yourself."

It was a hard winter that year. Rainfall was plentiful, while sections of Moss Rock Creek overflowed its swollen banks. A massive snowstorm in December iced the surrounding landscape with its thick white frosting. The unexpected snowfall lingered for weeks, making travel difficult. Farmers found it challenging to haul feed for their livestock into the fields. Major deliveries to and from the town were halted by necessity. At Kellwood, John and Kyzer spent a great deal of time cutting and splitting firewood, while stockpiling it for daily use.

Hopefully, there was enough meat hanging in the smokehouse and canned vegetables in the pantry to get the Kelseys through the winter. Aurelia made sure the fruit cellar was always stocked with a good supply of Irish and sweet potatoes and onions, as well as an ample assortment of dried fruits. Aurelia had the knack for taking bits of potatoes, carrots, and onions, along with a few scraps of meat, and turning out a delicious stew or soup, whenever necessary. While Elizabeth was alive, on the Sundays whenever Reverend Jennings came for dinner, Aurelia would kill and fry up a chicken. John remembered those wonderful plantation days of joy and happiness. Those days were gone now. There wasn't a day gone by that John Kelsey didn't think about Elizabeth. He often felt her warm, gentle spirit but all the mirth and joy he had known with her at Kellwood had been extinguished by her absence. He had tried to blame God for his misery. Shortly after her death, John's heartfelt prayer gave him peace.

"Father, God, I pray you forgive the sins and shortcomings of the one who brings this petition before you. I am saddened over the loss of my dearest Elizabeth, your devoted servant, faithful and true. Please, grant me the understanding I need to accept this as your perfect will, while my heart lies broken and crushed. Father, lift my spirit to do your will and help me to find the peace I so desperately need. Thank you for the blessings of life and the watch care over my family. Amen."

John Kelsey found his peace with God that day.

Loneliness ... ... it would remain a struggle.

CHAPTER 20

At the end of January, Aurelia died early in the morning. The frost still lay on the ground, shining white in the sunlight like the brilliant color of her hair. Aurelia had remained ill throughout the bleak months of winter, longing to find her granddaughter Epsy and to see her before she died. Suddenly, the pneumonia took her last breath. After three days of mourning, John Kelsey had her buried beside her boy, Jesse, in the little cemetery on the edge of town.

After a lengthy discussion with his daughter, Richard Braxton finally consented for Dinah and Nathaniel to come live and work for the Kelsey family at Kellwood. The Braxtons simply hired two more servants to take their places. Dellanna was more than happy to have Dinah back close to her again to help with her children. Lydia was quite healthy, but Jared proved to be a sickly little boy.

"Dinah, I don't know what I'm going to do with this baby. He's so fretfully, crying all the time," Dellanna said.

"Your milk's not satisfying him when you nurse," Dinah said. "He needs more. Maybe some goat's milk will help." Within a week, the addition of the goat's milk brought satisfaction and eventually growth to baby Jared.

With Aurelia's personal things packed away, Dinah and Nathaniel settled into her former little house out back. Kyzer had been good to help move their things from Chandalar to the new location with Dellanna's persistent persuasion.

For the past few months, the overall economy was on the rise once again in the South, and things were going well with the Kelsey family. Kyzer began working days every week with the additional overtime shift on any given Saturday. Business was good at Kelsey Tobacco.

Dr. John Kelsey was semi-retired from the Hastings Infirmary. He assisted Dr. Vincent whenever necessary, but no longer kept regular work hours. He was still physically able to help out with the work around Kellwood, but he spent most of his time reading and playing with his grandchildren. Some days, he sat on the bench in the shade of the magnolia trees surrounding the Kelsey Family Cemetery. He would think about Elizabeth and Rob sometimes while he whittled out a toy for Lydia or Jared. Quite often, he began to wonder why he never told Kyzer about his mother. He always reasoned it out by convincing himself that it really didn't matter now. Why dredge up the past after all this time? After all, Kyzer was happy with Dellanna and his own family, and he didn't want to upset him with the truth. What would be the point? John knew how badly he personally felt about it, though. Still he thought that nobody needed to know.

By the middle of the summer, Dellanna announced she was pregnant again. Kyzer was happy when she told him that the baby would probably come during his birth month in April. Conceived in love, this little one would be their love child. This time, it really didn't matter to him if the baby was to be a boy or girl, as long as it was healthy. Kyzer worked hard while he strived to be a good father to his children and a loving husband to Dellanna. He loved her so much; but in the next few months, he felt she was somehow changing. Although he wasn't a doctor like his father, he could sense something about her very different, strangely different.

Dellanna's declining energy level was the first thing Kyzer noticed about her. She complained about being tired all the time, while she forced herself to stay up when she didn't feel like it. Some days after Kyzer left for work, she would go back to bed, arising shortly before he returned home. She left Dinah to care for Lydia and Jared whenever she didn't have the strength to do it herself. Kyzer soon caught on to what she was doing. It wasn't long until he confronted her about it.

"Darling, I realize that you are probably uncomfortable to have my father examine you, but I want you to have Doctor Vincent to take a look at you before long. No more Dinah says this or Dinah says that, all right?" She nodded in agreement.

By the next week, Doctor Vincent had confirmed that everything was fine with the pregnancy. The baby was in the proper position. Dellanna was most likely experiencing a vitamin deficiency. An increased amount of fresh fruits and vegetables would prove to be the best medicine. Soon, Dellanna began to feel much better. Her color and much needed physical stamina returned to her body. She was able now to return to help Dinah with the daily chores as they both tried to carry out all the duties that Aurelia had done so masterfully over the past years of her service.

Severe thunderstorms began in late afternoon on the eleventh of April while the bright lightning flashed the sky and the rolling thunder rumbled nearby. By nightfall, the heavens erupted as the heavy rain abundantly showered down onto the rooftop of Kellwood. It seemed to her as though it wasn't going to let up anytime soon when Dinah vacated her station momentarily. She needed to find a small pail to catch the water from the leak in the ceiling. Dinah returned to sit with Kyzer on the landing outside Dellanna's bedroom. Declining to call upon Doctor Vincent during the turbulent storm at two o'clock in the morning, the emergency delivery would be attended by Dr. John Kelsey. Dinah left once again to check on the sleeping children while she made a quick check on Nathaniel. When she discovered him asleep in his room, she was soon back sitting across from Kyzer.

"Everything okay?" he asked.

"Lydia and Jared, they's fast asleep. I's worried 'bout Nathaniel. He scared of storms, but he still sleeping," Dinah said. "At least, the rain let up for a while."

"This is taking too long for me. I'm going down to the parlor. Dinah, please come for me when it's time," Kyzer said.

"You go on back to sleep, Mr. Kyzer. I come for you when it's time."

Dinah stood there in the candlelight, her back pressed against the wall while she waited. Judging from the sounds now coming from within the bedroom, she could hardly stand it. A loud sudden scream from Dellanna was all it took to signal Dinah to thrust open the door. Once through the door way, her body fell back against the door slamming it shut. Dinah rushed to the bedside as she fell on the floor by Dellanna's side. Up again, falling prostrate across her in a consoling embrace, Dinah cried, "Oh, dear child! My God in Heaven, how can this be?"

As she stood by the bed, Dinah took a cloth and began wiping Dellanna's sweating brow while she tried to understand what she was seeing. Dr. John Kelsey tearfully bent over Dellanna's stillborn baby while he cut the cord.

"I'll clean her up," Dinah said.

"Let me hold him," Dellanna said as she reached out her hands.

Dr. John quickly wiped him with a clean towel and placed the baby with his mother. Leaning down, his mouth against her ear, John Kelsey whispered his secret to Dellanna. Tears began to roll down her face while she lay there trembling as she listened. Then, crying aloud as he finished, she held tightly to her little brown baby dead in her arms.

"I'm going for Kyzer," he said.

"Dellanna, sweet baby, now give him to me," Dinah said while Dellanna refused her command. "Child, this little baby done winged it's way to his heavenly home. He's asleep in the Lord. You let me take him and put him in the cradle over there. You hear, Miss Dellanna? Give him to me, baby."

Dellanna slowly responded as she allowed Dinah to take the baby. "Let's get you and this bed straightened up before Mister Kyzer gets here. He'll be coming any minute," Dinah said.

John Kelsey opened the door to the parlor and walked in while Kyzer arose from his nap on the sofa. "Is it time already? The baby's here?"

"Just a minute before we go. Kyzer, I have to tell you something before you see Dellanna."

"She's all right, isn't she?"

"Yes, son, but she's terribly upset. It's a boy. He was stillborn, and the baby is … …"

Kyzer ran from the room and headed up the stairs before John could finish or stop him. He stood at the door as he firmly knocked. Dinah opened the door and stepped back. He didn't move while gazing across at a tearful Dellanna now propped in the bed with pillows at her back.

"I'm so sorry," she said.

He walked over to her. "Don't worry, my darling. We will try again," he said as he knelt to kiss her. "You're all right. That's all that matters now."

"I feel so … .so very tired," she said.

"You just rest. We'll talk later," he said as he walked to the other side of the bed and looked into the cradle. John Kelsey had reached the bedroom as he stopped short in the doorway.

Kyzer turned toward him, looking as though he had just seen a ghost.

"What? What is this?" He fell back against a small table, his stumbling sending Dellanna's favorite vase crashing onto the floor while it shattered into pieces. "Oh, I get it now. Your little secret, huh, Dellanna? You and Nathaniel, well I'll be damned! You just had to let him get to you, or were you going to try to tell me that he took advantage of you? Is that it? Did he rape you?"

"No, no, no," she screamed. "That's not true."

"Well, how do you explain it then?" he asked in a rage. "It must be God's punishment for your adultery with a retarded slave boy, leaving you with a black baby born dead."

"You're wrong, Kyzer. I have kept myself only for you," Dellanna cried.

"I don't believe you. You're lying to me. It's Nathaniel. I'm going to kill him," Kyzer yelled.

"Oh no, wait Kyzer," Dinah pleaded. "Stop him, Dr. Kelsey. He's gonna kill my boy."

"Listen, son," John Kelsey said as he tried to block the doorway. "For God's sakes, listen to me."

"Out of my way, old man," Kyzer said while he shoved his father roughly onto the floor and stepped over him. Fighting back tears, the angry Kyzer fled the room as fast as he could move, hobbling on his bad leg down the staircase.

Dr. John and Dinah followed right behind him while she screamed out. "Mister Kyzer, stop! Please stop! Don't hurt Nathaniel. He's got nothing to do with this."

By the time John and Dinah arrived in Nathaniel's room, Kyzer was all over him, beating Nathaniel in the face with his fists and pounding him in the chest with his strong arms. Nathaniel, scared from the sudden blows that had awakened him from a dead sleep, babbled and mumbled as he felt the pain. "It was you, wasn't it, boy?" Kyzer continued the beating.

"Kyzer, damn it. Stop it now," John yelled as he and Dinah

fought to pull him off Nathaniel. "Listen to me. Calm down, son. Sit here and let me tell you something."

Dinah began to sing softly to Nathaniel, caressing him while stopping to say gently, "It's all right, baby. It's all right."

Kyzer wiped the sweat from his face and took a seat across from John.

"Kyzer, remember when you were eleven and found out that you were adopted? I wanted to tell you the complete truth at that time. You were so upset, I just couldn't bring myself to do it. Regrets, life is so full of them. I fully realize now that it will be most difficult for you to accept what I'm going to tell you, but I promise this time what I say will be the truth so help me God. Son, are you ready for the truth? Look at me, son, I'm going to tell you everything. Before you judge me for the wrong that I have done toward you, imagine yourself in my place after you hear my story. Would you please listen?"

"Yeah, let's hear it, Father," Kyzer said.

"First of all, Nathaniel over there is not the father of Dellanna's baby. You owe him an apology for the beating you gave him. You could have killed him, and you would have been wrong in doing that. Now, here's what really happened." John sat next to him while Kyzer stared across the room.

"The day before I was to move my family from Jonesboro to Kellwood in 1841, the servant girl of a family friend, Mrs. Rachel Petersen, came to my office. She was crying and upset. She told me that she had been raped by Mrs. Petersen's son, had become pregnant by him, and had given birth to a baby boy who appeared physically to be white. She begged and pleaded for me to take the baby and raise him as white. After thinking about it overnight, I promised her I would and that I would never tell anyone about it. Elizabeth and I adopted that baby. That baby is you, Kyzer." He paused.

"Your father was Matt Petersen. He died a young man, age thirty-two. A gambler most of his life, he was robbed and murdered on a river boat somewhere along the Mississippi

River some years back. Your mother told me she was seventeen when she had you. Merely, a child herself, small and thin, she had very light colored skin. I recall, her name was Delilah, Delilah James."

"Where is she now? What happened to her?"

"Mrs. Rachel Petersen never knew she was your grandmother; and after she died, Delilah was sent to work for a family in Atlanta. The last time I saw Delilah was at Matt Petersen's funeral. She kept you for us while we attended the service. That was probably the last time she ever saw you. That's all I know. I don't know if she is still alive. That's how you are able to be the father of Dellanna's baby. What I did, I now regret, but not in caring for you all this time. I felt I did this accordingly to your mother's wishes. She sacrificed for you, loving you so much. She wanted you to have a different life. A life she would never be able to give you by herself."

Kyzer got up and walked toward the door. He turned to look at a pitiful John Kelsey sitting there in tears. "I hate you, old man. You deceived me in a way I never dreamed possible or could ever imagine. God damn you!" He walked out toward the house in the pouring rain. John Kelsey remained there for a while just staring across the room at Dinah and Nathaniel.

Kyzer spent the rest of the night in Dellanna's room while he sat in a chair by her bedside. On the other side of the bed, the baby lay in the cradle. Kyzer and Dellanna talked briefly in a subdued whisper until she drifted into sleep. The last words she said to him, 'Promise me this … .I love you.'

The morning sun peeked through the windows spreading its rays across the foot of the bed. Late in the morning, Kyzer was awakened by the gentle knocking on the door.

"Go away," he yelled.

"Mr. Kyzer, it's Dinah. Please let me in to check on Miss Dellanna."

"She's asleep. Don't bother us."

"Please, sir, I need to see her."

"Leave us alone. Go away, you hear?"

"I'm not leaving, sir. Please let me in."

The door slowly opened. Kyzer turned and walked back to his chair.

"Miss Dellanna, wake up child. I've come to bathe you," Dinah said.

No response.

"Miss Dellanna, wake up. Answer me. Oh my God, Mister Kyzer, she's dead!" Dinah screamed.

"No," he yelled. "Oh God, no!" He tore the covers back, revealing the blood soaked bed all around her. He dropped down, looking under the bed to see the blood dripping from the mattress and puddling onto the floor. Rising, he stepped into a pool of blood at the edge of the bed.

"How could I have let this happen? I thought she was asleep, just resting, and all the while, she was bleeding to death, Oh, my darling Dellanna, I'm so sorry."

Dinah was crying as she put her hand on his shoulder as he knelt on the floor. "Mr. Kyzer, you go out on the porch and take some fresh air. There's nothing more you can do for her now. Miss Dellana just crossed over into Glory Land," Dinah said. Kyzer left immediately to go downstairs to the front porch veranda.

"I've just come from her room," John Kelsey said as he walked across the veranda and stopped beside Kyzer. "I'm sorry, son. Is there anything I can do for you?"

"Hell, no. You've done enough already," Kyzer snapped.

"All right, go ahead and stay mad. It'll just eat you up, and you know it," John said.

"I guess that's for me to worry about. Just leave me alone."

"What about Dellanna? You want me to contact Uriah Priester?"

"No, I'm going to take care of Dellanna. Let me alone so I can think," Kyzer said.

"Very well," John said as he walked down the steps and headed for the barn.

Kyzer sat there for almost an hour until he went upstairs to the bedroom. He walked in while Dinah was bathing Dellanna. "Dinah, I'm sorry for my attack on Nathaniel. Please convey to him my sincere apology."

"Yes, sir."

"Would you do something else for me or rather for Dellanna, I should say?"

"Why, yes sir, anything I can," Dinah said.

"After you finish bathing her, dress her in the pale green dress, her wedding dress, brush her hair, and make up her face. Could you do that? Leave her lying on the bed."

"What about the baby?" she asked.

"Wrap him in one of Jared's old blankets and leave him in the cradle for now. I'll be back in a while," Kyzer said.

By the time Kyzer got to the barn, John had the wagon hitched ready to go.

"I figured you'd be coming for the wagon. I have it ready for you," John said.

"All right," Kyzer nodded while he took the reins. "Be back in a while. I'm going into town and then to Chandalar."

Kyzer drove to the bank and withdrew fifteen hundred dollars from his savings. He put the bills into a money clip and poked it into his front trouser pocket. From there, he went to the hardware store for a small load of lumber and a sack of nails. He stopped by Kelsey Tobacco and asked Mr. Caufield for a leave of absence. After explaining his situation, a three month's absence was granted. On the way home, he drove by Chandalar to break the sad news about their daughter's death to Richard and Anne Braxton.

Kyzer returned home and pulled the wagon to the side of the barn stopping in the shade. He went inside for his hammer, hand saw, shovel, and two bundles of rope. Returning to the wagon, he placed the tools and rope next to the lumber and drove around the house to the cemetery, stopping as near to the gate as possible. While Kyzer was unloading the wood, John Kelsey walked up.

"I'll be glad to help, if you want," he said.

Kyzer continued unloading without acknowledging him for a few minutes. John stood there watching him. "All right, start digging while I work on the coffin," Kyzer said. The two men worked together all afternoon, hardly speaking a word, until the grave had been dug and the coffin completed. John sat in silence beside Kyzer as he drove the wagon back to the barn.

At sunset, John Kelsey opened the front door of Kellwood. He walked onto the veranda carrying Elizabeth's Bible in his hand. Kyzer followed as he carried Dellanna down the steps toward the cemetery. Her neck and limbs now stiffened as rigor mortis was setting in. A gentle wind blew through her hair as it fell across her pretty face. Dinah held the baby wrapped in a pale blue blanket while she helped Lydia and Jared down the front steps. At the bottom, Dinah put Jared's hand into Nathaniel's while Lydia held onto Jared; and Dinah took Lydia's hand while they walked behind. Richard Braxton held onto his wife Anne while she struggled to walk down the stairs toward the cemetery.

When they arrived at the grave site, Kyzer placed Dellanna gently into the handcrafted pine box. He pulled and bent her arms into a cradling position before brushing the hair from across her face with his fingertips. Turning to Dinah, he took the baby and placed him in his mother's arms.

"Lydia, Jared, say goodbye to your Mama," Kyzer said as he lifted them up overlooking a sleeping Dellanna.

"Bye-bye, Mommy," said Lydia as she climbed down from his arms. Walking over to a nearby gardenia bush, she pulled a blossom and tossed it over the side into the coffin. Then, she ran and jumped into Dinah's arms.

Richard Braxton had to pull his wife away as she fell grief-stricken across her daughter's body. Kyzer bent down and kissed

Dellanna for the last time. While Kyzer nailed the lid onto the coffin, John read the Twenty-third Psalm aloud from the Bible.

"Dinah, please take the children back to the house. I'll be there to talk with you after a while," Kyzer said. Richard and Anne Braxton left with Dinah and the children.

When they were gone into the house, Kyzer took the two ropes and tied one end to the iron fence. He stretched them across the open grave. Motioning to John, they positioned the coffin at the edge of the grave, lifting and sliding it onto the ropes. Kyzer and John each took a rope as they held it tightly; and using their feet, they pushed the coffin directly over the open pit. Letting loose the slack, they lowered the coffin into the ground. Kyzer untied the ropes from the fence and threw them into the grave. It was nearly dark by the time they finished with their shoveling.

A screech owl began to hoot in the darkness while father and son made their way toward the barn, Kyzer's muddy shovel slung over his shoulder. At last, Kyzer knew what he had to do.

Kyzer was up the next morning at daybreak out in the barn saddling Cimarron. He was a comparable riding horse but never as good as Captain Midnight had been. Kyzer regretted that the very year he had returned from Andersonville, he had to put Midnight down, following the discovery of his broken leg. With the bridle secured on his horse, Kyzer led him around outside to the kitchen and tied him to the porch. Dinah and Nathaniel were busy preparing breakfast when he walked in. Nathaniel appeared to be a little wary about Kyzer's sudden presence.

"Is the coffee ready?" he asked.

"Why don't you sit at the table while I get a cup for you? The eggs will be ready in a few minutes," Dinah said. "Here's a warm biscuit for you."

"I'm not very hungry," he said.

"Well, Dinah thinks you need to eat a little something. Where you going so early this morning?"

"Today, I will begin the quest to find my mama. I'm headed to Georgia for a start. I wanted to ask you to look after Lydia and Jared. Could you do that for me?"

"I would be glad to take care of them. They're no trouble. How long you gonna be gone?"

"That, I don't know, depends," he said. "I can send letters along. I can write, you know."

"Yes, but I can't read very well. I would have to get someone to read the letter for me," she said.

"I've got about everything ready for my trip. Just have to get it all in the saddle bags and then I'm gone," he said.

"You want me to go get the children up where you can tell them goodbye?"

"I don't think so. I'll peek into their rooms before I leave. They've been through enough, losing their mama. They don't need to hear their father say goodbye. It's probably better this way. You can tell them later that I'm on a trip, and I'll be home again as soon as I can."

"Mister Kyzer, it nearly broke my heart about Miss Dellanna. I keep thinking she's up in her room just waiting for me to open her curtains and bring her breakfast tray." Dinah sat there crying.

"I know. I'm going to miss her. I'm so ashamed that I nearly lost it, accusing her with Nathaniel. Now, to think about my mama as a slave girl. It's hard to realize that I'm not much different than you or Nathaniel. My skin is so light that I appear white; but with just one drop of her blood, I am considered a negro."

"Well, Mr. Kyzer, nobody really knows that about you. You can just keep on like you've always been," Dinah said.

"Yes, but now I know; and I'll have to deal with it. Maybe if I can find her, it will help me decide what to do," Kyzer said.

"My daddy's brother passed as white down in New Orleans,

but his children were black. They all got sold off as slaves. It was sad for him to lose his children," she said.

"Now, look at my children," Kyzer said. "When Lydia and Jared grow up, they could possibly have negro children. See, that's something else I'll have to face. Now, I've got to go. The sun is already up. Thank you for the breakfast and for taking charge of my children. I'm very grateful."

After looking in on the children, with his belongings and rifle packed away on Cimarron, Kyzer swung himself into the saddle and headed him down the drive.

"Where's Kyzer off to so early this morning?" John Kelsey asked as he walked into the kitchen. "I heard him ride away."

"He's gone lookin' for his mama," she said.

John Kelsey sat down at the table and cried.

By nightfall, Kyzer was already in North Carolina. He was hoping to make it to Raleigh the next day. He made his camp for overnight underneath a gigantic railroad trestle. He tied Cimarron to one of the supports while he unloaded his gear. After gathering and arranging a few sticks of wood, he used his flint to start a fire. He spread out his bedroll and, while he sat, unwrapped the piece of oilcloth that contained two leftover biscuits and a piece of salt pork for his supper. He took a drink of water from the canteen, pulled off his boots, and settled into the bedroll for the night, his rifle lying beside him. As he lay on the ground looking up at the stars, he tried to find all the constellations he had known as a boy until sleep gradually overtook him.

At daylight, Kyzer awoke from a fairly good night's sleep. Standing to scratch himself, he observed the campfire now smouldering with a few remaining embers. The experience brought to his mind all those nights under the stars at Andersonville. Only this time, there were no walls of the stockade to hold him prisoner. He scattered the ashes from the fire making certain that it was completely out as he finished packing up. He pulled a ripe red apple out of his pocket, took a bite, and held it between his teeth while he unbuttoned his fly. He watched as the warm yellow stream foamed upon the ground as it disappeared into the smooth sandy soil. Finishing the apple, he put the core into the mouth of his trusty mount. "Hey boy, I'll get you some oats when we get to Raleigh," he said.

The city was bustling in the afternoon when Kyzer arrived in the middle of town. He found a livery stable to board his horse along with a cheap hotel across the street for himself. At least, the bed looked clean as he propped his rifle beside it. Sleeping in it, he thought, would be another experience. Right now, he wanted to get out on the streets and see as much of the city as he could. His first visit to Raleigh, he bought a handful of boiled peanuts from a vendor on the street to hold him over until supper. He had already spotted a nice restaurant in the next block that he was hoping he could afford.

Kyzer began walking up and down the streets trying to reach the state capitol building. He could see its ornate cupola rising above the city skyline. It was interesting, he thought, as he finished his afternoon tour. Now, he had to get back across town for supper. It was no surprise for him to be ushered and seated at the table at Delmonico's. But now, somehow he felt uncomfortable. Looking around, white people were everywhere. The only blacks he saw were the cooks and some who cleaned the tables.

Kyzer enjoyed a delicious beef steak dinner with a glass of wine. He figured if he had one good meal a day, he would survive until he got to Jonesboro. When Kyzer left the restaurant for his hotel, he overheard two cooks talking outside the kitchen entrance. He had to chuckle to himself when he heard the words spoken by the young black man. "Yassir, we spits in their food and they's don't even know it." That made Kyzer think twice about the delicious meal he had just devoured.

After breakfast the next morning, Kyzer walked across the street to get his horse. Before leaving Raleigh, he stopped at the general store to purchase some additional food supplies for himself and a small bag of oats for Cimarron. For the next three days, Kyzer made his journey down through South Carolina, camping at night, until he reached the Georgia state line. By tomorrow afternoon, he planned to arrive in Jonesboro.

"Why Kyzer, what are you doing here? Come on into the house," Mary McArdle said. "Are you alone?"

"Yes ma'am, I'm alone," he said.

"Wait. Let me get George. Have a seat over there," she said.

In a few minutes, George and Mary McArdle appeared as George reached to shake Kyzer's hand.

"Hello there, Kyzer. It's been a while. How's your family?"

"Dellanna is dead. Her baby is dead," he said.

"Dear Jesus," Mary said. "How awful! I'm so sorry."

"My God, son, what happened?" George asked.

"Last week, Dellanna had the baby. He was stillborn. During the night, when I thought she was asleep, just resting, Dellanna hemorrhaged to death. That's not all, our baby was black," he said.

George fell back into his chair. "Whatever do you mean?"

"John Kelsey, your son-in-law, just told me the most astonishing news about myself. He finally confessed to me that my father was Matt Petersen and my mother is Delilah James," Kyzer said while Mary McArdle fainted on her sofa. "Don't guess he told you either, huh?"

"My dear boy, I'm shocked. Please allow me to see about Mary," he said.

"I'll just wait out on the front porch," Kyzer said.

A few minutes later, George and Mary returned to find him sitting there smoking his pipe. He looked at them, despairingly. "The startling discovery for me is the revelation that I was born a negro in a white man's body and didn't even know it. He never told me, and I can hardly forgive him. I'm so angry, just totally devastated. My life is ruined."

"Oh Kyzer, I'm so sorry, son. I wish I could say or do something to comfort you, but I don't know what that would be," George said.

"I'm here for one reason. I want to find Delilah. Do you think she is alive, and where do I need to start looking for her?" Kyzer stood to leave.

"Let me see, after Rachel Petersen died, Delilah was sent to the McGuire family in Atlanta. I'm really sorry, but that's all I know," Mary said.

"Thank you both. Guess I'll be riding to Atlanta this afternoon," Kyzer said.

"Won't you stay and have supper with us?" Mary asked.

"I need to go. I believe I can get there before dark," he said.

"At least, I told him the truth," Mary said to her husband after Kyzer left. "Anything he finds out now about Sabra McGuire, he will have to discover himself."

Kyzer decided to camp out on the Jonesboro Road before heading into Atlanta on Sunday.

◀▶◀▶

"Excuse me, sir, I'm looking for the McGuire residence," Kyzer said to the man standing on the street corner.

"Can't help you, sorry," he said.

Positioned conveniently just up the street, Kyzer saw the sign *UNITED STATES POST OFFICE - ATLANTA, GEORGIA*. He tied his horse to the hitching post there and went inside. "Could you direct me to the McGuire residence, please?" Kyzer asked the postal clerk.

"Sorry, sir, Atlanta's a big town; and I haven't been working here very long. The only McGuire I know is Mrs. Magnus McGuire over on Calhoun Avenue."

"Where's that?" Kyzer asked the stout little man with the barrel chest.

"Three blocks down that way," he pointed. "The house is a big two story painted slate blue. You can't miss it."

"Thank you for your help," Kyzer said while he turned to leave the post office.

A knock at the house on Calhoun brought a genteel elderly lady to the door. "Good afternoon, ma'am. Are you Mrs. McGuire?" Kyzer asked.

"Yes, I am and you, sir. Who might you be?"

"Kelsey, ma'am. I'm trying to locate someone, and I was directed here. Would you happen to employ a servant by the name of Delilah?"

"No sir, I have no servants. I'm a widow, and I live here with my sister."

"Are you acquainted with any other McGuires in town, may I ask?"

"Well, there's Sabra McGuire over on Peachtree Street. Thank goodness, she's no kin to me. You know, she's the one who paid to have her husband shot and killed after her torrid love affair with a married man years ago. No one hardly sees her. They say she rarely goes out in public, especially after her husband cut up her face the way he did. Terrible, it was just terrible, I do declare. The sinful goings on of some people today. I reckon it's a force they just can't control," she said.

"How do I get to Peachtree?"

Mrs. Magnus McGuire stood there as though she already expected him to know. "Why, that's the main street through town. You know where the post office is located, don't you?"

"Yes ma'am, I've already been there," he said.

"Well then, the post office is on Peachtree Street. As you head north going out of town, there is a nice residential area beginning there. There are many trees and sidewalks with gaslights on the corner of each block. You'll be able to recognize it when you see it. The McGuire mansion covers a complete city block setting there gloriously on the left in all it's splendor," she said.

"I thank you for your time, ma'am, and your helpful information. Good day, Mrs. McGuire."

"I hope you are able to find the person for whom you are looking," she said while he went on his way.

◀▶◀▶

Kyzer stepped back, slowly looking the place over after he rang the bell. He stood before the massive front door with its ornate overhead transom and sidelight panels fashioned of leaded cut glass. Through the door, he could see a large gas lighted crystal chandelier suspended there as it illuminated the vibrant blue entrance foyer. In a few minutes, the door was opened and pulled back by a small framed, light skinned negress who Kyzer thought looked to be middle-aged.

"Yes, sir." She stood before him in a long black dress with its crisp white ruffled apron flowing down the front. Behind her, beautiful stained glass windows crowned the second floor level. A grand winding staircase came floating down to rest against the white marble floor. Kyzer was at a loss for words as he stood before her. "Yes, may I help you, sir?" she repeated.

"Are you Delilah?" he finally asked.

Slowly, she answered, "Why, no sir, I'm Hattie."

"Is Delilah here?"

"No sir, there's no one named Delilah around here."

"Then, may I see Mrs. McGuire, please?"

"Miss Sabra cannot be disturbed at this time. I'm sorry, sir. What business do you have with her? She's not expecting anyone today."

"My name is Kyzer. I'm the adopted son of John and Elizabeth Kelsey formerly of Jonesboro. Delilah is my mother's name. I'm trying to find her."

Moments later, Kyzer was surprised when he heard the

voice from within the parlor. "Who is it, Hattie? Who's that at the door?"

"Wait here," Hattie said. It took both hands for her to close the door. She walked and stood between the tall mahogany paneled pocket doors of the parlor. "There's a young white man on the porch. Looks like a beggar if you ask me. Named Kyzer. Says he's looking for his mother, Delilah."

Calmly, she spoke again, "Hattie, I want you to dim all the lights in this room and kindly invite our guest in to see me. When he steps into the parlor, you are to pull the doors closed, understand?"

"Yes'sum," she said returning to the front door to invite the waiting Kyzer inside.

As Kyzer stood just inside the doorway of the large stately parlor, the doors were closed behind him as Hattie made her exit. From the corner of the room, an elegantly dressed woman in blue satin lounged upon her chaise with a folding fan spread across her face just below her eyes. The position of her body extended almost in silhouette as the dim lighting surrounded her partially hidden face.

"Mrs. McGuire, thank you for seeing me."

"Tell me who you are, and where is your home?" she asked peering over the shield of her fan.

"My name is Kyzer Kelsey, ma'am. Sadly to say, my wife Dellanna has just died in childbirth, and the baby stillborn. I have two small children back home, Lydia and Jared. I have ridden here all the way from Hastings, Virginia. It has taken over a week to get here."

"I am certainly distressed to learn just now of your sorrow and loss. You have my sincere sympathy; but why, may I ask, are you visiting at this time? I should think one would not be considering such a journey after such a tragic event," she said.

"I am trying to locate my real mother. You see, I'm adopted."

"Really? Then, who are your adoptive parents?"

"Dr. John and Elizabeth Kelsey from Jonesboro, but we moved to Hastings when I was a baby. Elizabeth died suddenly last year."

"I'm sorry. Your grandparents?"

"George and Mary McArdle, also of Jonesboro. They have another daughter named Katharine."

"Oh, I see. And, you think your real mother is named ... ." Her eyes began to moisten, as he interrupted.

"Delilah. Yes, I believe so, but John Kelsey has lied to me before."

"Your name again, please?"

"Kyzer."

"Well Kyzer, as I remember years ago, I had a maid named Delilah. I never heard her mention having a baby let alone a white one."

"That's just it. You see, Delilah worked for Mrs. Rachel Petersen before coming to you. Her son, Matt, is supposed to be my father. It was Delilah who gave me up to the Kelsey family. I just want to find her, if she's still alive."

"Walk closer. Would you mind coming a little closer?" Kyzer advanced a few steps at Sabra's request. "I see you walk with a limp in your left leg. Do you mind my asking what happened to you to cause the injury?"

"I was shot and taken prisoner during the siege of Petersburg. Lucky for me, I didn't lose the leg, but I did lose a brother. I was sent to the stockade at Andersonville where I found Rob. He was John and Elizabeth's son. Poor Rob died there."

"I'm sorry for you both, and for your entire family. You seem to have been through so much. I really do sympathize with you although I feel at this time, I'm not able to be much help."

"I appreciate you seeing me, anyway. I can find my way out," he said.

Kyzer was nearing the front door when she hurriedly walked into the foyer. Sabra lowered the fan from her face and folded it, allowing full exposure of her once very beautiful face. Kyzer turned to see her hideous face revealed now in its present state after years of aging and wrinkling. He found it hard not to stare as she asked him to return to the parlor once again.

"I need you to do something you might find uncomfortable. You might even refuse me. If so, I understand." She paused. "Would you please turn around and remove your shirt? Only for a moment, that's all I ask. Please, do not feel embarrassed. I will not be offended by you."

Kyzer stood there before her frozen in the moment. He had to think. Slowly, he turned while unbuttoning his shirt, dropping it to the waist.

"Thank you, I've seen all I need to see. You may put your shirt back on."

Kyzer turned to face her while never questioning her sudden request for him to bare his back.

"If you can remain in Atlanta for another week, come here again next Sunday afternoon bathed and dressed in clean clothes. Get yourself a fresh haircut and shave. I will look forward to seeing you then. Goodbye, Kyzer."

Kyzer left the McGuire mansion feeling disappointed that he didn't find his mother there. However, he thought the meeting with Sabra McGuire seemed rather odd but quite interesting. As he remembered standing there half naked before her for an instant, he tried to imagine what she might have looked like years ago, years before the brutal attack inflicted upon herself by her now dead and murdered former husband. To be asked to take his shirt off before anyone other than Dellanna, well, if he had to do that over again, he would have just refused. That was strange, but then she seemed so familiar with some of the names that were mentioned in their conversation. She did have a maid named Delilah at one time, but what happened to her? Was she dead? Now, he was invited to come back next Sunday, all cleaned up, but for what reason? His cluttered mind was reeling. Guess he would have to find a boarding house and rent himself a room for another week, at least. Where else could he go?

Sabra McGuire sat most of the night at her writing desk as she carefully penned two letters. The first one written to her attorney, Mr. Michael Radcliffe, Esq. and the second one to Delilah James with no address. As she finished writing, Sabra placed the letters together in a single envelope, leaving it there on the corner of the desk while she prepared herself for bed.

Early the next morning, her carriage driver took Sabra McGuire to the rear entrance of the law offices of *Mitchell, Radcliffe, and White*. The firm had relocated there on Peachtree Street again following the burning of Atlanta during the war. Sabra met with Attorney Radcliffe for nearly two hours as she made her request while leaving the letters of explanation with him. Her mission accomplished, she emerged once again, her short black veil pulled over her face as she returned to the mansion. Keeping a positive outlook, all she could do now was wait.

CHAPTER 21

Delilah slightly opened the door of her little house as she peered through the crack at the well dressed gentleman standing on the porch.

"Are you Delilah James?"

"Yes, sir, but it's Jefferson now." She opened the door.

"I am Tyler Whitfield, representing a Mr. Michael Radcliffe from the firm of *Mitchell, Radcliffe, and White* in Atlanta. I'm here today on behalf of Mrs. Sabra McGuire who sends you this letter." He presented her the envelope from his satchel. "It has been most difficult to locate you this week. I must say now time is of the uttermost importance."

"Would you like to sit on my porch, sir?" she asked.

"Very well," he said while he sat and took off his hat.

She opened the envelope and began reading to herself from the letter dated April 18, 1869.

Dear Delilah,

I am trusting this letter finds you well after all these years. I have an urgent need to contact you as soon as possible about a very important matter. I believe I may have some wonderful news for you about your son.

I am asking you to please come to Atlanta at once. A representative from my attorney's office, the firm of Mr. Michael Radcliffe, will be delivering my letter to you in person. The expenses for your train fare will be provided as well as any additional costs that may arise from the trip. Please consider traveling with the man who will personally escort you to my home by this coming Sunday morning. Please do whatever you need to do accordingly to insure your prompt arrival on this date.

If you really want to see your son, I am convinced that he is diligently seeking to find you now. I believe the young man I have recently met is indeed he. I have seen the birthmark on his back that confirms his story. You will remember it many years ago when you were with me in Atlanta.

I believe you will be proud to see the fine man he seems to have become. My heart is filled with joy for you while I await the occasion we will have in meeting again for this grand reunion. I will look forward to your much anticipated arrival very soon.

Kindest regards,
Sabra McGuire

Tears were flowing down her face as Delilah pulled up the edge of her apron to dab at her eyes. She immediately began to think of any reason that would hinder her from traveling to Atlanta, and she could think of absolutely nothing.

"When do I need to be ready?" she asked Mr. Whitfield.

"We could leave on Friday morning, if you would like," he said.

"I'll be ready then, just have to take care of a few things," she said.

"I'm leaving now to purchase the tickets. I'll come for you on Friday," Tyler Whitfield said as he put on his stylish black hat and walked away, whistling down the street.

Delilah went inside and fell across her bed. "Kyzer, oh my Kyzer, I am longing to see you in four more days."

Delilah sat on the porch that afternoon waiting for her husband to come home from work. She could hardly wait to tell Lovell Jefferson about her surprising good news. He was still almost a block away when she ran from the porch down the street and hurled herself into his big arms. A hug and a kiss, along with a radiant smile from her, was his warm reception.

"All right, what's going on? You ain't been this happy since my mama moved out," he said.

"It's Kyzer. He's come to Atlanta looking for me. A nice man, Mr. Whitfield, is taking me there to meet him. The train's leaving on Friday, and I will see Kyzer on Sunday at Sabra McGuire's. She has arranged everything for us. Isn't that wonderful? I told you I used to work for Miss Sabra after I left Jonesboro, remember?"

"What about me? Who's gonna take care of me?" Lovell asked.

"Well, I'm a lookin' at a grown man who I know can take care of himself for a few days. I won't be gone for very long," she said.

"Don't be expectin' me to take on any more hungry mouths to feed. Kyzer may have seven or eight young'uns by now," he said.

"So what, yo' mama could eat that much. Get on in the bedroom, Lovell, we might have to take us a little nap before supper," she said, as she sat grinning on the side of the bed while rolling her stockings down.

Friday morning at nine o'clock, Delilah sat on the train across the aisle from Tyler Whitfield as she looked out the window. She waved goodbye to Lovell standing there at the depot underneath the sign *VALDOSTA, GEORGIA* while she said under her breath, "He's probably glad to see me go for a few days. He knows for sure, I can make his life pure hell."

Kyzer arrived precisely at three o'clock on Sunday afternoon at the McGuire mansion. He was dressed nicely in a solid grey suit with black leather shoes, the new clothes he bought just three days ago while shopping in Atlanta. For the five dollars he spent at the barber shop, he received a fresh haircut and shave along with a hot tub bath. His dark hair, cut to a medium length, was neatly combed into place. He stood nervously on the porch still trying to figure out why he was here again as he rang the bell. Hattie came to the door and opened it. She stood there smiling at him.

"Good afternoon, Hattie. I don't know if I'm early or late, but I'm here," he said.

"Miss Sabra say for you to stand over there at the bottom of the staircase. She'll be down, directly," she said while she left the foyer.

All alone for several minutes while he waited, Kyzer began to turn and look the place over. On his last visit, he failed to notice all the large portraits and beautiful landscapes framed along the wall. Now, he saw the golden sconces, curios filled with porcelain figurines, a silk fan collection, and crystal vases filled with fresh cut flowers set on French styled tables. He also noted a huge silver candelabra, now with lighted white tapers, the furnishings gracefully filling the main entrance. It looked like a room in a museum, he thought, standing underneath the grandeur of the sparkling chandelier with hundreds of pieces of fine cut crystal shimmering above his head. The shiny Italian white marble floor glistened under the gaslight. It was almost too much to take in all at once, and this was only the entrance foyer. Kyzer could only imagine what some of the other rooms must look like.

As he turned to look up again at the stained glass windows across the second level, at the top of the grand staircase, he knew at once it was her. Delilah was standing with her right hand resting on the ornate mahogany bannister. She stood like a petite statue dressed in a flowing gown of periwinkle blue muslin, long sleeved and high collared. Her long black hair was straightened as it hung shoulder length and clipped at the back of her neck with a matching blue bow. Large, golden hoop earrings peeked out underneath the loose hair framing her face. Big dark brown eyes sparkled, with a wide smile gleaming, just for him. If this was his mother, she wasn't at all like he expected. Her light colored skin would almost allow her also to pass for white were it not for her slightly widened nose.

As Delilah started her descent, Kyzer rushed up the stairs to meet her about halfway down while he put his strong arms around her. "Happy Birthday! It's your birthday, remember?" She reminded him through her tears.

"The twenty-fifth of April and I haven't even thought about it. I'm twenty-eight today," he said.

"I can't believe it's really you, Kyzer. Let's go down to the parlor. Miss Sabra told me to sit there where we could be alone to talk. She will be joining us for supper later on," she said.

"We've got a lifetime of catching up to do, don't we? Where do we start?" he asked.

"Let me sit down for a few minutes and just look at you. You are real nice looking for a white man," she laughed. "When did you find out?"

"That you were my mother? Oh, just a couple of weeks ago, I reckon. My Dellanna just died in childbirth," he said.

"Oh Kyzer, I'm so sorry. Then, you're married?"

"Yes ma'am. I married Dellanna Braxton almost four years ago. Our daughter, Lydia, was born before we were ever married. She's already four. Jared was born in 1867. He's two. My children are both white. I lost Dellanna nearly two weeks ago. She bled to death overnight after giving birth to our son. He was born dead, and he was black. John Kelsey had to confess everything after that. You see, that's how I found out about you. Tell me about yourself."

"I want you to know that I never stopped loving or caring for you. At the time, when I was seventeen, Dr. Kelsey was the only one I thought could help me. Are you angry with him?"

"I told him I hated him when I first found out about everything, but now I don't know."

"If you're angry at anybody, it should probably be me, don't you think? I was the one who gave you up and begged him not to tell anyone. We both suffered for what I swore him to do in the first place. When I look back, I realize he only did what I told him to do. I was scared and alone."

"What about my father, Matt Petersen?"

"I'm sorry he was murdered, but I've always been glad that he's gone out of my life. I was terrified of him. Kyzer, yes, he was your father, but I never loved him that way. After you were born, I felt so different because you were different. We can talk about him later."

"Where do you live?" he asked.

"After Mrs. Rachel passed, I guess you already know that I went to Atlanta to work for Miss Sabra. Later, I met my husband; and after a few years, we moved to Valdosta. His name is Lovell Jefferson, and he works as a brick mason. Lovell's really good to me. I wanted a family, but I was never able to have anymore children. Now, I've got you back if you'll have me as your mother."

"Why would I have come looking for you, if I didn't want you? Of course, I do. You're all I've got except for Lydia and Jared," he said.

Delilah and Kyzer remained lost in conversation and each other over the course of the late afternoon while they continued the renewal of their newly found relationship. A gentle rap at the door caused a break while they turned their attention to the parlor door as it opened. Hattie stood there. "Miss Sabra asks you both to join her for supper. If you would, please follow me," she said.

Sabra McGuire met her guests while she stood at her place in her elegant and elaborate dining room. "I hope I've given you both enough time to get reacquainted; but if not, you're welcomed to stay for as long as you want. Kyzer, your mother is staying here with me tonight. You are invited also as I have plenty of room which you must well imagine," she said.

"Thank you, but I'll need to go back into town. I'm not prepared to stay overnight. I have to check on my horse, Cimarron, and I'm already paid at the Gleason's boarding house," he said. "May I come back in the morning?"

"Certainly. Delilah will be with me for a few more days. Well, Delilah, what do you think about Kyzer?"

"He's more than I could have ever imagined. I'm very pleased at how well he looks and how he has turned out. Dr. John and Elizabeth Kelsey did a wonderful job with him," she said.

"Kyzer, what about your mama? Were you surprised?"

"She's wonderful. I can't wait to take her back to Kellwood," he said without thinking.

Delilah looked surprised. "Oh, we'll have to talk about that later," she said.

Kyzer sat there through the meal wondering what Delilah thought when he blurted out, 'I can't wait to take her back to Kellwood.'

As their time together ended in Atlanta for those three short days, Delilah and Kyzer thanked Sabra for all she had done in reuniting them. Kyzer never thought it possible for such a kind, generous, and mysterious lady to play such an integral part in helping him to find his mother. In spite of all her past misfortune, Kyzer would always be grateful for Sabra McGuire.

Kyzer and Delilah stood at the Atlanta Depot saying their goodbyes. They were unable to reach an agreement before they parted. Delilah knew that Lovell would never agree to move to Virginia, and Kyzer had so many things to sort out and decide himself. How could he leave the only home that he had ever known? They would have to wait for another time to see each other again. Kyzer waved goodbye as he watched the train gradually pull away from the station. It was taking his mother home to Valdosta. When the train was out of sight, Kyzer headed his horse northeast out of Atlanta. He already knew it would take him over a week to return home.

In the meantime, Kyzer thought about all the things he needed to do and the changes he was going to have to make in the near future. For the first time, he felt joy, happiness, and fulfillment in life, especially after seeing and meeting his mother. There were two questions that remained, questions he needed to answer in order to give him peace. Could he ever forgive John Kelsey? How was he going to live the rest of his life, white or black?

He prayed to God for help to decide what to do. Right now, he was anxious to get home to see Lydia and Jared. He remembered his dead baby as he crossed over the Virginia state line.

I will call his name Ethan.

◀▶◀▶

Kyzer arrived at Kellwood before dark and led his horse to the barn. After taking the saddlebags and pitching them aside, he removed the bridle and saddle. He gave Cimarron some feed and fresh water and put him into the stall. He picked up the bags and his rifle and headed toward the back of the house.

The house was still and darkened. It was time to light the lamps, he thought. Actually, it was much too quiet. Where was everyone? Kyzer placed his gear on the porch and walked toward the kitchen. He could hear a faint sound coming from within, and he could see a light under the closed door. Dinah was busy placing several dishes of food on a tray when he opened the door.

"Hope I didn't scare you," he said.

"No sir, I knew it was you. I saw you go into the barn," she said.

"Where's Lydia and Jared?"

"The children are at Chandalar. Mrs. Anne's been keeping

them for me. They're all right, except for crying and missing Miss Dellanna, I mean. I've had my hands full here since the first week you've been gone. I've got Nathaniel to care for and now Mister John."

"What's happened?"

"Mister John had a stroke. He's up in his room. I'm ready to go up and feed him his supper," she said as she finished up with the tray.

"How is he?"

"He's just lying in his bed. He can barely move much less walk. Can't talk, either. Just mumbles, kinda like Nathaniel, you know, except I can't understand him. I think he can hear me at times, but I'm not sure. He's in a pitiful state, Lord, have mercy," she said.

"Can I help you with anything before I go up?"

"If you don't mind, Mr. Kyzer, let me take this tray upstairs and try to feed him. I'm afraid if he sees you, he won't eat anything. You can see him after while. It'll be all right," she said. "You can light the lamps in the hallway and the parlor, if you want. I don't think we'll need anymore lights in the house tonight."

"Dinah, I've decided to ride over to Chandalar and spend the night with Lydia and Jared. I'll bring them home with me in the morning after breakfast. I want to see them before they go to bed. I'll see him tomorrow."

"That's good, Mr. Kyzer. They need to see their father," Dinah said.

"And, I don't want you to worry, I'm going to get you some help. I'll hire somebody to sit with him and take care of him. It's not your place to have to do it," Kyzer said.

"I'll do what I can. I don't mind," she said.

"I've got a couple of days to see about it before I have to go back to work. We'll get it all worked out before long. Dinah, I found my mama. I really did. I sat with her and talked to her in Atlanta. She's been living in Valdosta all this time. She's married but doesn't have anymore children. Dinah, she's really nice," he said.

"Mr. Kyzer, that's wonderful. I'm happy for you. I'm sure she was glad to see you. Must have been a glad reunion," Dinah said.

"It was. It really was. I hope she can come here to live one day," he said. "I'll let you get upstairs with that tray. I'm leaving now. Good night."

The morning brought Kyzer back to Kellwood with his children. He asked Dinah to watch them while he went upstairs to the bedroom of John Kelsey. He opened the door slowly and pushed it back, closing it quietly. He saw him lying there slightly twitching, but sleeping. His matted hair lay disheveled with loose strands falling across his forehead. His head was thrown back on the pillow with his chin up, mouth opening and shutting with very irregular breathing. His body was drawn down the left side, arm pulled inward. One side of his face was pulled downward, lowering his closed eyes, one below the other. His nightshirt was stained with vomit and dried food particles. The bed smelled of urine and feces. Just three weeks had passed, and now he looked like a completely different man so different from the father he had known.

Kyzer sat in the chair by the bed and waited. He sat, staring at him until he dozed off for a while. He didn't remember how long. Maybe it was a few minutes. A mumbling sound awakened him, and when Kyzer opened his eyes, John Kelsey was staring back. Kyzer stood and walked over to the side of the bed. He reached to touch his hand. It felt cold. Kyzer looked into his eyes.

"Hey, old man, I'm home. I found my mama. I'm happy now. I leave for a while and look what happens to you." Kyzer saw John trying to move a bit and point, but John couldn't control his movement. Kyzer continued to watch his eyes. "Can you hear me? Do you know who I am?"

"Uhhh, ahh," John Kelsey moaned.

"Blink. Blink your eyes if you hear me. Good job, I see you. All right, look here. One long blink is 'yes' and two short ones is 'no'. Got it? Let's try it then. Look at me. Over here. Now keep your eyes looking this way," Kyzer said.

"Is Rob Kelsey your son?" One blink.

"Is Susannah Hollis your daughter?" One blink.

"Is my name Kyzer?" One blink.

"Were you married to Katharine?" Two blinks.

"Were you married to Elizabeth?" One blink.

"Dinah tells me that Dr. Vincent is coming back today to see you. Do you know Dr. Vincent?" One blink. "I've got something I want to tell you. I need to tell you about something that's really important. Do you think you can listen for a few minutes?" One blink. "And, you can see me, all right?" One blink.

"You'll remember, a long time ago I told you something soon after I found out I was adopted. I went on to say how grateful I was to have been adopted by you and Elizabeth. Knowing that, as I grew older, I wanted to learn more about where I came from and who my real parents were. Deep within my soul, I held hard feelings against you after the sudden revelation of it all. It was a shocking discovery when I had to find out about my mother and father through the birth of my own dead baby. Can you begin to imagine the pain from that? I see your blink. That's okay. Just listen to me right now. You see, I realize because of my circumstances, I am going to be faced with the same thing with my children. Lydia and Jared are going to have to be told one day that they have negro blood flowing in them. When do I tell them? I certainly can't wait until they are grown. That hurt me so bad. It made me angry that I felt I had to tell you how much I hated you. I want to tell you that I am sorry you have had this stroke and assure you that I am going to take care of you. All of us are praying that you will soon recover and be well again. I want you to know that I have forgiven you. I'm sorry I said all those things to you. I have just returned from Atlanta where I saw my mother. Delilah told me about my father. She told me she was really to blame because she made you promise her that you would never tell anyone. It was you who kept that part of the bargain. What about Elizabeth? Did she ever know the truth? I see, two blinks. You never even told her. I am astounded. But, you see, that's where I'm going to have to be different. My children are going to have to know, and I will be sure to tell them. The final question I am going to have to decide is really tough for me. Do I continue to pass myself off as completely white, or can I accept myself as having some negro blood and live accordingly. I guess only time will tell, especially as the children grow older. I want them to know the truth about their roots. No more lies and deceptions."

From where Kyzer was standing, it looked like tears were running from John Kelsey's eyes as he began mumbling. Kyzer slid his hand onto John's. "Rest for a while. I'll be back to see you later."

Despite everything that could be done for him, Dr. John Kelsey died in September, after lingering nearly six months. Under the provisions of his last will and testament, Susannah and Kyzer jointly inherited Kellwood and its twelve acres. Susannah received Elizabeth's china cabinet, along with all her china, crystal, silver, and jewelry. She also inherited her parent's bedroom furniture. Kyzer received John's rifles, shotguns, household furnishings, and personal effects. Later, he struck a deal with Susannah, buying out her share of the estate, eventually becoming the sole heir and owner of Kellwood Plantation.

The new year of 1870 brought more bad news. In the summer, Kyzer received a letter from Delilah. Her husband, Lovell, was killed in an accident at work. While bricking the side of the new Catholic church in Valdosta, he fell from the scaffolding to his untimely death. Delilah was heartbroken and alone.

Kyzer knew immediately what he intended to do. He would ask Delilah to sell her house and move to Kellwood. He had wanted this for so long. So what, if people started calling him a negro, he would have his family together and be happy. After all, white or black, he was thirty years old and the proud owner of Kellwood. He was quite satisfied. He counted it a blessing to be born as one of God's special children. Suddenly, at last, he found the peace in his life that passes all understanding.

That was Kyzer's destiny — my destiny!

◆▶◀▶

"What is it you wanted to tell me?" Lydia asked, while her father finished telling her the story.

"Oh, it's about a special promise I made to your mother. She wanted to be sure that I would tell you one day. I'll tell you as soon as we finish our supper," he said.

Quietly, a small figure appeared at the massive front doorway on the majestic white columned veranda. In silhouette against the backdrop of dusk, she stood there in her long white apron covering her brightly colored calico dress. She had a radiant smile while her outstretched arms reached for Lydia. Flowing black hair fell across her shoulders when she bent to pick up her granddaughter.

"Kyzer, son, you come in for supper now."

"I've waited all my life to hear you say that. I love you, Mama." He rose from the rocking chair and followed them into the great hallway of Kellwood. "Tobacco ought to go sky high next year. I must remember to buy plenty of stock in the Kelsey Tobacco Company of Virginia."

Kyzer smiled while he placed a strong arm around Delilah and drew her close to his side.

AFTERWORD

Soon after May 4, 1865, when the last of the prisoners were released, history would record the final outcome. Between February-1864 and May-1865, more than 45,000 Union soldiers were imprisoned at Andersonville. From that great number, 12,913 died there. As far as the prisoner exchange itself, it failed in negotiation and never happened. On November 10, 1865, Captain Henry Wirz, Interior Prison Commandant of Camp Sumter at Andersonville was hanged in Washington. He was destined to become the only soldier to be tried and executed for war crimes committed during the civil war.

On July 25, 1865, U.S. Secretary of War, Edwin M. Stanton commissioned a group to assist Supt. W.A. Griffith in preserving and marking the graves in the prison cemetery. Among those in the group mainly responsible for that tremendous task were Clara Barton, founder of the American Red Cross, and former prison inmate Dorance Atwater. It was through the sole efforts of Atwater's records for him to keep and maintain his unofficial death list. Those records provided the much needed information to supply the names, rank, and home state of thousands of men with the simple assignment of a number.

Since that very day on August 13, 1864, when the miraculous spring came gushing forth in the Andersonville prison yard, Providence Spring still flows there today. A beautiful monument erected in 1901 marks the spot of its origin.   JHH

There are any number of books, pamphlets, and other sources for those interested in further information about Captain Wirz and Andersonville located in Macon County / Sumter County. For a quick study, I recommend the following: *CAMP SUMTER - The Pictorial History of Andersonville* by Ken Drew. (ISBN#0-9622714-0-3)

Visit the website www.AndersonvilleNationalHistoricSite.com

Visit Andersonville National Cemetery and Prison Site located near Americus, Georgia.

ACKNOWLEDGMENTS

I would like to offer thanks to several people for their support during the writing of *Kyzer's Destiny*. There were thirteen special individuals who consented to become models by allowing me to personally photograph them and use their physical likeness to create and develop some of the characters. I appreciate the willingness and spirit of their efforts to help me stay focused.

Thank you so much to Gene Kyzer, Michele Criswell, Ronnie Tucker, Shelley O'Brien, Angelia Neelley, Chad Carpenter, Erich Schnee, Lauren Evans, Jeremy Evans, Justin Northam, Matt Dupree, Chris Glassing, and Billy Kirkpatrick. You were all great!

For your words of encouragement, guidance, and opinions, I am deeply indebted to Carmen Goldwaithe, Kelly McClymer, Phyllis Harris, Jim and Myra Wallace for your valuable services during the writing of the manuscript. Lynn Pass, your great work of editing significantly improved the final outcome. To Erin Sullivan, Sarah Wilkinson, Lacey Perry, Monica Butler, and Jeff Fuson at iUniverse Publishing who worked with me and helped me immensely, I am very grateful. Thank you so much, Sonya Sherer, for all you've done and continue to do for me. Your assistance is greatly appreciated. To countless family and friends who offer their love and support, you have encouraged me to fulfill my dream and reach my destiny. To the readers who will read me, I sincerely hope you are inspired to be that special person that God intends you to be.

The following books and other materials were helpful in developing the cultural and historical background for the novel: *The World Book Encyclopedia* (1957) J. Morris Jones, B.A. Editor in Chief; *Andersonville* (1955) MacKinlay Kantor; *Cold Mountain* (1997) Charles Frazier; *One Drop* (2007) Bliss

Broyard; *Gone With The Wind* (1936) Margaret Mitchell; *Scarlett* (1991) Alexandra Ripley; *Camp Sumter - The Pictorial History of Andersonville* by Ken Drew; and *Andersonville - The Great Untold Story of the Civil War* (1996) DVD-ROM - John Frankenheimer and David W. Rintels.

Finally, I have to list the places mentioned in the novel. Without you there wouldn't have been a story to write. I salute the following: Montgomery, Alabama - Natchez, Mississippi - New Orleans, Louisiana - Atlanta, Savannah, Andersonville, Jonesboro, Clayton County, Valdosta, Georgia - Richmond, Petersburg, Lexington, Fredericksburg, Chancellorsville, Rockbridge County, Chesterfield County, and the fictional town of Hastings, Virginia - Raleigh, North Carolina - Charleston, South Carolina - Philadelphia, Harrisburg, Gettysburg, Pennsylvania - Boston, Massachusetts - Washington D.C.

Jon Howard Hall
jonhall@windstream.net

CPSIA information can be obtained
at www.ICGtesting.com
Printed in the USA
LVHW092341280323
742902LV00022B/542